Splat!!
Hugo Miller Mysteries 7

Joseph Allen

Dedication

For my family, especially my beloved children, Angus and John, and my wonderful grandchildren, Isabelle and Xixi.

Chapter One

It wasn't the first time it had happened.

Since the impressive glass-faced high rise had been finished less than eighteen months before, two men had committed suicide by plunging off the roof and crashing into the pavement twenty stories below. As it happens, nearly two-thirds of all suicides are men, twice the number of women who choose to end their lives. What was different about this time was that the guy who flew off the edge of the roof landed on an elderly man who was apparently out for a walk, and—voila!—there were two men dead, not just one.

Some youngish guy—Latino, I would guess, from his last name, which was Barrio—apparently threw himself off the roof of the building, obviously intending to kill himself—unless he was pushed over the edge (and there was no evidence of a fight or scuffle). Only he landed on Robert J "Bob" Bliss, a 75-year-old man out for a night-time walk. Both of them were dead. Murder-suicide? There was, in fact, a handgun on the floor of the roof story; it looked like it had been tossed or dropped after it had been fired, and was found wedged up against a bricked-in chimney-type structure that housed an exhaust pipe that was part of the HVAC system. Obviously intended to prevent people from getting burned if they touched the pipe.

The Yonkers PD Crime Scene Investigators (CSIs) said there were some blurred fingerprints on the gun, but the grip was covered completely with cross-hatched metal, which made it difficult to find—or lift—prints, even when they dusted the whole weapon, including the trigger. It also interfered with collecting traces of DNA that might have been deposited from sweat or body oil. According to the Forensic Lab, Mr. Barrio's fingerprints were not a match for anything on the gun that was found on the roof, although some of the prints were blurred enough that it made matching impossible.

"The cross-hatch and the general shape of the gun makes it look like a Stoner CNC Beretta 92," one of the CSIs offered. He flashed a picture of the gun on his smartphone. I didn't recall ever having seen a gun like it.

Of course, there was a swarm of police cars on the death scene almost immediately. Yonkers is not a small city, though it's also not huge, just over a quarter of a million people in its population—about the same size, population-wise, as Irvine, California, which is where my kids grew up. Still, it's the fourth-largest city in the State of New York. It goes like this: NYC is the biggest, then Buffalo, then Rochester, then Yonkers. There's a large Police Department, and the street was choking with sedans with flashing lights—and a lot of sirens coming closer all the time.

Yonkers was founded by a Dutch fellow in the seventeenth century, before the whole territory was grabbed by the English in 1664. He was named something like Adrian Van der Donck, who apparently didn't get along well with Peter Stuyvesant, the longtime governor of the New Amsterdam Dutch colony. Stuyvesant was a former soldier who had lost a leg in a sea battle in the Caribbean. He had a wooden leg, so he was called "Peg-Leg" by the English-speakers. Van der Donck fled from Stuyvesant's Manhattan and traveled up the Hudson River (which was called the North River at the time—the South River being the Delaware River that today forms the border between New Jersey and Delaware as it empties into the Atlantic Ocean) to buy some land; he ventured out of Stuyvesant's territory into what seemed like an endless forest that is now Westchester County. I've been told that he was a *Jonkheer*, which was then, as I understand it, a polite term in Dutch for a person we might call a "gentleman" in English (not an aristocrat). The J was pronounced like a Y, and that's how the city became Yonkers, because it was the Jonkheer's home. At least that's how the story goes, the way it was told to me.

The ambulances drowned out the sirens from the police cars, but the police cars had more flashing lights. The two men's bodies were loaded up and sent off to hospitals, where both were pronounced dead on arrival. A suicide and an accidental homicide, they decided at the coroner's office of Westchester County (which isn't in Yonkers, but in a county office in a town called Valhalla, well north of Yonkers).

Almost immediately, the Bliss family hired Mike di Saronno to help them sort out who was responsible for Bob Bliss's demise—because several of the Blisses had read where Mike had been written up in the local papers for his work on then-recent homicides, most of which were in "downtown" Yonkers—an area called Getty Square that, in spite of being modernized and re-zoned for higher luxury buildings, was rife with drug dealers and various kinds of petty criminals.

In this case, the deaths were in the northwest corner of Yonkers—not anywhere near Getty Square, but close to a newly subdivided area on a new street called Executive Boulevard. It was not far from the next town north of Yonkers, called Hastings-on-the-Hudson (to distinguish it from the Hastings where William the Conqueror beat the crap out of the English in 1066, thereby winning what schoolteachers call the Norman Conquest).

My old friend Mike di Saronno called me and asked me to work with him on the case. I had worked with Mike for years when he was the highest-ranking detective in the NYPD, but he had retired and taken his pension a year or so earlier, and hung out a shingle—in Manhattan—for his services as an attorney (he has a Columbia University law degree). His fee would probably be paid nearly 100% from insurance of some kind—most likely from winning a negligence suit from the owners of the building for not restricting traffic on the roof of their building. He said he would split it—whatever it was—60% for himself, 40% for me and my team, and he would also reimburse us for any expenses that we incurred—with his pre-approval. That included a monthly allotment for gasoline and car expense, which was figured in dollars per mile. The fee would probably be smallish, he said, because he didn't want to overcharge anyone, and Mr. Bliss was way past his prime when the falling body killed him. Mike's a prince of a guy, and volunteers his time and experience to help people who have been accused of some crime and are unable to make bail, so they are remanded to jail cells pending trials, which sometimes take months to be scheduled.

Mike also volunteers for the Innocence Project, a nonprofit legal organization committed to exonerating individuals—the majority of whom are minorities—who have been wrongly convicted of felonies and imprisoned. Sometimes these incarcerated individuals had already served decades for crimes they didn't commit. Mike has been successful in getting prisoners released from prison because of DNA evidence that was either unavailable at the time of their trials, or was beyond the ability of forensic labs. A lot of his clients in the Innocence Project had been convicted of sexual violence or homicides, and were cleared because DNA found in trial evidence lockers proved they were nowhere near the crimes they were convicted for. Many of his clients were people of color—Black or LatinX (what we used to call Latino, but allowing for racial mixtures that didn't fit the word Latino—like a guy whose mother was Peruvian and his father was Japanese. Tiger Woods might be an example of LatinX).

I also called my friends Gabriele and Ruth—both of them experienced in working with Mike and me, mostly on homicide or terrorism cases, which had been Mike's specialties when he was in the NYPD. Both of them had seen coverage of the suicide and the innocent bystander elderly walker on Channel 12, a local all-news TV channel that is included with a lot of cable TV packages.

Both Gabriele and Ruth signed on immediately. How often does this happen, that a falling body kills somebody on the street? Good TV, no matter how rare or common it was. It probably happened in the 1929 Market Crash, and for sure on 9-11 in 2001, when people were jumping from the burning upper floors of the World Trade Center towers after huge commercial airplanes were crashed into them by Al-Qaida terrorists. Imagine plunging out of a burning building and knowing you'd be falling 90 floors to land on a sidewalk or a street!

Gabriele Cortese owns—with his cousin, Dante di Benedetto—an Italian-style restaurant called Ora di Pranzo (the name means "lunchtime," due to a miscalculation on the part of the owners, who anticipated that the crowds would be heaviest mid-day, since they were surrounded by office buildings). Turned out that it was more of a dinner or even after-the-theater joint, and the last customers tended to hang out until after 4AM, which by law in NYC is when "last call" signals the closing of an establishment that serves alcoholic drinks. The point was that restaurants were supposed to be closed from 4 until about 8AM—to make sure there was no around-the-clock drinking going on (of course, the law didn't prevent that, because people could go home or to a friend's house or a private club and keep drinking there—London isn't the only city where drunks sleep off their hangovers on the sidewalks).

Anyway, although Gabriele was in his fifties, he was far and away the most handsome man in whatever room he was in. He was originally from the Isle of Capri, which is part of Italy, nearest to Naples of all Italian cities. Dante, his cousin, was originally from Napoli itself; he's the chef of Ora di Pranzo, with (of course) a specialty in pastas and pizzas, since both of those dishes originated in southern Italy (and were not brought back from China by Marco Polo, who was Venetian). Gabriele was—and is—a celebrity restaurateur like Danny Meyer, and he is always—ALWAYS—comped for anything he eats or drinks (and anyone with him, which at times like this includes helpers like Ruth and Gabriele and me.

I am close as well with Ruth "the Sleuth" Jenson, and with Gabriele, who had been a sex worker in my neighborhood in the Theater District for years (so I would see him on the street and at restaurants, but we seldom said anything—just a wave here and there). I started off on a homicide case where I was a "person of interest," due to having been in an apartment under question. A fairly well-known keyboard musician died as a result of a drug overdose and a related intoxicated fall from a window in his then apartment built in a group over the roof of Carnegie Hall. Andrew Carnegie built the apartments because he believed it would be impossible for Carnegie Hall to support itself on ticket sales. Ha!

I have worked with the NYPD on a string of what turned out to be high-profile homicide cases. All of those were due to my boss and friend, Mike di Saronno, who used to be the highest-ranking detective in the department. But five years ago, my ex-wife had a ruptured aneurysm in her brain, which changed both her brain and my life.

Chapter Two

My name is Hugo Miller, and I am nearly 100% British (English-Irish-Scots) genetically, except that one of my grandfathers was pure German on both sides—his parents were immigrants from Prussia (yes, it was that long ago), so I guess I'm notionally 25% German (DNA analysis is more complicated, because sperms aren't nationalistic—not only that, but they're all different, and apparently there are really tens of millions of them in a normal ejaculation, so it's like a lottery, what a baby ends up looking like and growing up like).

In my case, I grew up in small towns in the eastern half of Texas until I was twelve. It was then that my dad got a great job offer in southern California and decided to move us all to a town near Los Angeles, close to the beach, where he would be working. I spent my teenage years in a beautiful seaside town called Palos Verdes Estates (*palos verdes* means "green sticks" in Spanish, and refers to a specific type of plant that I don't think I've ever seen, at least not live, maybe in pictures).

I was born when my dad was overseas, busy in the Normandy invasion on Omaha Beach right after D-Day. I think my mom was fairly certain he was dead when I was born, because the newspapers covered the invasion itself, and she knew he had been shipped out to England, so it seemed obvious that he was cannon-fodder on the beach with the other dead soldiers that the Nazis shot. So, although he was Catholic, she had me baptized in the Methodist church, which was how she had been raised.

As it turned out, he wasn't dead, wasn't shot, was all in one piece, even though he had been in the Normandy invasion, and then the Battle of the Bulge with Patton's troops. I think he had what we would call PTSD, but what would have been called then just "shell shock." He was always a drinker, and eventually Mom joined him in that.

I went to church twice every Sunday when I was a kid. First to the

Methodist church, frequently with my Texas grandparents, where I was put in Sunday School, and shuttled from the kids' area over to the church itself when it got to hymn-singing time, because I had a nice high boy-soprano voice. Then when I got home, Dad dragged me to Our Lady Queen of Peace, the Catholic Church, where I became fascinated with the magic of the Latin language. I remember thinking it was like a secret code of some kind. I would follow everything the priest said during mass in a book called a Missal, which had English translations and the Latin originals in columns next to each other.

When we moved to Los Angeles County, I was twelve and in the sixth grade, so it wasn't long before I was enrolled in a Catholic (Franciscan) high school, where I had four full years of Latin and two of Greek. My school was new and probably not fully accredited, but my grades were accepted by the University of California and I was accepted by UCLA, which was the school I wanted to go to. I originally wanted to go to Georgetown, so I could work in the Foreign Service—maybe be an ambassador to some fancy city in Europe. But Georgetown was too far away from California, according to my dad. That wasn't a time when people traveled by air at the drop of a hat. It took a lot of planning and money, and you wore a suit and tie when you got on a plane.

Yes, there were plane flights, but they were few and expensive, so I understood when my dad put the kibosh on my going to Georgetown or Fordham, which was close to where my NY grandparents (my dad's parents) lived. He also refused to pay for UCLA, because it was a "communist" school in his view. He wanted me to go to Notre Dame, which was where he graduated from, but I had no interest in living in winter-cold landlocked Indiana, having grown up in mild climates and near water—first, the Gulf of Mexico near Galveston, then within a hundred paces (and a nearly vertical cliff) of the Pacific Ocean in southern California. The Eisenhower years were a time when "communist" was a fairly common insult that maybe didn't really mean much in reality.

It was like calling a girl a name like "bitch," which had no specific meaning, but was still an insult. Americans worried about communists when Stalin was running the Soviet Union. I remember Senators McCarthy and Richard Nixon as commie hunters, trying to protect

Americans from totalitarianism. We had duck-and-cover practices in schools, where we learned to get under our desks if there was a bombing attack. I remember when Julius and Ethel Rosenberg were executed; I was destroyed because the Rosenberg kids' mom was killed by the government—and how could they live without their mom? I couldn't imagine what life would be like without my mom, and it made me cry a lot that the Rosenberg boys would lose their mother to the electric chair.

By the time we moved to California, that was all over. It was a year or so after Disneyland opened, and it was a big deal that we got to go to Disneyland, and write letters to our relatives about how wonderful it was, and what an E Ticket was. The theme song on TV was "When you wish upon a star, makes no difference who you are," and I remember singing that when we moved into our new house near a tall cliff where the Pacific Ocean lapped at the base in a small bay that was full of seaweed, anemones and mussels. The flats at the top of the cliff had wild anise plants—what the Italians call *finocchio*, almost like the little wooden puppet with the fast-growing nose in the animated movie, which I think is where the song I learned came from.

I studied Latin and Greek at UCLA, and took a full major in English literature (not American, just English), and had to read the same novels several times for different classes, including *Brideshead Revisited* and *Vanity Fair*. I managed to never read *Tristram Shandy* and *Ulysses;* neither of them made sense when I tried to dig into them.

It was the sixties, and education was all about self-fulfillment in those days. I had read that Shakespeare was poorly educated ("small Latin and less Greek"), and wanted to write plays, so I tried to improve myself by getting a more classical education. Sometime after I left UCLA, I discovered my favorite historian, John Julius Norwich, a Brit (of course) with the most elegant and easily understandable writing style of any nonfiction writer I've ever read.

I admired Tacitus when I read some of his work in Latin classes—especially the parts about Nero and Agrippina—but nobody has ever been as easy to learn from as Lord Norwich. His multi-volume history of Byzantium taught me more about the history of Christianity than I ever learned at either of the churches my family took me to—or catechism, for that matter. I'm still convinced that Constantine the Great shaped Christianity—the hierarchy, the centralization of doctrine and persecution of heretics, even the use of a cross on the tops of churches.

I also learned a lot about the history of Islam from Lord Norwich—not about dogma or sharia (religious law), but about the spread of Islam in the 7th and 8th centuries, when it burst out of Arabia and took over North Africa, the Middle East, not to mention Spain and even what we call Afghanistan and India, including the world's oldest civilizations in Egypt and Mesopotamia.

My first job after college was with a small educational publisher in Beverly Hills. I was a production editor, and later an acquisitions editor—which was a little boring, since the only books we published were in social science (sociology, criminology, anthropology, stuff like that). Nothing romantic, no fiction of any kind.

Eventually, I was able to parlay my experience in editing at a publishing house to a job with a big petroleum company that was headquartered in downtown Los Angeles, and was plopped down in their Public Affairs Department (most companies would have called it Public Relations), where I finally learned how to do something useful—I wrote speeches and quarterly reports for the shareholders, as well as editing some political papers to tone down criticism of the Alaska Pipeline, which was super controversial all over the United States. What if it sprang a leak? That was the question that all the nay-sayers wanted to get an answer to. By the way, I don't think it ever did spring a leak, at least not one I read about in the papers. There was a big oil spill in the ocean off Alaska; it was named after the ship that was carrying the oil, the Exxon Valdez.

Due to my big oil experience, I was hired by an international PR and Advertising company to head up the southern California territory that they were trying to become a leader in. The company was headquartered in the Midwest (Omaha), with offices all over the world, including places like London and Singapore, that I never thought I would ever see. My office was in Newport Beach, convenient to my Orange County home, but I had to drive three times a week to an office in Westwood, which, as it happens, is where UCLA is, so I was real familiar with it—but the traffic on the freeway made it a couple of hours in each direction. Eventually the southern California territory got enough of a boost to start growing of its own accord.

When that happened, I took a small real estate company that I was particularly close to, and left to start my own little company, where I decided to specialize in what was called "financial relations," where the chief line of business was writing Annual Reports and/or Shareholder Letters for public companies. That evolved into what got to be called "investor relations," and then we realized that we were most useful to our clients if we concentrated on bringing institutional investors and investment banks to small-cap companies at a time when small-cap companies were still really small, like under $100 million in market cap.

At that time, there were very few companies with a market capitalization in the hundreds of millions of dollars, much less billions or trillions, like there are today—and remember, all those mega-cap companies are built on the Internet, which we didn't have at all when I started my own investor relations company. It was a big deal for us when we helped a client raise a public offering of $6 million. Today, no investment bank would even consider a raise that small. We specialized in technology, which at that point meant healthcare (contact lenses were the latest and greatest, but we also took on gadgets for heart surgery, like oxygenators).

We also made a dent in another very young industry: computers, which had always been what they called "mainframes," but were starting to get smaller and more useful on the desktop. There were even "portable" "micro" computers the size and weight of a Singer sewing machine—that was the leading edge of technology, along with the silicon chips that ran them—mostly from Intel, where we did a major project for the famous CEO, Andy Grove. By the numbers though, we mostly dealt with "minicomputers," where one computer serviced many terminals that were called "slaves." Our clients were companies like General Automation, Digital Equipment Corp/DEC, Prime Computing, and software "operating system" companies like Pick Computing (founded by a guy named Dick Pick). We also worked with brand new companies near San Jose that were developing computers designed for a single desk, with

10

enough memory to replace a whole file cabinet. Those computers were what made the Internet a possibility.

There was no Internet. That was only thirty or forty years ago! I remember climbing under desks in hotels on the road to plug in a modem to a telephone line so I could send information and documents to our own home office; there was no way to send anything to clients. Documents had to be printed out and faxed if clients needed to see them.

We used what they called "wire services" to get our news releases disseminated. We'd fax them to the wire services, who would disseminate them on hard-wired networks to newspapers, radio/TV stations, magazines, and so forth. One of our clients was *Businessweek* magazine, which needed our help to get headlines of their new articles to radio commentators, who could help draw potential readers to McGraw-Hill. Radio and TV—particularly radio—were the kingpins of that part of the business back then, when magazines were still being read—magazines like *TIME* and *U.S. News & World Report*—names that still exist, but the magazines themselves have gone the way of all flesh.

Long story short, my wife and I were bickering pretty constantly at home. We hadn't been getting along well for a while (although we remained very friendly until she died, even after she was way deep in dementia over the last nearly seven years of her life). We lived separately for years, although it was unofficial (we stayed married, because neither of us wanted to divorce—I just traveled most of the time on business). Our two children were both over eighteen and no longer living at home. There was no reason why we had to maintain the concept of a small, close family, and I ended up opening an office in Manhattan, which we needed for the business we were in. But I couldn't find anyone capable of running that office, so I ended up just moving to Manhattan, to an apartment, which seemed temporary enough that I could still be married and my dwelling could still be in California.

We'd been married for more than 25 years when I moved to Manhattan. It wasn't as though we were a flash in the pan as a couple.

She had a terrible pain in her head one day when I was living in New York City. We were talking on the phone because I had just returned to NYC from visiting her and our granddaughters. I thought she was

11

having a stroke, but it turned out to be a ruptured blood vessel in her brain. When she got out of the hospital after a couple of long, complicated brain surgeries, she was clearly going to be damaged goods for as long as she stayed alive.

She had almost no short-term memory, although her long-term memory was more intact, at least for a while. She could remember her grandmother's maiden name, for instance. But she was increasingly delusional—the rehab hospital/nursing home where she was staying was, in her mind, a ship that was sinking, and she was afraid she would drown because she never learned how to swim. That level of delusion became less common and less scary over a couple of years, but it would have been clear to any sane person that she could never live without 24-7 skilled nursing care.

I took to visiting her with lunch in a bag, so we could eat together. Over the years, we had good experiences having dinner together, and she was always very happy when I took Chinese food or Mexican food for lunch, because the food in the nursing home was bland and repetitious— lots of mashed potatoes with little or no salt, and roasted chicken with no flavorings other than what was natural in the chicken skin.

Because of rising rents, I had moved away from Manhattan, to save money. I ended up in Long Island City, which is a historic community in the NYC borough of Queens. It has, however, more the look and feel of Manhattan than what they call the "outer boroughs." High-rises, upwardly-mobile youngish people in the apartments. Diverse racially and ethnically, as I had become used to living near Times Square for half a decade. I loved living in the Theater District, but it was much too expensive to keep shelling out for, at least for me. My apartment was about $2000 per month when I moved in. Ten years later, it was going to be $15,000 per month. Who could pay that? Not me. So I left Manhattan and moved to Queens.

Living just off Times Square had become fashionable. And the more fashionable it got, the higher the rent got. My beautiful apartment was on the 34th floor of a newish building, and had more windows than any apartment I had ever seen before. Lots of sunlight, and views to the north (some treetops in Central Park), west (the Hudson River and New

Jersey Palisades) and south (Times Square), with windows on three sides of the building. The master bedroom, where I slept, had windows on two of the four walls. Heaven.

But the rent went straight up, year after year, and finally was no longer tolerable. I ended up in Long Island City, which was a place where wannabe Manhattanites could live in a Manhattan-type style, but without the Manhattan rents that were no joke, no matter where on that freaking island you wanted to live. Alphabet City (the East Village) was overpriced. FiDi was overpriced (FiDi = Financial District/Wall Street area, wayyyyy downtown). The Upper West was not only overpriced—it had a critical lack of garage spaces, because zoning hadn't required underground parking to be built into the apartments and condos there. Find street parking or get rid of your car. Imagine a Californian without a car. Ha!

The standard get-up for Manhattanite men at that point was jeans and a black T-shirt, and that's what I wore (still do). I knew that when I saw a guy in a black T-shirt, he was a local, so to speak. Local girls wore blue jeans and T-shirts of a variety of colors and patterns, but nothing with advertising on it.

The apartment I moved into in LIC was about the same size, but it also had a clothes washer and dryer, so I didn't have to go to a basement laundry room in order to do a load of wash. Most of all, the rent was close to the $2,000 I had started with in my 34th-floor cliff dwelling in the Theater District—which I had rented because I could walk to work.

From LIC, I had to take a subway to get to work. We had moved the office from 30 Rock to near Madison Square (a gentrifying part of Manhattan with the gay Chelsea district on the west, and the famous Flatiron Building in the middle). Our office was at 5th Avenue and 20th Street. So I could take a subway train from LIC's Vernon-Jackson station to Grand Central, and then take a reasonable, like 20-minute, walk from there (42nd Street) to 20th Street. A city block in Manhattan is 20 blocks to the mile, so it was just over a mile—flat, not hilly—from the train to the office. Not bad, weather permitting. I tried to travel in the winter, to get better weather.

Anyway, when my wife was still in the hospital in California, I packed up everything in the house, gave a lot of it away to relatives and even more to charities—like thousands of LP records to the library, and shipped most of my favorite paintings and rugs to myself in LIC.

Then I put the house on the block. Fortunately for me, it sold quickly, but for a price that was not even close to what I had expected (we were in a real estate dip—or depression). You can't turn a house into money unless you sell it. Otherwise houses are money-pits, even while you have them on the market for sale.

Be that as it may, I thought I might be able to take care of my wife's sadly diminished body and mind at my apartment in LIC.

Not.

The first night we were at my apartment in Long Island City, she set fire to the kitchen while she was trying to make some coffee. There were still boxes everywhere in the living room and bedrooms. There were paintings leaning on the hallway walls, waiting to be mounted someplace. She had tried to make some coffee in a percolator on the stove, and left a dishtowel on top of the range, where it caught fire. When I realized what had happened, there were small flaming pieces of cloth floating all around the kitchen. I grabbed a couple of wet towels from the bathroom and swatted the fires and embers out, and—breathing hard—I realized I couldn't take care of her by myself. I also knew I might not ever fall asleep again if she was in the house.

Fortunately, because I had an aunt who was a nun, we were able to get her right away into a good Catholic nursing home in Westchester County. Upshot was that I moved her to the nursing home, and moved myself from LIC to Yonkers, which isn't even in NYC. But it was close to where the nursing home was, so I could visit and be a real Health Proxy. I was still in an apartment, but this time it was a co-op, which is a New York invention that's more complicated than advanced algebra. Suffice it to say, you don't rent your apartment—you buy shares in the building and then pay a maintenance fee every month to continue in the apartment, where there is technically no rent. Sound odd? It is.

Chapter Three

So the question at the Excalibre building in Yonkers was actually two questions. Why did the Latino guy jump or fall off the roof? And why was Mr. Bliss out for a walk at exactly that time? Did he do it every day at exactly the same time? If he heard a scream or a yell, why didn't he duck out of the way? If he had moved four feet in any direction, he would have been okay. Not that it was his fault that he was killed, but it was just a crying shame that it happened. It would have been the same if somebody lost control of a car and hit him after running up onto the sidewalk.

The Latino suicide fellow had a family name from El Salvador—most of his family, though, lived in Yonkers—his name was Felipe Barrio. He owned an apartment in the building in his own name—with no mortgage—on the 14th floor, which he shared with a pretty White girl named Lela Swann, who told the cops she was his fiancée; in other words, that they were engaged to be married.

No, she said, they had not set a date for the marriage, and she was not wearing an engagement ring. But they were engaged, and planned to marry and have children. When the cops asked her in an interrogation room at the local precinct near the subway station, she told them she hadn't noticed him acting strangely, and she hadn't seen him hanging out with any new people she'd never seen before, but she knew that he had money problems and was having trouble paying his monthly bills.

Was he abusive?

No, not even once.

Did he use any drugs? No. At least that's what she told the cops.

Danny O'Toole and Mike both wondered if she was pregnant. She seemed very emotional, but her fiancée had just been killed, so maybe that was it. If she was pregnant, it could be very early. Did she have a brother or a father who might have been pissed off with her hanging out with Felipe?

No.

Was she seeing any other guys while she was dating Felipe?

That last question got a sexy smile, but a negative shake of the head, accompanied by a very firm "No." She looked at the cop like he might be flirting with her, and kept a ghost of the sexy smile on her face, with the corners of her mouth turned up and her dimples showing.

Did he ever get drunk? Not that she could remember, just a drink here and there, mostly scotch, she thought, and only at restaurants—no bottles of scotch at home. Or sometimes he would order a Stella Artois beer, but not ever more than one, and there was usually beer in the fridge at home, too. He was a fitness junkie, and worked out at LA Fitness at the Ridge Hill shopping area there in Yonkers. He also did push-ups and crunches every morning at home. Several sets of both.

The DA's office took the case to the Grand Jury, which quickly decided that this was a suicide with a possible accidental homicide attached. Nobody to prosecute yet, until the handgun gave them some further hints as to who else was there when Felipe fell off the edge of the roof.

After Mike di Saronno resigned from the NYPD during the Asian Hate and Black Lives Matter times in New York City, he rented a small office at the corner of 5th Avenue and 20th Street, on the 5th floor of the same building I had an office in once upon a time. It was a landmark building at 156 5th Avenue. Beautiful lobby with a fancy ceiling, very antique and European-looking. Nice big windows in the office, but only with views basically of the exteriors of the building across 20th Street on the downtown side of the building. The southern exposure meant that there would almost never be an afternoon sun beating through the windows, so the AC didn't have to work hard to keep the office comfortable even on hot, muggy days. He had his own conference room *en suite*, and splurged on a big conference table with a wooden top and modern-looking ergonomic black chairs with open-net backs to keep people cool. No sweat, as they say.

Mike asked me to come over with Ruth and Gabriele to talk about the suicide in Yonkers. He had been hired by the Bliss family, who picked his name up out of the newspaper, to look into what happened, and to advise them on whether to sue somebody for negligence—maybe like the building itself, for not adequately locking up the exits to the roof.

"Do the three of you have time to head up to Yonkers and have a look at the roof where this happened?" he asked us, as though there were a possibility that we wouldn't do what he wanted.

"You're the boss," I said to him. "Obviously, we're going to do what you want us to do. We can take a train from Grand Central this afternoon if you can arrange for us to get into the building and onto the roof."

The train station was Greystone on the Metro-North Hudson Line, less than 40 minutes each way, and a lot less if the trains didn't stop at all the stations. Could be just over a half-hour ride each way, depending on which trains we took.

The four of us walked to Grand Central from Mike's office, up Madison Avenue all the way, going past the Morgan Library about halfway there. JP Morgan's actual home. He was the one man who ever prevented a market crash by posting his own fortune to back up the markets. That's what JP did when the Panic of 1907 was frightening banks and businesses all across America. The Panic took place over a three-week period, when the New York Stock Exchange fell by almost half its value. It was a time of full-blown recession, and there were numerous runs on banks and trust companies. Panic spread from sea to shining sea when banks and businesses started filing for bankruptcy.

The Panic was triggered by a failed attempt to corner the market on stock of the then-blue-chip United Copper Company. When that attempt failed, banks that had lent money to the cornering scheme suffered runs on deposits that later spread to many other banks and trusts, leading quickly to the crash of the Knickerbocker Trust Company, a leading national depository trust. It was one of the largest plunges in U.S. stock market history.

Morgan was able to arrest additional panic by pledging his own money, which led other bankers to do the same. The banking system was stabilized and saved. And today his home and his personal library are open to the public on Madison Avenue and 36th Street. Wow. Only in

New York.

Well, we got to Greystone and took an Uber car to the co-op tower where Felipe Barrio had fallen twenty stories to the street, hitting Mr. Bliss, who was out for his morning constitutional at exactly the wrong moment. Mike had arranged for us to get onto the roof through the same route that Barrio had probably used—up the elevator to the top apartment floor and then a short flight of stairs to the roof level.

The roof at the top of the stairs was flat like a terrace, but was covered with fine crushed white stone—shiny like quartz, that crunched under our shoes as we walked. There were cigarette butts everywhere, like this was a place you could go for a smoke when you didn't want to risk going for a walk on the street. A Yonkers cop Mike had talked to showed us where the handgun was found.

"Why would they have that crushed stone on the floor?" I asked.

"Probably to keep it from being slippery," Danny the cop said. "You know if it rains, a painted cement-sheathed floor like this can be like ice on a sidewalk. Either you add fine gravel to the cement before it's poured, so that the surface is rough and not slippery. Or if you prefer, you can put something like this crushed stone down so that even leather-bottom shoes will not slip and slide around, especially if it rains. Problem with the crushed stone is that it's uncomfortable for people wearing flip-flops or if they get a stone in their shoe. There's always a layer of dust on a surface like this, and that dust can turn to mud if it's not kept really clean all the time. Ice is more slippery than mud, but mud can be pretty goddamn slippery by itself when it's wet."

He was staring at the floor, and added, "Cigarette butts can be slippery if they're wet, too. Leather-bottom shoes can be dangerous on a surface like that.

"The gun is in the Yonkers PD evidence lock-up now," he said. "We can arrange for you to see it if you need to, in order for Mr. di Saronno to move forward with his case. It just has to stay on the premises, and one of our evidence guys has to watch while you handle it, to keep the chain of evidence from being violated."

He told us that the YPD had total trust in Mike, based on his long service to the NYPD, and his sterling law degree from Columbia

University, not to mention his work for the Innocence Project.

We told him that we didn't need to see the gun, but we would need to see any forensic materials that might be used in a civil trial as to who was responsible for what happened. There wasn't a lot to see on the roof, just the corner where Felipe fell from, and the bricked-in pony wall where the gun was found. And the tons of cigarette butts

We were back at Grand Central just in time to hit the Oyster Bar for a quick cocktail. Then Ruth walked off to the Lexington Avenue subway to take a train to 59th Street, so she could get home to her apartment at Park Avenue and 61st Street. Gabriele called an Uber to take him to Ora di Pranzo. I walked up to the Frick Collection for a quick walk-through to see some of my favorite paintings, and later made my way back to Yonkers to my apartment, boarding this time at 125th Street instead of Grand Central. I ordered some food for an early dinner from DoorDash®—a Caesar salad and some tortellini Alfredo. There was a corked-up but already opened bottle of Montepulciano d'Abruzzo on the dining table. It was a perfect companion for the food that arrived via the Dasher, whom I tipped in cash when I went downstairs to meet him. When I used to visit Mary at the nursing home, it was always for lunch, because I didn't want to interfere with the dinnertime routine that the dementia patients were used to. I almost always had dinner at home, because of the pandemic, and tried to keep enough ingredients to be able to make my own dinners a lot of evenings.

Since I don't eat red meat (not for over 30 years now), I keep spicy turkey sausages for Italian dishes—one of my favorites is those sausages, with lots of sauteed chopped garlic cooked with fresh chopped rapini (broccoli rabe), smothered with pecorino romano cheese. I probably have that two or three times a week. Very nutritious, and very tasty. I love the taste of the rapini, in particular. The garlic gets stuck in my teeth, so I have to floss for quite a while after I have it.

Chapter Four

"Hey, did you see the cigarette stubs on the roof when we were there?" Gabriele asked me when he called during the seven o'clock news on CNBC (I've always been a news junkie, and keep the TV turned on to the latest news whenever I can find it). CNBC was founded as a stock-market channel—originally called the Financial News Network (FNN), but changed its name to CNBC when it was acquired by NBC, along about the time of their deal with Microsoft to form MSNBC, another news-only business plan that took off soon after being announced. Now it has a superb news hour on weekday evenings at 7PM NY time, featuring a fine anchor/reporter named Shepard Smith. He covers the waterfront, so even after I watch the ABC World News at 6:30, there's always something new on the CNBC news at 7PM.

Yes, I had taken note of the cigarette butts, but it wasn't the only time I had seen a place people go to smoke. I told him that I see cigarette butts in lots of places, and don't always pay attention. There are places in all the city parks in Manhattan where people go to smoke. Sometimes you can tell where you are by the smells of stale cigarette butts.

"I just wondered if whoever was there on the roof with Mr. Barrio was smoking," Gabriele said. "I talked to Ruth, and she said she thought it was worth looking into. After all, there could be DNA on the butts, from saliva on the filtered ends. DNA is even better evidence than fingerprints sometimes. Like on a cigarette butt, if you can find the person whose saliva is on the cigarette."

I agreed.

He asked me if I had eaten.

"I ordered food delivered from the local pizza joint," I told him. "Not pizza, but a salad and some pasta."

He asked what kind of salad and pasta. I told him.

"Not good," he said. "Caesar salad and alfredo sauce too much same food, like eating pasta to start and pasta to end. Too much dairy product. Next time have pasta with red sauce, or some kind *zuppa*, instead of salad," he told me.

"Yes, Mommy," I answered. I could see him smiling at the other end of the phone. "You at Ora di Pranzo?"

Yes, he said—he was at the restaurant. I told him I would be there as soon as I could get there after the news was over at 8PM. I was thinking of having some blackberries and blueberries with milk for dessert. But I also just wanted to talk, and I'm old enough that telephone talk just isn't the same thing as face-to-face talk. I volunteer at a local park on the weekends, so I can talk to real people, because I get tired of just talking on the phone.

"Good," he said. "Ruth coming over, too."

I had been end-run, but it was okay. "Is Mike going to be there?"

No.

I changed my shirt because I had sweated profusely earlier in the day and I didn't want to stink. So I put on a fresh T-shirt and a lightweight rayon button-front shirt over it, with an abstract pattern of lines and boxes. I try not to wear Hawaiian flowered prints, because I'm afraid it will make me look like a tourist from Iowa. Even with a quick sponge bath, I was in my car in less than 10 minutes, and heading toward Manhattan. In the evening, cars are better than waiting for trains, which tend to only leave about once an hour. I'd have to pay for a parking garage, but since Gabriele never charges me for anything, it would be okay no matter what it cost to park.

There was almost no traffic on the Saw Mill Parkway or on the West Side Highway. I was really looking forward to being with Gabriele and Ruth and having my berries for dessert. They usually have the dark-colored berries that I like. I don't favor the red berries, like raspberries or strawberries—and the dark ones are super-foods, super-nutritious and worth eating, even with milk on them (lactic acid is not great nutritionally). I'm getting old enough that I try to only eat things that are worthwhile putting in my stomach. Seldom eat ice cream anymore, which is a sure mark of aging, at least in my case.

21

Splat!!

I was walking into Ora di Pranzo a little more than 45 minutes after I walked out the door of my apartment, so it wasn't even nine o'clock when I got there. Gabriele was waiting for me with a huge bear hug. I'm not attracted to him sexually—too straight, I guess, to even think about it. But I grew up being a hugger and I still am one. Hugging is life-prolonging. Ruth was already there (she was only coming from Park and 61st, and using the subway, which is the fastest way to get anywhere in the City except Staten Island, which has no subways). Ruth and I did the double-cheek-kiss thing, like Europeans. No hugs.

When Gabriele put us at a table in the back of the restaurant, I said to the two of them, "So, cigarette butts?"

Ruth nodded, and Gabriele said, "I see many on roof, on floor in white rocks. Different kinds, some filter, some no filter. I hate cigarette, smell bad and make room smell bad." H pulled a baggie out of his breast pocket and showed it to us. It had several cigarette butts in it. A couple were just tobacco butts, but most of them were distinctive-looking filters that looked like Marlboro Lights or Viceroys.

"Are there more still there?" I asked him.

He nodded vigorously. "Many more."

"Because the ones you collected wouldn't be good as evidence anymore," I said, "because we only have your word that they're from the roof area where Felipe went over the edge. Near where the gun was found."

He looked abashed.

"Evidence found at the scene has to be very carefully handled and packaged according to police procedures, and submitted to the evidence files, usually without ever being touched by human hands, except with latex gloves on," I said. "You can't take them home and show them to us later, and still think they're good as evidence."

He frowned and called a busboy over to the table. When he got there, Gabriele put the butts back in the baggie and handed it to the busboy, telling him to trash the baggie.

Sad, but it seemed like the right thing to do.

I used to smoke when I was a teenager, most likely because I grew up with smokers. My mother smoked like a chimney, and her father (my grandfather) the same, but he wasn't a chain smoker, didn't light one cigarette from the one he had been smoking before. My mom was a chain smoker, seldom using matches, lighting a new cigarette from the last one. All her butts went into ash trays though, which guaranteed that every room in the house smelled like tobacco ashes. I got used to it by the time I was a teenager, and started smoking myself. I smoked for about ten or twenty years, and then quit when Mary and I had kids. After that I would have one every once in a while, but they made me cough, so I stopped completely.

My dad jumped all over me when he saw me with a cigarette when I was about sixteen. He had smoked Lucky Strikes when I was little (an Army habit, I think, because neither of his parents smoked, at least not cigarettes). My NY grandfather smoked cigars sometimes and a pipe other times, but no cigarettes. Neither of my grandmothers smoked anything—it wasn't ladylike, and they were both ladies for sure. My NY grandmother had emphysema anyway, and had lots of what they called "small" strokes. She died younger than one would have expected, in her early 70s. Maybe it was related to the secondary smoke from the cigars and pipes—or maybe the fires in the fireplaces, of which there were many in that old house—for heating purposes principally. But even with two heavy smokers in the house, my Texas grandmother lived to be nearly 90 and never had lung problems. Go figure.

American Indians must have had a high incidence of COPD because they all had fires in their dwellings to fend off the winter chills. Imagine living in a wigwam with a fire in the middle of it. Makes my eyes water just thinking about it.

I dialed Mike's new number on my cellphone and briefly told him when he answered about Gabriele's collection of cigarette butts. Like I figured, he was not pleased, but he was also not angry.

"Most of the cigarette butts in places like that wouldn't tell us much anyway. The roof is usually a place to go to smoke when you can't smoke where you are. And it might be one of the last places where you could stamp the butts out on the floor," he said. "Tell Gabriele it's okay, just not to do it again. Next time he sees something like that, he should tell the cops, and not take it into his own hands."

Chapter Five

Mike promptly sent a text to all three of us, telling us to try to plan to be back at the scene the next day by 1PM, so that the local cops could have a look around, and Gabriele could point out what he had seen. Both Gabriele and Ruth replied that they would be there on time. I replied that I would not be there, because I didn't think I had anything to add to the situation.

Mike was cool with that. He said he would have to tell his clients in the Bliss family what had happened, but otherwise things should be okay.

Mike suggested that he might stop by my apartment later, to have a chat. He realized that I was living in Yonkers, and that wasn't a problem. He suggested that he would try to be there by 8PM, and asked what parking was like where I lived.

"There's usually street parking," I told him. "But if you can't find anything, I can show you a parking slot where you can leave your car safely and not get towed away. Do you still have an NYPD sticker on your car?"

Yes, he did.

"Well," I said, "you'll probably be generally okay wherever you park."

Mike showed up on the dot. I poured him a dirty vodka, and one for myself. I had gorged myself on blackberries and blueberries at Ora di Pranzo the night before, with whipped cream slathered all over them. Even though I had eaten abstemiously all day, I felt like my stomach was still distended, and the vodka would help me relax.

"Look," I said to him, "I knew that the cigarette ends he collected wouldn't be of any use, and I was there when he told the busboy to throw them in the garbage. Sorry, boss."

24

"Not a problem," he said. "I doubt they would have been any help. You said they were of several different types, some with filters of various kinds, and some with no filters at all."

I nodded.

"So they had most likely been there for a while, and not just dropped on the floor that same day," he said. "It's the gun that we need to concentrate on. We need to see if it was fired, and if it was, see whether there's a slug someplace. We also need to alert the coroner that a gun may have been fired, so if there is a flesh wound that could have been caused by a bullet, we need to know."

I sipped on my vodka, and realized that he was concentrating hard on making me feel better." I said something to that effect to him, like "Mike, don't worry about me. I'm okay."

"I'm not worried about you," he said slowly and carefully. "What I'm worried about is whether I can help my clients find any evidence that would allow them to file some kind of civil suit against either Excalibre Properties or the Yonkers PD, for mis-handling evidence." I pointed out that the Yonkers PD cops didn't see the butts, and consequently didn't collect any of them. If they were really all over the place, it would have been obvious that the roof was an unofficial smokers' lounge, and would have nothing to do with the suicide or the accidental homicide.

"According to the autopsy, the only grunge in Barrio's lungs would have matched just breathing the everyday air in Yonkers, where the air is as polluted as it would be in midtown Manhattan, due to auto exhaust and the frequent lack of wind and/or rain that might have cleaned up the air somewhat."

"You're right," I said. "We haven't had much rain in a couple of weeks." My windowsills were covered with dust and grunge. So was the roof of my car, which I had left in the parking lot for several days. I could have written my name on the car—or I could have written 'WASH ME' in all caps if I wanted to be a smart-alec.

"I'm not a cop anymore," he said. "Don't forget that. My duty is to my client, in this case all the relatives of Bob Bliss, who was hit and killed by Felipe Barrio when he fell, which I personally am inclined to think was an accident, not a suicide." He said he thought it would be a very difficult suit to win unless there was some kind of dramatic change in the evidence—not just a few cigarette butts.

He stared out the window at the hills and trees, which were directly behind my television. The TV is a flat-screen that sits on the flat top of a mahogany buffet that was backed up to a wall below a window, which allowed me to see the beautiful verdant landscape any time I looked up from whatever was on TV.

He was leaning against the buffet while he stared out the window. It didn't bother me, but he realized all of a sudden that he was leaning on it, and jerked back so that he wasn't touching it anymore. The buffet itself contained some of my parents' fancy china that had been given to them at the time they were married during World War 2. The buffet was heavy to start off with, and even heavier with a Lenox service for ten or twelve stacked inside it. I leaned on the chest very obviously.

"This chest is unlikely to move without movers and a moving van," I said. Then I opened the small doors on the front of the buffet and showed him the stacks of china. "I have to figure out who to give this to when I die. I'm afraid nobody in the family will want it. It's for sure from a different time in history. Who's going to set a table with china like that these days? I used to use it at Thanksgiving, but these days it's impossible to have a traditional Thanksgiving family feast—because of COVID-19 if nothing else."

He smiled. "We're even, then," he said. "No amount of cigarette butts is going to help the Bliss family pay for a funeral," he said. "It's like you worrying about that beautiful china, and not knowing what to do with it. Sweating it doesn't help. It's possible that if we could check for DNA from all the butts on the roof, we could come up with something. More likely if we see who's smoking up there tonight, it's more likely that the same people were there when Felipe fell. Maybe somebody heard a gunshot. That would help." He cleared his throat.

"Let me change the subject, sorry," he said. "You've met Danny O'Toole, who is the head detective from the Yonkers PD. We're going to be working with him on this case. And I think it would be just as well if the two of you could shake hands or elbow-bump, or whatever is in vogue that doesn't spread the coronavirus."

I agreed, and asked when and where he thought it might work. "I think Danny ought to meet Gabriele and Ruth, too, just in case they run into each other along the way to figuring out who did what to whom when Barrio sailed off the roof—and what kind of settlement the Bliss family ought to get from Excalibre Properties."

I told Mike that I knew for a fact that Gabriele knew the guy who ran an Italian restaurant in the downtown part of Yonkers. "It's called Zuppa," I said, "and Gabriele told me it's a high point in the foodie part of Yonkers. Soup is like *pasta e fagioli* or *minestrone.* The one is all dried beans and dried pasta, and the other one is all vegetables and dried beans, maybe some pieces of pasta, like orzo—small pastas, not long stringy ones like spaghetti or linguine—and no meat. Zuppa is frequently a bowl of stewed fresh vegetables, but it can also be a bowl of seafood, with some reddish broth that keeps it wet and succulent. Shrimps and fish and mussels, stuff like that. Onions. Fun to eat, and tasty as it comes. Sprinkle some cheese over it and it gets even better. Anyway, that's the name of the restaurant, Zuppa.

"Then there's what the Italians call Zuppa Inglese, which means English Soup. But that one is a very sweet dessert dish full of sugar, fruit, custard and ladyfingers."

Chapter Six

Danny O'Toole was short and stocky: the opposite of tall, slim Mike di Saronno. But they were both from families of cops—just that Danny was Irish and Mike was Italian. They looked like Mutt and Jeff.

"Same difference," Danny said. "Both of us are mackerel-snappers. We eat fish on Fridays, and so did our grandparents and their grandparents. The big Vatican Counsel that suspended the fish on Friday rule—it has always been ignored in families like ours. In our house, Friday means shrimp, for instance. Shrimp don't stink like fish. Kids don't refuse to taste them, or screw up their faces when you even mention it."

Mike nodded. "Only difference is that all Irish food is boiled, and Italian food is made all different types of ways. Look at pizza, for instance. There's nothing that's less boiled-tasting than pizza."

"Not true," Danny fired back. "We have shepherd's pie, which is in a crust with leftover mashed potatoes on top. Best of the best. But corned beef is boiled for sure—with cabbage. Heaven. And in Italy, all that soup is boiled, I'd have to say."

When they dropped the subject of the food they grew up with, pretty soon we were standing on the sidewalk, looking up at the twenty-story high-rise where Felipe Barrio took a dive onto the pavement.

"Glad I wasn't here when it happened. Must have been a mess," I said.

"Not as bad as you think," Danny said. "What's really a mess is when a jumper lands on a car. Totals the car, and splatters of blood and stuff everywhere. Ever seen an eye that's not in a body anymore? They're bigger than you expect them to be."

I remembered reading a newspaper article when I was a kid about President Kennedy's wife being served a calf's eye, "Armenian." I felt like throwing up when I read the paper that day. It was raw, and the writer said it was tough to chew. Ugh.

I asked Danny if Barrio had any record of arrests.

No, and he had spent his whole life in Yonkers, although he was born in El Salvador or someplace south of the border. His family took him to the USA to visit his mother's brother—Uncle Steve, in the family—in New Rochelle when he was still a toddler. During that trip, Felipe was invited to live with a friend of Uncle Steve's in Yonkers, near the Bronx River Parkway, which was basically the border between Yonkers and Mount Vernon, a smaller neighboring town to the east of Yonkers. Mount Vernon is mostly between Yonkers and New Rochelle— but they're not very far apart.

His pretty girlfriend, Lela, edged her way into the interrogation room we were in at the precinct where Danny was officed. From elementary school through high school, Lela said, "He was a Yonkers boy all the way. He went to college at Iona College in New Rochelle. When he was there, it was a boys-only college, with a sister school called New Rochelle College that was all-girls—and that was where I was going to school. We used to go to dances that our two schools were putting on. I loved dancing with him."

These days Iona is co-ed, so the girls who might have been at New Rochelle a few years before might be going to school at Iona with the guys, or to Mercy College in Dobbs Ferry, which the College of New Rochelle had merged with before the New Rochelle buildings were torn down and sold for residential development. Mercy College was originally run by Mercy Sisters, but starting before 2010, it became strictly secular, no more nuns anywhere. And it's entirely co-ed, both males and females—but with a main campus close to the Hudson River, on the other side of the County from New Rochelle.

Lela stared at Danny and said that Felipe had worked in various eateries as a cook, a bartender and a waiter, depending on which type of work you asked him about.

Lela had known him for well over half her life, although they only started really spending all their time together when she was in college. She had been his girlfriend off and on since high school. "He tried to get hired at the high-end restaurants in town," she said, "like one on an old barge that was anchored or tied up close to Main Street downtown and called X20 or Xavier's (either one), but it never happened. He thought it was because he was Latino-looking with tan or light-brown skin. Today you could sue a place for that kind of discrimination, and you would win, of course.

"He thought if he could work at the higher-class places, he would be better paid. But as it turned out, he was still always short of money," Lela said. "We were going to get married, but he wanted to have a real wedding—in a church, with a priest. And he wanted to get me a ring," she said, showing her ringless left hand.

"The rings were all expensive," she said, "so we didn't get there because he wanted to save up to get a ring that he would be proud for me to wear."

Both Lela and Felipe were Catholic, and both were church-goers every Sunday and holy days of obligation. Felipe did a novena of First Fridays once a year, too.

"He always put money in the collection basket when they brought it around," she said. "He was a good man, and he supported the church we went to." That was St Anthony's; it was on a street that ran parallel to the Saw Mill Parkway in the middle of Yonkers—not far from where that magazine, *Consumer Reports*, has its offices. There aren't a lot of famous companies in Yonkers. It's where Otis Elevators came from, in the old downtown area around Getty Square, but Otis was bought by some big conglomerate years before, she told us. "The real Saint Anthony was from Spain or Portugal, but he spent a lot of time in Italy, and they call him St Anthony of Padua, but the church is just called St Anthony's.

"He worried about paying the bills," she said, sounding a little chattier. "I don't know why we moved into that building. It was too expensive, but Felipe wanted to be middle-class. We couldn't afford it. I was studying accounting at nights, and had a full-time job as a clerk with a CPA company. But even with my salary every two weeks, we couldn't pay everything we needed to pay. I was getting paid more than minimum wage, but no real benefits—no health insurance, for instance. I think if he did what the police think he did, it was because he was going crazy worrying about where to get the money he needed to pay bills with."

She put her hands on her neck and scratched her chin, then said, "There was a portrait of Padre Pio there at St Anthony's. He liked that," she told us, referring to a twentieth century holy man and priest from Italy. She clearly wanted to change the subject away from money and bills.

"He had the stigmata, Padre Pio," she said. "He had the same wounds that Jesus had in his hands and feet—just like St Francis did a long time ago. Padre Pio was a Franciscan priest some place in Italy. He was canonized by Pope John Paul II when Felipe and I were in high school, so he was a saint, and we could pray to him to help us. But Felipe needed more help than Padre Pio sent him from Heaven."

She started to bite on the nails of her right hand, like she was trying to trim them down. It looked like she was biting her cuticle on the sides of her fingers, too. Nerves.

"Is it possible he was doing some work on the side that might have got him in trouble?" Danny asked her. "Maybe helping guys he knew sell watches or things that somebody might have picked up someplace or even stolen? Or selling some small-time drugs, like marijuana? Those things might have fit right in with his work at restaurants."

She shrugged. "He would roll some grass sometimes and smoke it, but he never did any real drugs, and I never saw him drink a lot either. Father John at St Anthony's said it wasn't sinful to smoke some weed once in a while; it was like having a glass of wine with dinner. He may have been selling grass to some of the guys in the neighborhood. I don't think he was doing anything illegal though. Marijuana isn't, like, legal— but it's not really illegal anymore." She said the word like: "IL-legal."

"She means the cops won't arrest anybody for grass these days," Danny said under his breath. "Unless there's a truckload of it."

Then he took me aside and told me that they had a warrant issued and they'd had a look at Felipe's bank account.

Lela seemed to know where Danny was headed, and added, "He had a very low balance in his checking account most of the time; sometimes he would write bad checks and end up paying really expensive fees for checks that bounced. Whenever he would get paid and make a deposit, he'd write checks to pay bills right away—TV cable, electricity, or there was a monthly maintenance cost of the apartment. He was getting a lot of overdue charges to his checking account, too."

"There's nothing that leaves raw skin like money problems," Mike said. "I can see how that might make him step off the roof, even if he wasn't planning to do it."

"Accidental suicide?" Ruth asked. "Is there such a thing? Like accidental homicide?"

Mike responded. "Suicide determination is not standardized in the law, and a lot of suicides are later classified as 'accidental' or 'undetermined.' Sometimes there are psychiatric issues that need to be taken into account. That kind of suicide is likely to be male, and violent, maybe with a family history of suicide. He wasn't ill, as far as we know. Was he in pain ever? Did he need drugs to help him sleep?"

"He took some pills, but I don't really know what they were for," Lela said. "I didn't go to the doctor with him. The pills are probably in the drawer by the bed, or in the medicine cabinet in the bathroom," she said. "Have a look. Don't worry about me."

Danny rummaged around after putting a pair of blue nitrile gloves on, and came up with two orange plastic pill containers that had CVS pharmacy logos on them. He put them into a manila envelope and handed them to one of the CSIs to be logged in.

"Anti-depressants and sedatives," Danny said to Mike and the three of us who were with Mike. "Valium, nothing unusual or expensive. It looks to me like he was on Medicaid anyway, so he wouldn't have had to pay for prescriptions like Valium. But Valium might make it easier to step over the edge of the roof, I guess. It wouldn't encourage him to do it, but it might make him feel like everything would work out, no matter what he did."

"I wouldn't know," Mike said. "I'm not a doctor."

"Neither am I," Danny said. "Not trying to accuse anybody of anything, just collecting evidence." He sounded like he was defending himself.

Lela looked back and forth from Danny to Mike and back again to Danny.

"When I was in the hospital after my kidney surgery," I said, "they gave me Valium to help me sleep at night. I didn't feel like I was getting hit with a sledge-hammer, but I did go to sleep a heck of a lot more easily when they gave me the Valium pills. They also fed Tylenol into my arm through my IV, and that made it easier, too." Tylenol, hmmm. Interesting how much more potent it seemed to be in the IV, as opposed to taking tablets by mouth. I guess it was because it went straight into the bloodstream, instead of going into the digestive tract, and making its way to the bloodstream later on.

"I think we should find out if Lela would be willing to testify to the Grand Jury," Danny said to Mike. I overheard what he said, and thought Mike should ignore what he was being told.

"None of my business," Mike said. "If she's going to testify, in my experience it's always a good idea to talk to a good lawyer before she goes in to answer questions from some ADA. A little practice or preparation or rehearsal never hurts, especially if it gives you an idea of what the questions might be, and how you might want to answer. It's scary when a witness trips over their own tongue trying to answer a surprise question."

"Any *informazione* about *pistola* where Barrio stand *quando è saltato giù dal tetto* ("when he fell off the roof")?" Gabriele asked Danny directly, mixing some Italian words with some English words. There are times when he speaks English with no accent and commonplace American grammar, but there are also times when he mixes them up, maybe to get extra attention. Something he does at Ora di Pranzo, where he conveys more Italian-ness than he does otherwise. It's hard to tell if he is doing it on purpose or not, in any given situation. Fortunately, Danny seemed to understand what Gabriele was asking him.

"Nothing new that I've been told," Danny said. "As far as I know, the CSIs aren't acting optimistic about lifting fingerprints from the gun. Problems with the cross-hatching, and problems with the smearing or blurring of the bits of prints that they could see on the scope when they were examining the gun. They did get prints from Mr. Barrio's hands at the morgue, though, so that end is taken care of. If he held the gun, it might be possible to tell. Except that the prints we found there were all smeared and blurry, and most of them in small bits and pieces that would be hard to work with, even if they were pristine and clear."

Mike added, "If the CSIs try to restore them or backtrack them to see what the prints looked like before they were smeared, the ADA or the plaintiff in a civil trial might be likely to argue that the evidence was being tampered with."

Chapter Seven

"Have you ever seen a case like this where somebody was killed by a body falling from a cliff or a rooftop or a balcony when it might have been a suicide?" Mike asked Danny.

Danny shook his head, and said, "I think I remember something like that happening in Manhattan on the West Side, but I only knew about it from the TV news, and there were no pictures, as far as I can remember. But it might be worth checking out."

Mike said the Bliss family had said something about a similar incident in Manhattan, too. "Hard to check on it without any dates or names."

Danny volunteered that the only similar thing he had heard of was a woman who was killed by a piece of a building that fell on her. "She was from a rich family of real estate people, I think," he said. "It got a lot of coverage because she was a rich socialite. I think that was only a couple of years back, maybe around the time just before the COVID-19 pandemic hit us in Manhattan, and about the same time in New Rochelle—hit us real hard in New Rochelle."

"Anybody have any idea where Felipe Barrio was from originally?" Ruth asked. "I heard someone say Mexico, but that's not very specific, and I bet it's just generic anyway. You know, tan skin must be Mexican."

Lela piped up. "He told me he was born in San Salvador," she said. "But he had relatives in Westchester County who got him admitted to the United States when he was still a baby. I think he told a lot of people he was from Los Angeles, or maybe that he grew up in Los Angeles. I know he has family out there."

She looked like she was chewing on her lip while she stared at the floor.

"Then he moved in with some cousins in New Rochelle. Their last name was Barrio, too, so maybe they were related on his father's side, but I have no idea," she said. "They don't live in New York anymore—haven't lived here for a long time, I think. I don't remember ever meeting them. I think they moved to Central America, maybe they're back in El Salvador, but Pipo was talking about going to see relatives in Acapulco. We used to get mail addressed to them from time to time, but as far as I know, Felipe had no letters or telephone calls with them—ever. His Spanish was rusty, too, so trying to carry on a conversation with them on the telephone might not have done much for him—or them. His strong language was always English, and he sounded like an American when he talked, not a foreigner. That's something that got us together in the first place. We were reading the same books, taking the same classes."

She started staring out the window, looking like she wished she was someplace else.

"We went to Acapulco when I was a kid, but that's the only Hispanic vacation spot I've ever been to, that I remember," Ruth said. "I was thinking about going to Belize to do some SCUBA diving, but it never happened," Ruth said, looking directly at Lela. "It was super-exotic to have a chance to go to Acapulco when we were living every day on the 10th floor of an apartment building in Crown Heights, Brooklyn. We stayed in a place called Las Brisas that wasn't really in the downtown part of Acapulco. It was on a hill near the airport, and was more or less like a hotel. You registered at the front desk like a hotel, but the layout was actually a bunch of thick-walled white cabins with red-tiled roofs, and each one had its own swimming pool," she said.

"Beautiful place, and they had pink jeeps that they charged us an arm and a leg for, so we could drive around, because it was up on a hill, not real near the beach," she said, "and of course everybody wanted to get in the water and lie down on the sand."

She looked dreamy and added, "Maybe that's why there was always a breeze, because it was on a hill, because I think the name means something about a breeze. There was also a place where you could sit and watch bats fly out from everywhere when the sun was going down. They eat the insects, like mosquitoes.

"Barrio is a common name," she said. "There's no such a thing as telephone directories anymore, but if there was, there would probably be pages of Barrios."

"Barrio has to be a fairly common name," Mike said, agreeing with Ruth. "It's a common word in Spanish, I think. Means something like 'neighborhood.' I doubt we'd be able to track the family we're interested in down, without leaving a lot of shoe leather on the sidewalks of Acapulco. It's probably like looking for everybody named Smith and Johnson here in the states. Besides, I think they've been having a crime wave in Acapulco, if I remember right from newspaper stories I've been reading. Drugs, I think, combined with money and sandy beaches, and multiplied by ease of transportation between Mexico City and Acapulco."

I told them I doubted whether it would help even if we could find them. "If they left New York a long time back, and Lela never even met them, they probably wouldn't know much that would help us," I said to them. "I have been at that same hotel a bunch of times, and it doesn't make me an expert on anything. I saw the cliff divers that made Acapulco famous. Yes, they were fabulous, but trying to look in Acapulco for Felipe's relatives, knowing nothing but a common last name—Felipe himself hadn't seen or talked to them in years—it would probably just be a waste of time."

A gum-chewing woman with long brown hair appeared on the edge of my field of vision. She looked like a reporter, but she didn't have a cameraman following her around. She walked toward Ruth, who was standing next to me. She hailed us like a cab, and held her hand out for a shake.

"No handshakes during the pandemic," Ruth said. I appreciated that she did that, and stepped back, indicating my agreement with what she said—although I might have shaken hands if the approaching woman was a guy.

"I'm Caroline Kashevsky, and I'm a reporter for 2020 WINR, everybody's favorite all-news radio station," she said to both of us, dropping her hand to her side as soon as she realized there wasn't going to be any body contact with us.

"No prob," she said. "You guys with the police?"

"Depends on what you mean by that question," I said, and then pointed at Danny O'Toole. "He's with the police department—in other words, he's a cop. We're here with him, so yes, we're with the police. But we're not police. I'm a Civilian Criminalist with the NYPD, and don't have any jurisdiction here in Yonkers." I was speaking loudly, and Danny moseyed on over when he heard me, stopping smack in the middle of the space between Caroline and me.

"What can I help you with, ma'am?" he said to her. He showed her his shield.

"Hi, detective," she said. "We've met before."

"Sorry, I didn't realize," Danny said.

"I'm with 2020 WINR," she said. "Westchester County and the Hudson Valley are my beat," she said. "Radio, so no cameras, although if there's something worth looking at, we can change that. I can call a cameraman, and then I'd be working for Channel 12, local news."

"Looks like we're going to get some publicity," Danny said, and Ruth was nodding. I stepped farther back, and almost bumped into Gabriele, who caught Caroline's eye.

"You here on that guy who fell on the old man the other day?" she asked Danny.

He nodded. Mike walked up.

"And you?" she said to Mike. "You a cop, too? You look like a cop."

"I used to be a cop," he said. "NYPD. But I retired last month, and now I'm a lawyer, and I'm representing the older man's family—the old man you were asking about. His name was Bliss, Robert or Bob Bliss. He went out for a walk, and ended up dead."

Caroline whipped out a microphone that said 2020 WINR on a plaque that sat on top of the mesh surrounding the microphone itself.

"Your name?" she asked.

"Michael di Saronno," he said. "Attorney at law, office in Manhattan on 5th Avenue and 20th Street. Chelsea area."

"You a gay guy?" she asked.

He shook his head negatively, but didn't answer. "Whatever we're talking about, it's not about my sex life," he said. "You a lesbo?"

She smiled a professional smile, like she was endorsing a bar of lavender soap. But she didn't have any soap in her hand.

"So what's the Bliss family after?"

"I'm not going to discuss that with you," he said. "But if Mr. Bliss was killed by Mr. Barrio when he jumped off the building, there may be room for a judgment that would help pay for Mr. Bliss's funeral, at least, depending on what evidence we have and if anyone was negligent in letting this happen. Could be the owner of the building. Who knows?"

"And you think the jumper had enough money to pay your fees and have something left over for the burial costs?"

Mike smiled and shook his head without saying anything. "I didn't say that," he said. "I just think it ought to be safer to walk down the street than it apparently was here yesterday when Mr. Bliss was killed by a falling body while he was out for his walk."

"Well, I'm going to do a piece on this," Caroline said. "And I think my angle may be just what you said—Mr. Bliss was the victim here. Maybe the city will have to cough up some moolah for the family."

"The City of Yonkers?" Mike asked. "Why the city?"

"Why not?" she held out her microphone.

"No idea whatsoever," Mike said into the mesh on the microphone.

Ruth stepped up.

"And you are?" Caroline said.

"Also a Civilian Criminalist with the NYPD," she said, "like him," she said, pointing at me. "We're friends of Mike di Saronno, the Bliss family lawyer, just here to see the sights."

"I heard there was a handgun up there on the roof," Caroline said. "You suppose somebody up there was holding up the jumper?"

"Do tell," Danny said. "A gun?"

"That's what my source told me," she said.

"And who was your source?" Danny asked.

"A cop," she said. "A guy in blue with a badge."

Danny stared at Caroline. "And if there was a gun up there, what would you think that might mean? A holdup of some kind?"

"I'm just a reporter," she said. "Don't ask me. I'm looking for

39

facts, not speculation. I need to go on the radio and tell the listeners the news. Just because it's Yonkers and not New York City doesn't mean it doesn't matter."

She smiled and swished her way back toward the other side of the street.

"She must have got what she wanted," Ruth said.

"She thinks you verified for her that there was a gun on the roof," Mike said. "Which you didn't, although you could have. She's gonna tell her listeners that you said there was a gun on the roof."

"If she does, she'll be right, although I didn't tell her that."

"Apparently another cop told her, or that's what she said. You backed up the other guy by not denying what she said," Ruth said with a silly grin. "It's not TV, so you're not in hot water. You're not even wearing a name tag, and she didn't ask your name."

"No, she said we had met before."

"Had you met her?'

"Not that I know of," he said.

"Then no prob," she said. "I think you're in the cat bird's seat," she said. "She's got nothing on you. She already knew there was a gun, and unless I'm wrong, she was going to use that to headline her story anyway." She waved at the reporter across the street, and Caroline waved back. "The Caroline Kashevsky news hour," Ruth said. "She's got a nose for it, and maybe that's all she has, but it's enough for her to get some exciting headlines from time to time. She's gonna be able to dine out on that gun for a while, as they used to say."

Sure enough, her story went out from where she was standing. She had a good strong voice, lots of excitement in her delivery, too.

"Was there a gun pointed at the guy who fell off the building in Yonkers yesterday? My sources tell me yes, there was a gun, a handgun, like a robber would be holding. Like a drug dealer would be holding. Like a gang-banger would be holding. Stick with me, this is Caroline Kashevsky reporting from downtown Yonkers. The Yonkers cops have the gun, and maybe that will rip this whole thing wide open. Stay tuned."

Chapter Eight

The next day, we went back to the scene in Yonkers, and up to the roof.

"It's creepy," Ruth said, "to be standing where Felipe was standing before he went over the side of the building."

"Look at *mozziconi (*cigarette butts)," Gabriele said, pointing at the floor, which was peppered with filters and bits of cigarettes between the white quartz-ish pebbles that were intended to cover the floor by themselves. "Hundreds."

I was already staring at the floor of the roof level. It was like a giant ashtray, although I didn't see any ashes.

"I'm not seeing any ashes," I said. "To the extent they were there at some point, they could have gotten washed away by rain. Maybe by one heavy rain, like we got when Hurricane Ida blew through here and flooded streets and basements all over town. Maybe that's why it doesn't smell like cigarettes either. The rain, lots of light showers over the last week or so."

Danny remembered, and said to the others, "Nepperhan Avenue was totally closed off for a couple of days, maybe longer. It was a mess—mud and trash, tree limbs and garbage everywhere—splintered furniture, too. I kept wondering how the markets could get delivery trucks through with food and cleaning stuff to put on the shelves."

"Anyway," Mike said, "it doesn't look to me like there would be anything to be gained by collecting all those cigarette butts and checking them for DNA. It would cost a fortune, too. I don't know what the budgets are like here in Westchester, but if we were in the city, the whole thing would have been laughed out of the lab. You'd have to take them to the lab in a shopping bag, not to mention the latex gloves that you'd go through picking them all up."

Splat!!

"Where was the gun?" Gabriele asked.

Danny walked over to a pony wall that was blocking the way to a series of exhaust pipes, and pointed with his shoe down at the floor where it joined the edge of the wall. "Right about there," he said. "Can't tell you exactly, but there are some photos of it before it was collected for evidence." He shot a knowing look at Mike.

"Does it have a serial number on it?" Mike asked.

"Filed off," Danny answered. "That may be why it was thrown on the floor, because it was so clearly illegal.

"I doubt it had anything to do with what happened, but I realize we have to follow it all the way, and see what comes of it. It seems logical that Barrio could have been backed up to the edge by a guy with a gun, and then lost his balance."

We took the elevator down to the ground floor and then out to the sidewalk and looked at the bloodstains on the cement. Two brown blotches from two bodies. "I guess either the old man ricocheted off Mr. Barrio, or for some other reason the old man landed on the ground away from Mr. Barrio afterward," Mike said.

Danny nodded. There were three other Yonkers cops looking around. One of them nodded, and said to Mike, with a long look at Danny, "You got it, chief."

"What kind of psych analysis do you have of Felipe Barrio?" Mike asked Danny. Then he turned to the cop who had spoken to him, and said, "I'm not a cop, and certainly not a chief."

Danny said that a psychologist who had testified several times on different cases had put together an analysis. "He was depressed a lot of the time, maybe bipolar—although he didn't seem to have any manic periods, according to his girlfriend and his family. He may have been using some drugs and some drinking to feel better, or at least that's what it looked like to me when I read through his report, but I'm not a scientist. There was marijuana in the apartment they lived in. And paraphernalia. A glass pipe, maybe hand-blown, and a couple of packets of Zig Zag brown cigarette papers. I don't remember what else, but it would all be in the evidence locker for the case."

Mike motioned to Gabriele to join the group, and Gabriele walked

42

over to where Mike and Danny were. "Do you know the restaurant people here in Yonkers?

"Some of them, *si,*" he said. "What you want?"

"I'd like to find out if any of the local restaurant owners knew Felipe Barrio. His girlfriend said he was looking for high-end restaurant work."

"I talk to some of them," Gabriele said. "And I tell you what they tell me." He pulled out his cellphone. "I have some names here." He sidled away and dialed something on his phone, shielding the mic with his hand, clearly trying not to have a conversation where he could be overheard. Pretty soon he was laughing and talking to somebody.

"Manager at Zuppa say Felipe Barrio work there with sous-chef sometimes. Chopping and slicing—is *molt'ostico* to do it like chef want," he said, using Italian to say the work is very difficult to do right. "Is good sign; Zuppa good chef, good food. Chef from Roma, make pasta like Roma—best *cacio e pepe* in Italia, cook with tonnarelli—is like spaghetti make with eggs, not break in pieces."

Cacio e pepe is a Roman pasta dish made with just black pepper and a wheel of Romano cheese. The hot pasta is rolled around in the wheel of cheese to pick up as much cheese as possible, then it's heavily covered with coarse-ground black pepper. Very basic and plain, but not easy to make and serve. Every Italian knows Rome is the center of the pasta world, and *cacio e pepe* is one of the basics in Rome. Like *carbonara*, which is a string pasta dish with a sauce of bacon or *pancetta*, egg yolk, cheese and garlic; it's one of the four basic dishes of Roman cooking.

It was obvious that Gabriele was going to make the rounds of the high end of restaurants in the area. He would be able to tell us what the managers thought of the guy. Could help us as we try to figure out what drove him off the roof. Did he fall or was he pushed?

I felt strongly, based on what Lela Swann had said, that Felipe was a sunny type of personality, an optimist who had his feet trapped in money problems. But as a practicing Catholic, suicide was just not an option.

"Ancient Romans committed suicide to avoid being shamed or embarrassed," Mike said. "All you have to do is read Shakespeare's

Julius Caesar," to know that Brutus 'fell' on his sword, when Mark Antony and his legions were closing in on him in Philippi. That was after he ran from Rome, after he and Cassius started the public gang-stabbing of Julius Caesar in the Senate on the Ides of March.

"Maybe the most famous murder in history," he added.

No kind of suicide has ever been permitted by Christianity, and Felipe would not have done it in his right mind—at least that's the way I was seeing it. His action had to be forced or accidental—either that or he had some drugs in his system, maybe hallucinogens or Angel Dust that made him think he could fly. That's what I would be looking for—some indication that if he didn't stumble and fall, and wasn't pushed, he wasn't in his right mind.

My second priority was that I wanted to know everything I could find out about the handgun that was just sitting against a wall on the floor of the roof level of the building. Would whoever had smoked those hundreds of cigarettes just leave an expensive and easily visible Beretta handgun sitting there on the roof if it had been there for a while? Probably not.

I thought Mike was looking at it like I was. After all, Mike was brought up Catholic all the way, so he had the same moral background as Felipe. I asked Mike if he'd have time to meet me for dinner to talk about this case. He said he would appreciate that.

Gabriele wanted us to meet at Ora di Pranzo if we were going to meet about the case. That way he could pass along to us what he was finding out about Felipe from the restaurant owners and chefs he was talking to. Mike said the sooner the better for him, and we decided to meet that evening whenever Gabriele said was a good time for us to get a table.

Seven PM was the best time. That worked for me and for Mike, too. I had a dirty vodka before I left my new Yonkers apartment, and fell asleep on the Metro-North train, but woke up with a start when it came to a stop in Grand Central. I felt brand new and sharp as a tack when I got on the number 6 subway to head to Ora di Pranzo. I was yawning when I walked from the subway station to the restaurant, but it was a short walk, and the cool night air was bracing. When Gabriele showed me to the table, there was a dirty vodka already sitting at one place on the table and Ruth and Mike already seated with their own drinks in front of them.

"I'm guessing that's for me?" I asked Gabriele. He smiled and nodded. I took a sip and sat down, determined not to drink it after having downed one already at home. I thought, *If I'd've known, I wouldn't have had that martini glass of vodka at home.*

"Maybe I'll trade it in on a glass of red wine," I told Gabriele, who gave me a cross-eyed look, clearly puzzled. "I'm driving tonight," I said, and he looked like he understood. "When I was living in Long Island City I could take the subway the whole way," I said. "Now I have to drive from my apartment to the station, and park in the lot there, which costs an arm and a leg, or find street parking—which there isn't any—but if there was a space, I'd need a magician or a witch to fit into it. It's all parallel parking, no nose-in parking."

"If you take Metro-North," Mike said. "it's easier, and you can hop on a subway at Grand Central, too."

"It's expensive to park at the station when I take the train, but that's what I did tonight. I thought about taking driving," I said. "But I didn't." I realized I was thinking out loud. "What's for dinner?"

Gabriele smiled broadly, "*Il tuo perferito* (your favorite)," he said.

"Sausage and rapini and garlic?" I asked, as though I didn't already know the answer. "I'll never know, as simple as that dish is, why yours tastes so much better than mine."

"Is how I cook it," he said. "Crush garlic, then chop it, use plenty olive oil, and mix all ingredients together when cook with good *olio extravergine d'oliva.*"

Ruth grinned.

It really is my favorite dish—even better than the pan-fried chicken I grew up with in Texas. Lots of olive oil and freshly peeled garlic too, good for the body and the digestive system.

Ruth was still smiling, and looking like she was reading my mind, and knew that I didn't want to get soused, that night of all nights. The waiter brought a glass of red wine and removed the vodka. I looked questioningly at Gabriele, who said one word, "Montepulciano," an everyday wine with a rich, deep taste of southern Italy, from an area just to the east of Rome itself.

I wish we could come up with an angle that would let us take a field trip to Italy.

"I think we need another field trip," Ruth said, again reading my mind, like the witch that she probably was.

"To Rome?" I asked.

"Sure, any time we can figure an angle, but this time, probably not," she answered. "Trying to find an angle that would let us go to Italy for this case would be impossible. More likely to Los Angeles, to do some fact-finding on Felipe Barrio when he was a youngster. I think we were told he told people he was brought up in southern California, but that a lot of his family lives near Acapulco."

"I take time off, talk to Dante about it," Gabriele said. "I want to go someplace new, not Los Angeles. If we go someplace it must be *bellissima,*" he said enthusiastically. I could see him in my mind, pressing buttons to raise and lower his seat in business class going from JFK to wherever we were headed.

"I might need to go along with you," Mike said, sipping at a glass of what looked like whiskey. "I think we can find some relatives of Felipe's family to talk to," he added. "One of the Yonkers CSIs said they had been poking around, and found some cousins and aunts."

That's when a steaming plate of sausage and rapini arrived with a waiter, who smiled broadly and put it in front of me. *It's not on the menu, and that's probably what the waiter is thinking.*

Chapter Nine

As it turned out, Gabriele got his way and Acapulco it was, in spite of my strong misgivings about trying to find a needle in a haystack with a common name like Barrio in a Spanish-speaking city. Acapulco was the good news—because who wouldn't want to spend a couple of days in Acapulco? The bad news was the itinerary; we had to fly from LaGuardia to Chicago and change to another flight to Seattle, then transfer to Alaska Air in Seattle, then make stops in Los Angeles and Mexico City before finally landing in Acapulco. It took nearly a full twenty-four hours from LaGuardia before we were walking off the plane on the jetway in Acapulco. Fortunately, I can sleep on planes, so I didn't feel like I was going to fall asleep while I was dragging myself off the plane.

"We could have taken a direct flight from JFK to Acapulco if we flew on Delta," Ruth said, "but the AAdvantage miles only work with American, not Delta."

Mike beamed, and turned to Ruth. "Can you take care of this?" he asked. "How much will you need from me?"

"Probably not much, maybe seventy-five bucks total," she said. "And, yes, I still have plenty of Murray's miles to get us there and back, with still lots left over in the account with no expiration date." She blinked theatrically, and added, "Remember, we don't check luggage. Everything in the overhead bins; there's plenty of overhead bin room when you fly in business or first class."

Mike had never flown with us before, but he was looking like a kid in a candy store while we were talking about the trip. He's tall, so flying in coach must have always been a trial for him—because the NYPD wouldn't even pick up the tab on business class. He would have had to struggle and been lucky to boot, just to get seated in an exit row

47

for some extra leg room. Business class seats on wide body planes recline to flat, like a bed, and there are soft comforters and pillows to make it possible to fall asleep without waking up with a sore neck afterward.

We took a flight that left around dinnertime from LaGuardia. Since we were flying westward, we gained some time, and had dinner while we were in flight going to Seattle from Chicago. Like most airplane food, it was bland, and in no way exceptional, but it was getting dark as we flew, and we all knew we would have to change planes—and probably terminals as well—in Seattle. We'd be moving from American to Alaska Air.

I was sitting next to Gabriele, who had learned to sleep on his side to make the most of the flattened seat, which wasn't, after all, very wide. He used the buttons on the armrest to move himself up and down several times until he got comfortable. He wasn't interested in the food. I watched Mike, who was across the aisle from me. He was much less active in terms of moving around, but he threw back a couple of Dewar's scotches on the rocks, and looked to be asleep pretty quickly. He looked to have the TV turned on to a football game, where the Tampa Bay Buccaneers were beating the Dallas Cowboys. I'm not at all sure that Mike was aware of what was happening. His mouth was open, and there was some drool dripping out of the corner, so he was probably deep asleep.

Gabriele was on his side facing me, and although the armrest separated us, he managed to get close enough that I could feel his body warmth and hear his breathing. Ruth was in the middle section next to Mike, with someone else to her left, but she seldom fully reclines her seat, and she usually eats virtually everything that is put in front of her, including a Caprese-type salad with fresh mozzarella cheese, basil leaves and slices of what looked like long slim Roma tomatoes, with small containers of olive oil on the side to pour over the salad. And coarse Kosher-type salt, always for a salad. Like me, Ruth doesn't eat red meat, so she was having a pasta dish with large shell pasta, and what looked like a cheesy tomato sauce.

I was watching CNN, which was delayed from earlier in the day—but news is news, and I'm a news junkie, so it was fine, and I slept off and on, waking up with kernels of "sleep" in the corners of my eyes when we started to descend toward Sea-Tac airport. The flight attendant picked up my tray and the small screw-top bottle of red wine she had left for me, which I had not opened—it was Sangiovese-based chianti, which is very smooth and not a favorite of mine (I like the rougher, more southern Italian reds, like *nero d'avola* or *aglianico*, made from ancient grapes originally planted near the southern coast of Italy by ancient Greek settlers from the seventh or sixth centuries BC). Very dark red ("black" or "nero") grapes have been grown there for millennia, and are considered to be treasures of the Italian wine industry. Nero d'avola grapes are from Sicily (theoretically from a town to the west of Siracusa named Avola). Most of the best aglianico wines are from the area known as Basilicata (from a Greek word, *basileus,* meaning "king," like the herb that is used to complete a lot of Italian dishes—the "king" of herbs). Basilicata is the "instep" of the boot shape of the Italian peninsula, the raised part (Gulf of Taranto) between the toe (Calabria) and the heel (the south end of Apulia). There are also some aglianico wines from Campania, which is the area of Italy around and to the south of Napoli—to my taste, markedly inferior to the Basilicata wines.

When we transferred to Alaska Air, we were put on a Boeing 737 plane, with no business class cabin, so we were in what they labeled first class, but the seats reclined only partially, with one aisle and just eight rows of two seats on each side—the ninth row was the front of the coach cabin—much smaller than the spacious 777 plane we had been on from LaGuardia to O'Hare, and from O'Hare to Sea-Tac.

Of course, the longest part of our journey would be on the smallest plane, because we flew in the 737 from Seattle to Los Angeles to Mexico City to Acapulco, landing three separate times. Acapulco is in the same time zone as Chicago and Houston, because the western coast curves eastward as it goes south. So we were on Pacific Time in Seattle and Los Angeles, and then on Central Time after that, losing an hour. The Acapulco airport is south of the city of Acapulco, close to the ocean, but the upside was that we were able to get taxis to Las Brisas easily. I shared a cottage with Mike; Gabriele and Ruth were nearby in a second cottage. Each cottage had two queen-sized beds—and its very own swimming pool. If you went for a swim when you woke up in the morning, the management would leave a pot of coffee and a bottle of orange juice, and some *pan dulce* with butter ("sweet bread" similar to what the Italians have with their coffee, or the sweet buttery croissants from France).

The big surprise for people who stay at Las Brisas is that when you come back to your room in the afternoon or evening, there will be dozens of hibiscus flowers floating in the swimming pool, courtesy of whoever made the bed and cleaned the room. A little extra treat—and an extra memory to take home. When my wife and I first stayed there, she was charmed, although she wouldn't go in the swimming pool because she had never learned to swim, and was afraid to go in the pool, except if she could stand on the floor of the pool and have her shoulders above the surface of the water. She was terrified of putting her face in the water, even with the hot sun beating down on her back. Go figure.

As it turned out, Mike's decades on the NYPD stood us in good stead.

"I worked on a lot of cases over the years where there were reasons to be in touch with Mexican police," he said. "So I called some friends to see if they could help us find some of Felipe's family. Apparently, they were able to find a bunch of them quickly. Some of them were in Taxco, which, although it's in the mountains, isn't far from Acapulco."

One of the people who showed up was a cousin of Felipe Barrio who was married to a girl from the famous Taxco family of Castillo—silversmiths known around the world. His name was Gonzalo Acosta, and he had gone to school in the United States, so his English was fluent.

"I went to high school near Los Angeles," Gonzalo told us. "Then I went to college at San Fernando Valley State College, which is now called Cal State Northridge. I studied Hispanic literature and American history, so I had connections in the Spanish Department and the History Department—two different buildings on the campus: the Humanities Building for History, and the Languages Building for Spanish."

He sounded American when he spoke English.

"I remember Felipe. We had two aunts we were both related to, so we were second cousins. He lived in southern California for a couple of years when he was a kid and when he went to college. I think he went to UCLA, and he lived in Venice, right on the beach next to Santa Monica," Gonzalo said. "I was living in Topanga Canyon, and since I had a car, I spent a fair amount of time with Felipe when he was staying near the Venice Canals."

He told us that when Felipe left UCLA without graduating, he moved to New York City to look for work. He also wanted to meet a girl and have a family.

"Was he religious?" Ruth asked him.

Gonzalo nodded vigorously. "A lot of us went to church once in a while," he said. "But Felipe—he went to Mass every Sunday, and usually several times during the week, too."

I told him what had happened. Gonzalo's immediate reaction was that Felipe couldn't ever have killed himself.

Gonzalo guided us to Zibu Acapulco, a restaurant that had a mix of Mexican and Thai food—a delicious combination if ever there was one. They called it MexThai Fusion on the neon sign above the front door. Several of Gonzalo's and Felipe's relatives met us there, and the general consensus was like Gonzalo had said. Felipe was a devout Catholic, they told us—no way he could have jumped off the roof to kill himself because of money problems.

We told them about Lela Swann, Felipe's girlfriend. "She said the same thing," I told them while we were all sitting at a long table. I toasted them with a glass of beer.

Mike told the group that he was representing the Bliss family, and explained about Felipe crashing into Bob Bliss when he fell.

"So the question we have to answer is whether Felipe was a suicide, and if he was, was the death of Bob Bliss an accident, or was it the fault of the owners of the building, for letting people onto the roof?" Mike told them. "I'm trying to get a judgement for them that would at least cover the funeral costs."

The reaction of the relatives was unanimous. "No way, no how did Felipe kill himself. Either he was pushed or lost his balance. If that's what happened, then he fell by mistake. No mortal sin. He should be buried in sacred ground in a Catholic cemetery."

Mike told them that there had been suicides from that same

rooftop in the past. "It was twenty stories down from the roof, so it was a slam-dunk that if you jumped off, you would be dead when you hit the sidewalk. One hundred percent certain."

"You said there was a gun found on the roof?" Gonzalo asked. "Maybe Felipe was being robbed."

"Felipe was broke," Mike said. "At least that's what Lela told us. He couldn't pay his bills, and was having nightmares every month about it."

The food at Zibu Acapulco, which was close to Las Brisas, was excellent. I had some blue-fin ceviche, which means fish that is soaked in lemon juice and chopped onion and other things, so it looks and tastes like it was cooked, when, in fact, it's not cooked at all. It's raw. The acid in the lemon changes the taste and texture like it had been roasted in an oven.

I found myself remembering that when I was in high school I used to go sport fishing when I could afford it, and had boat-made ceviche several times.

The crews would try to find a school of tuna, and if we caught a couple, they could cut one of them up and make ceviche—they would always have a bag of lemons and onions, and it took a couple of hours of soaking the fish in the lemon and onion mixture for it to be ready to eat. After that one fish turned into lunch, the others—if there were others— were bait for sport fish like marlin or what I would call mahi-mahi (called dorado because they're a metallic gold color when you bring them up alongside the boat). I never caught a marlin, but I fought with several dorado over the years, landed three or four after what seemed like titanic struggles that left my arms and shoulders sore.

I've never eaten any marlin, but when I saw one being cleaned, the meat looked brown, like it would taste fishy. Ugh. Dorado or mahi-mahi I had eaten in Hawaii a couple of times, but it was no treat in my book either. I like white flaky fish like cod or hake or anything that would be called scrod in Boston.

That ceviche dinner and beer with hot tortillas and butter was all we needed, given the number of family members that showed up.

"Is clear Felipe not jump off roof," Gabriele said. "He pushed, or fall in accident."

It seemed that way to me, too.

I could tell that Mike was leaning toward suing the building for the Bliss family.

I went for a quick swim when I got back to the hotel. I thought Mike was going to join me, but he didn't; he was fast asleep when I got out of the shower. He had a book called *Rome* by an author named Robert Hughes, which I recognized, having started it myself (but never finished it, sadly) open on his chest. I lifted it off his sheet and put it on the side table on his side of the bed. He never moved.

Chapter Ten

We were all tired after the long flights and the late dinner, but we were on our way back to New York the next day. Fortunately, we were able to fly non-stop to Dallas-Fort Worth and from there directly to LaGuardia in New York, so we didn't spend a full day on the plane again. More like five hours on the plane and nearly two in DFW changing planes (two different terminals where we had to take a monorail shuttle to get from one side of the airport to the other, going from Terminal B to Terminal A—sounds like they would be close to each other, but in reality they were on opposite sides of the airport.

I slept like a baby in the 777 from Acapulco to Dallas. My wife used to get annoyed with me for the way I could fall asleep on airplanes, frequently asleep before the plane even took off, no matter what kind of plane I was on, or what cabin I was in. I only had trouble if the person next to me was too fat, and I couldn't find a way to situate myself where I wasn't rubbing on their arms or legs or whatever part of the body was hanging over into my space.

From Dallas to LaGuardia, we were on an older 737, with only partially reclining seats (but plenty of leg room), and only eight rows of first-class seats. Row 9 started the main cabin. Fortunately, they started beverage service as soon as we were in the air, and they gave us a lunch, which was a choice of chicken or pasta. I chose the pasta, which was shells with a tomato and cheese sauce—nutritious but super-bland and difficult to swallow without wine—but they saved my bacon by giving me a California cabernet sauvignon in a screw-top bottle.

Both Mike and I sat up straight with a start when the flight attendant came by and woke us up, raised our seats so the backs were straight up and folded up our trays and removed the remaining beverages for landing. We also had to tighten our seat belts. It was about 8PM

Acapulco time, but 10PM New York time. Mike is one of those people who wake up fully or not at all. In this case, he was ready to dig into anything I had on my mind, and it was obvious that he was bright-eyed and bushy-tailed, as they say. I almost suggested that he try reading some more in his book on Rome, but I ditched the idea and kept my mouth shut.

I asked him when we might be able to talk to the Bliss family, to see what we could find out about Bob Bliss's daily routine, and why he happened to be in exactly the wrong place at the wrong time when Felipe Barrio crashed down on him.

"I already had that talk with them," Mike told me. "But if you want to go over what I found out, I'm willing."

"What did they tell you?" I asked.

"Morning routine there was he got up while it was still dark outside and drank two mugs of black coffee. Then he went for a walk—the same walk every day, which took him in front of the building where he died, but normally also took him to a city park, where he would have a sit-down with some of his buddies who met there every morning. Sometimes they'd just argue about the news in the day's paper; other times they played chess. Obviously, he didn't make it to the neighborly chat with his buds that morning, but he had been on the same routine since he retired, which was seven years earlier."

"And did his daughter-in-law have breakfast ready for him when he got home, normally?" I asked.

"As I recall, he liked to make his own bacon and eggs, but she washed up afterward," he said.

"No variance?"

"They were clear that every day followed the same routine. He did the same walk at twilight, had a talk with the same buds that he met in the mornings, at the same group of park benches."

"How many of his buds were there?"

"Funny you should ask," he said. "I asked Donna Bliss, his daughter-in-law that was his principal caregiver, that same question. There were a bunch of them, she told me, and once in a while a couple of them would walk back with him for a shot of whiskey."

"What kind of whiskey?" I asked, as the plane bumped onto the runway. "Was Bob a drinker?"

"That I didn't ask," Mike said, "because it seemed like it wouldn't matter, but it might be really offensive to ask a question like that."

We dropped the conversation when we pulled up to the jetway and the pilot told us we could get ready to disembark. I had two carry-on bags, because I usually packed to stay a week wherever I was going—just in case.

Mike had one small hanging bag, which clearly had his blue suit in it (he was wearing a pair of tan slacks and a blue blazer on the flight, so the suit he had worn to dinner the night before must have been packed). Ruth and Gabriele each carried a backpack and a small duffel bag. Gabriele is like me—he wears jeans unless there's an obvious reason not to. He was clad in a black V-neck T-shirt and Levis for the trip from Acapulco to DFW to LaGuardia. Ruth was dressed in classic Chanel. "Classic" for her meant that even though it was in mint condition, she bought it for a song, from a second-hand store, a Goodwill thrift shop or sometimes a garage sale. The upshot was that although she looked like a million bucks, she never dropped more than a few bucks on her Chanel wardrobe. All her clothes looked new to me, whatever she was wearing, but especially when she was wearing Chanel. This particular flight she was wearing a nubby white Chanel Eisenhower-length jacket that ended just barely below her waist. It had a black plaid pattern on top of the white base. She was wearing red leggings and a pair of black patent leather flats. She had a classic Chanel bag with a gold chain that was adjusted to be shoulder-length, and looked like she had just walked out of a Paris fashion show from a few years back.

Mike had arranged on his cellphone for an Uber car to pick us all up. That way we could go to our separate destinations, which meant that Mike, Ruth and Gabriele would get taken to the general vicinity of Times Square, and then the driver headed north and dropped me outside my apartment building in Yonkers. The driver was Asian (I could see him in the mirror), and I asked him if he was getting a bunch of crap because of the COVID pandemic.

"Some people start to give me a lot of junk, but I turn them off. After all, they're in my car, and I don't have to take them where they want to go if they're obnoxious," he said. "My mother was shoved in the subway, and I felt like hanging out in the subway to find the bastard that did it, but I didn't."

We didn't keep up the conversation after that, and I was tired anyway.

The Chinese Exclusion Act of 1882 is something that ought to be taught in our schools. It tried to prevent all Chinese immigration at a time when Chinese labor was the cheapest on the market, and there weren't any laws about minimum wages or overtime or the 5-day week, or any of the things we take for granted these days.

I grew up as a teenager in California, and almost always had Japanese friends at school. My best friend was married to a Japanese girl. Most of the Japanese people I knew had relatives who had been arrested after Pearl Harbor and interned in one of the infamous American concentration camps like Manzanar, in the desert, north of Lone Pine, California, and east of Sequoia and Kings Canyon National Park and Mt. Whitney.

Manzanar sprang up at the order of FDR in 1942, and was closed in 1945 after the War ended. Asian Hate has a long history in the United States of America. It was no surprise to anyone when the Chinatowns in various towns and cities across the country like the ones in San Francisco and Manhattan were hit hard by thugs and vandals after COVID-19 was connected to China in public by President Donald Trump. At least millions—maybe billions—of dollars of lost business and damage to buildings and stores.

My phone buzzed with a text message while I was in the Uber car. We were on the West Side Highway headed north—the West Side Highway changes names a couple of times. When it passes the George Washington Bridge, it becomes the Henry Hudson Parkway. Then from there, the Henry Hudson Parkway becomes the Saw Mill River Parkway when it enters Westchester County north of the Bronx. Then it runs right through Yonkers, and virtually all the way to the north of the county, where it merges with the Taconic Parkway and heads up toward Albany.

The text message was from Mike, saying that he would set something up with the Bliss family the next day, probably on the phone unless there was some reason that wouldn't fly for me. I replied that was okay, but I might try to meet the Blisses in the flesh in Yonkers, since we didn't live very far apart. It always helps me to actually meet people face-to-face. I'm just more a visual learner, I think, and I imprint faces with names. I don't have a photographic memory or anything like that, but people seem more real to me once I've actually met them, instead of just talking to them on a phone line.

Mike told me that Felipe's cousin, Jose-David, said that Felipe worked twelve to fifteen hours a day every day, seven days a week. They had a funeral with a full Requiem Mass for Felipe, who was buried afterward in the Catholic part of a cemetery in the town of Hastings-on-Hudson. Jose-David was working on getting a stone marker for the grave. Lela wore a below-the-knee black dress, I was told later, with a black mantilla over her head. It partly obscured her face, but she sobbed pretty much straight through the whole funeral and interment, so it was probably just as well.

Jose-David wondered if she was pregnant, but she gave him a super-hostile snarl when he said something about that.

Fortunately, Jose-David was able to get a group of Barrios to agree to meet me at my apartment in the northwest part of Yonkers, where a number 2 bus would drop them right in front of my building.

"Depending on how many people show up, I might be able to drive them home afterward," I told Jose-David on the phone. Then I went to the market and picked up an eight-pack of Cokes and one of Dr Pepper. While I was at the market, I walked by the juice aisle, and grabbed a six-pack of cran-apple, too, just in case somebody didn't want to drink a soda. When I got home, I threw a bottle of champagne in the fridge—also just in case. I don't drink champagne, or alcoholic beverages that are carbonated, because they give me a headache. So I can't have scotch and soda, for instance, or Sangria that has 7-Up or ginger ale in it. I usually stick with either a glass of red wine or coffee in a situation where I don't know all the other people beforehand. Or a soda in a bottle, like a Diet Coke.

Sure enough, the Barrio delegates arrived the next afternoon, and there were six of them. Jose-David was the family group leader—he and

Felipe were cousins, their mothers having been first cousins (so they shared grandparents). There were also Felipe's sister, Maria, and a brother, Rodrigo. There were three others, all of whom were female (all cousins, but more distant than Jose-David). They were all—including Jose-David—younger than Felipe had been when he died, so they had all looked up to him like a big brother or generational elder. Jose-David had also met Gonzalo Barrio, the fellow we met in Acapulco, during a time when Jose-David's family was living in the Los Angeles area.

"We flew down to Acapulco, where Gonzalo was thinking about moving," he said. "I got the creeps from some of the guys he knew in Acapulco, because I felt sure they were in the drug business, one way or another. Just from things they said, but I can't remember exactly enough to quote them."

One of the girls took the lead in the conversation after I poured her a Coke over ice, and said there was no way Felipe killed himself on purpose. She was named Tricia and looked White, while most of the others looked Latino, or what they call LatinX these days, indicating that more than one race was evident in their looks. One of the cousins was Blatino, meaning her skin was as dark as a Black person, but her features and her first language being Spanish—and her Latina mother—made her LatinX. Her name was Catalina, which I think is a Hispanic translation, or translated version of what the Irish would call Kathleen or Caitlin. Catalina was the one who told me about the funeral, including how Lela had dressed like a widow in a black dress with a black mantilla covering her head.

Somebody told me a few years back that eventually most human beings would look like today's Latinos, because the races would continue to merge and become impossible to tell apart.

The unanimous vote of the Barrio family was that Felipe's plunge off the roof must have been an accident, because suicide would have been a mortal sin.

"No way Felipe went to Hell," Jose-David declared, and the rest of the family agreed. "He's in Heaven. It's no sin to not have enough money to pay all your bills on time." Fortunately, Lela wasn't there; she was in mourning, the girls told me.

Mike had told me that the Bliss family didn't have a position on why or how Felipe fell to the street, at least nothing that they mentioned on a Zoom call with Mike. They wanted us to know that Bob Bliss was a devout Catholic, and went to Mass every morning at a small church that the family had been attending for decades. That church was Saints Peter and Paul, and was a short walking distance from the house where several of them lived, and some others had grown up in.

The eldest aunt said she had been going to Mass at Saints Peter and Paul all her life, and she was eighty. Although she was born near the southern California border near Mexico, she had spent her whole life in that same house in Yonkers from the time her parents moved to Yonkers when she was still an infant. Most everybody in the Bliss family had gone to the same elementary and high schools. Several of the men had attended Iona College in New Rochelle (which came within a mile of bordering on Yonkers). The family was, as a group, talking to Father John, the parish Franciscan priest, about trying to get Bob Bliss canonized, so there would be a saint in the family.

I didn't insist on a personal, face-to-face meeting with the Blisses. Mike seemed to have found out everything he needed to know, and I figured I could ask him if I needed to fill in some blanks.

I looked out the window after the phone call and saw that reporter, Caroline Kashevsky, on the sidewalk outside. I made a note to myself and stuck it on the fridge door with a magnet, reminding me to get in touch with Danny O'Toole and bring him up to date, and to mention that Caroline was hanging around, clearly looking for headlines. The worst thing I could do would have been to keep secrets from the detective in charge of the case in Yonkers.

Danny worked out of a precinct on Lake Street, less than a mile from where I was living. We could get together for a slice at lunchtime, if he was willing. The Palisade Pizza and Pasta joint was about halfway between where I live and where he works.

Chapter Eleven

I figured if I arranged a place and time to meet with Danny O'Toole, when I got there, Caroline would be there, too. I was right. She clearly had a bug—or some bugs—to tell her where to look for information. It seemed logical to me that she had either hacked into his phone or mine (or maybe both).

I wrote a message to Danny, but sent it to an email address that misspelled Yonkers (Yonkes—missing the final "r"). Sure enough, he didn't get it, but Caroline did.

"How the hell did that reporter woman hack my phone?" I asked Mike. He asked me to hand him the phone, and then he opened up my messaging service, which was owned by Facebook. I knew the password and User ID, and he changed both of them, letting me know the new ID and password.

"You should be okay now," he said. "Except if she knows how to get into your phone, she may be able to break in again, so change your password every day, and make sure to have some symbols in the password, too—you know, exclamation points or extra back-slashes," he said. "Don't just change a 1 to a 2 and think you have a new password."

"I have an email that I use if I want to prowl for porn," I said squeamishly. "It's the name of a beatnik writer from the sixties, with a couple of numbers on it. I think the writer died some years back, so I wouldn't be competing for his name, most likely." I felt like I shouldn't have told him as much as I did.

"Sounds like a plan, man," he said. "Just use AGinsberg76 and you're most likely home free—at least for today."

"How did you know it was Allen Ginsberg?"

"When you told me you were using the name of a writer from the sixties, I figured it would be either Ginsberg or Kerouac," he said. "So I used eenie-meenie-miney-mo and decided I'd bet on Ginsberg, since Kerouac was too obvious."

"I actually bought a half-size paperback copy of *Howl*," I told him, referring to a long confusing, semi-narrative poem by Ginsberg. "That was when I was in about tenth grade, I think. Hard to remember exactly. I think it was hallucinations, probably from peyote or some kind of magic mushrooms, because it was before the days of LSD. Then he wrote the poem while he was high. It never made sense to me, probably because I was not high, and was trying to make it make sense, which was impossible. I kept it because it was cool to have it, and the biggest thing in life I didn't want to be was not-cool. I bought it at a nightclub in Manhattan Beach called 'The Insomniac.' Only cool people went there, and as soon as I had a driver's license, I could go there and have a Coke."

I paused and then added, "I think it was published by City Light Books in San Francisco, which might mean that Ferlinghetti had something to do with it, since that was his stomping ground in the 60s." I remembered his name, but nothing about why he was famous. Maybe he was a writer, too, but I don't remember.

"So anyway, just do it," Mike told me very sternly, "and change the password every day, no fail, okay? Caroline will leave you alone, although if you send email to Danny O'Toole, she may be able to read your address that way, so it's important for you to change the password every day for sure."

I could see that he was working hard not to shake his finger at me, and he was successful—he didn't do it. He looked at me like he was being really parental, and said, "You can't let her jimmy the door of your email again. She's likely to find out something you really don't want her to know."

"Is it safer if I call him and talk to him?"

He nodded. "But nothing is really safe when she's already had the door open. She knows too much already. She knows where your lock is, the rest is just her or some hacker she works with, being patient and working toward breaking your code."

I said I understood what he was saying, which was a lie. I understood where he was going, but I had no idea what it would mean changing my password every day, come rain or come shine. I was worried that some kind of pattern in my passwords would make it easier to guess what the new passwords were, so I told Mike what worried me.

"Use the dictionary to get your passwords," he said. "Don't just trust your own cleverness to come up with something unsolvable every day. Just open the dictionary every day at random, and put your finger down on one of the pages. Whatever word your finger is resting on, that's the new password."

"How'm I going to remember the passwords?"

"Write them down in your checkbook register, or on the title page of the dictionary, and then rip it out, and add a new password every day," he said. "Your strongest position is when you write on a piece of paper that you keep in your possession," he said like a college professor.

"If you go online with anything, it's much easier to hack," he continued. "Nobody can pick your pocket every day. If they try, you're gonna feel hands in your pockets at some point. You have all the advantages if you write down your passwords, which are selected at random, and you have the only copy of your cheat sheet."

I decided to change the subject, because I thought I had listened as long as I could listen about passwords and locking out Caroline Kashevsky.

"Do you know if Danny O'Toole's team has interviewed any of the property managers of the company that owns the building where Felipe Barrio fell off the roof?" I asked. "I was surprised when we went up there to the roof, and it was obvious that it was a smoking parlor for anyone and everyone in the building that didn't want to smoke while they were going for a walk after dinner. There were hundreds—maybe thousands—of cigarette butts on the roof. And a Beretta that at least one of the CSIs thought had been fired recently. What kind of place are they running? Three suicides in six months? What's the likelihood of that? How many residential high-rise buildings have that many suicides in the first year after people start moving in for the first time?"

Mike perked up. After all, he was going to be filing a civil suit looking for damages. I poked at him. "Whether Felipe Barrio jumped off the building or was pushed off the edge of the roof could have to do with the way the building was being managed. Right?"

Mike nodded.

I added, "If there were no railings to protect people, and no way to prevent people from milling around on the roof whenever they wanted to have a ciggie, doesn't that spell potential damages to you?"

He nodded again, then added, "I've already got an appointment with the CEO of Excalibre Properties, the owner, which is listed on the New York Stock Exchange," he said. "It was a REIT when it was founded, but converted to a C Corp and listed on the NYSE last year," he said. The appointment was the following morning.

"I should also have set up to interview the property manager, which is City Management, but there I'd need to meet with the manager who was assigned to the specific building, moving on to the CEO after I'd already met with the underling. City Management is a privately held company, so there's no financial statement to look at online, and no way to calculate the value of the company like there would be if the stock was being traded every day—so there's no public market value. I'm guessing it's way more valuable than Excalibre, though. If they went public or got bought, it would be billions."

"So I was a day late and a dollar short," I said. "You were way ahead of me."

"Not way ahead, no. I don't have any kind of arrangement to talk to City Management, and my appointment with Aristotle Costas, who is the CEO of Excalibre, is this afternoon, but I think I'll be talking to his lawyer, even if he's in the room." He smiled. "You were on the right track anyway. Sometimes I still think like a cop, and I'm not a cop anymore. My instincts have to change so that I'm always concentrating on my client, instead of on the victim or the perp."

"Shouldn't you see if Danny O'Toole could join these interviews, since he's heading up the investigation?" I said, trying not to sound like a smarty-pants.

"You're right, but it might give us more leverage if we let Caroline Kashevsky in on the fun, too. It might throw Costas off his balance to have a reporter jotting things down," he said. "Only problem is you never know what she would be writing, what kind of headlines she'd be looking for."

"Record the conversation," I suggested. "Make sure she knows you're doing it, too, so she'll know if she makes things up, you have a come-back that'll give her a migraine."

Chapter Twelve

Excalibre Properties was headquartered in Rockefeller Center's most famous building—the one that the world knows as "30 Rock," like the TV show. The company's offices took up most of the nineteenth and twentieth floors, and had some space on the seventh and eighth floors as well, which included a lot of services, like the Mail Room, a print shop, a cafeteria, and an infirmary. Aristotle Costas's office was on the twentieth floor at the corner of the building that faced the skating rink and the Christmas Tree on the east side and a panoramic view of the Radio City Music Hall on the north side. The CEO's office looked to be eight hundred or so square feet, and included a conference room with seats for ten people, a big shiny conference table, and a really huge flat-screen TV mounted on the wall opposite the glass front of the room.

He could have been a wrestler, to look at him. Not particularly tall, but not short, maybe 5'10" or 11", but a very thick neck, maybe eighteen inches. His arms and thighs bulged with muscles. The arms looked like if he flexed them, they would rip the cloth of his shirt-sleeves, which were as tight as his skin anyway. Shaved head, or bald as a cue-ball, hard to tell which, because, like a lot of Greeks, he probably had fair hair if he let it grow out, even though his skin was very tanned from being in the sun, probably way too much. There were tattoos poking out, reaching for his hands from under his French cuffs, which were fastened with very large gold cufflinks with emeralds or some green gemstone in them.

There was a photo of him with a woman and a baby on a hutch behind where he was sitting as he faced us across his desk. I was staring at it.

"That's Olympia, my wife, and our son, Demetrios, when he was still a baby," he said to me.

I checked out what looked like a misspelling of the company's name. As it turned out, there were a variety of companies in housing and in recreation/leisure with the name Excalibur, which is the traditional spelling of the famous sword that in legend belonged to King Arthur, famous as the Sword in the Stone. Only Prince Arthur could remove it from the stone where it was wedged, due to what was apparently a magic spell—maybe something to do with the wizard, Merlin, who was living backward (something I couldn't understand, except that each day he was a day younger than he had been the day before). There was also the puzzle of the Lady of the Lake, whose magic reclaimed the sword when Arthur died. As I remember the story, the sword was thrown into the water, and an arm reached out of the water to catch it, then took it under the surface of the lake. Creepy.

I asked Mr. Costas about the spelling of the company's name, and he chuckled.

"We originally wanted to spell it the traditional way—like King Arthur's sword—and we put up some signs on a couple of our properties with that spelling," he said. "We should've talked to the lawyers before we took that first step. But when we did it, we quickly found out about the other companies using that same name, and decided to change the spelling," he smilingly said, "but then of course we needed new signs and a new logo with the new spelling."

"I bet people misspell it sometimes," Mike said to Mr. Costas, with a nod to Danny O'Toole. "I see that your logo incorporates the concept of a sword. Any problem with that?"

"When we listed on the NYSE," Costas said, "there was a fair amount of discussion about the name and the logo, including the sword. But we got through it, and now people spell it our way almost all the time." He said that, as it turns out, a lot of changes in spellings are used in situations like this—just like a lot of totally made-up names are used, and accepted by the public. He pointed out that Twitter was a word that had been adapted by a company, with nothing like the original meaning of the word. Twitter deals in "tweets," which is a word that means the noise that birds make, as Twitter's logo indicates. Does that make Twitter-users bird-brains?

He paused for a brief breath, and then continued. "Excalibre is high caliber," he said, with a grin. "People relate to that tagline, which is on all our signage, including on the buildings. We're a high-caliber outfit, and people are learning that."

"A bunch of suicides can't be helpful in making your brand name popular," Mike said.

Costas frowned, but said nothing.

Danny told Costas that he was leading the investigation for the Yonkers Police Department, and introduced Mike as an attorney representing the family of Mr. Bliss, "who was killed by accident when Mr. Barrio hit him after he fell off the edge of the roof."

Mike shook hands with Costas, and introduced me, saying that I was a Civilian Criminalist with the NYPD, but was not acting on behalf of the NYPD on this case, although he and I had worked together over the years on several homicide cases "when I was still a detective on the NYPD, which I retired from a few months back," he said. He told everyone in the room that my help was *pro bono*, and did not have to be compensated in any way.

"I have a lot of experience with this team, which also includes a well-known restaurant owner named Gabriele Cortese, and a socialite and fashion-plate named Ruth Jensen," he said. I shook Mr. Costas's hand and gave him my business card with my cellphone number for contact.

"Do people call you Hugo?" he asked.

I nodded, and added, "The number on the card is my cellphone, and usually I try to answer it any time somebody calls—but I don't take it to bed with me, or into the shower, so there are times when it's hard to get in touch with me. In a case like that, send me a text message, and I'll respond as soon as I see it."

"Do you take other clients?" Costas asked me. "Maybe Excalibre would be interested. We have to investigate people we sell co-ops to, especially when they are private corporations with no public listings. We're constantly poking around, looking for verification of facts and claims from companies we've been asked to work with. Maybe you could help."

"Sorry, not really into taking new clients," I said. "I work with

Mike here, because we're old friends. For the most part, I'm retired. I raise orchids and try hard to be a favorite uncle for the kids in my family."

"You sure?" he asked.

"I'm complimented, and thanks for the idea, but I'm busier than you might think," I said. "Don't really have a lot of extra time. Besides, Mike di Saronno has first call on me, just like he has first call on my buddies, Gabriele and Ruth. If he wants us to help out, we're pledged to do it. Besides, I'm still a Civilian Criminalist for the NYPD, so they have a hook in me, too. Between Mike and the NYPD, I'm spoken for. But I really appreciate your offer and thoughts."

Danny stood up, and said, "Sorry to interrupt a friendly conversation, but we need to talk to Excalibre and Mr. Costas about the roof of the Excalibre building on Waterton Street in Yonkers."

"Ask away," Costas said with a smile.

"Why aren't the exits to the roof locked?"

"Why should they be?" he responded. "There are lots of times during the year when there are reasons to want to look at the stars, particularly at night. Fireworks are one example, but mostly on Independence Day and New Year's Eve, and the people in the building like to go up there to see fireworks or shooting stars. Some people like to go upstairs and get some fresh air sometimes, too. This is still Yonkers, and not everyone feels safe going for a walk—like at night, for instance, when you want to see a meteor shower that's been on the news because it happens the same time every year. People who own these apartments like to go upstairs to look at the stars at night, and they'd be upset with us if we locked them out of the roof. There are railings all the way around the roof, and DANGER signs everywhere we could find to post them."

"And your insurance covers people who are on the roof? It looks like a lot of people go up there to smoke, for instance. There are hundreds, maybe thousands, of cigarette butts on the roof level floor up there. That's not to mention that our cops found a loaded handgun up there after the tragedy last week when Mr. Barrio fell over the edge of the roof and Mr. Bliss was killed on the street as a result."

"We have some liability insurance, but I can't disclose to you exactly what's covered and what isn't," Costas replied, sounding like an echo of a lawyer. "Sorry, it would invalidate my insurance if I started telling people what they could sue us for. But I'll personally make sure that there are no cigarette butts up there by this time tomorrow; we'll put a whole team on it. This is a no-smoking building, indoors and outdoors, so nobody should be smoking on the roof. If Mr. Barrio jumped off the roof, it would have been hard to know that was going to happen—and even harder to stop it from happening. The Board will have to decide right away if we should start locking the exit to the roof, to keep a few people from abusing the opportunity to go outside for the views. If there are a lot of cigarette butts on the roof, that's proof that there are a lot of people who enjoy the fresh air up there regularly. Of course, we will start enforcing the No Smoking rules more rigorously. That's a health issue, not to mention a matter of city and state laws."

Mike made a face that said the conversation wasn't going anyplace helpful, and he stood up and made a motion of zipping his mouth closed, pointed at Danny O'Toole.

Danny nodded, and said, "Thanks, Mr. Costas. We're going to be talking to your property manager at City Management."

"I'll tell them to expect you," Costas said, in a way that made it sound more like a threat than a friendly referral. "Anything we can do to help, let me know. We'll do our best to pave the way for you." Then he stood up with a look of finality, and said, "Thanks to all of you for coming over." Then he held out his hand and shook each of ours, one at a time. When it was my turn, we did an elbow bump to honor the potential of spreading the pandemic.

On the way out, I heard Mike and Danny talking. Danny was saying that he and his crew would handle a meeting with City Management, and report back. "I doubt they're going to be helpful. I didn't see any No Smoking signs in the building—also not on the roof. But I'll let you know what I find out—if anything."

Mike said he wanted to talk to some of the surviving Blisses, to see what—if anything—was going on there that we ought to know about. "I spoke with the wife of one of the Bliss boys," he said. "Her name was Donna, and the conversation was totally vanilla. I'd like to learn some more about the family, like how long they had lived in the neighborhood, what their financial position was like, everyday things like that."

The Bliss family was mostly named with common monikers. There was a John, a Joe, a Bill (Donna's husband), a Tricia, a Gail and a Susie. Three boys, three girls. Mike arranged a conference call just to complete his due diligence on the family.

Bill Bliss seemed to be the family spokesman; at least he talked the most on the call. It turned out there was an interesting piece of information that Mike fished out of their conversation. The decedent, Bob Bliss, had filed a suit against Excalibre Properties for blocking the family's view of the Hudson River, when the plans for the building were filed with the zoning commission. The law firm that represented them on that apparently didn't have a bright view of the potential for winning any compensation in a jury trial. There were several high-rise buildings in the neighborhood, and it was assumed that the Bliss house could have been put on the market instead of just getting its afternoon sunlight blocked by a new building. Given the obvious gentrification of the neighborhood, they could have picked up a pot of gold if they had sold the house. But they didn't sell it, and they didn't pursue the suit actively for blocking the view of the river from the slight hilltop where the house was situated.

As a result of the way the suit was handled, there had never been a mutually agreed-upon end to the suit, so it was theoretically still active. It would probably also encourage the Barrio family to file a similar suit, since their house was almost next door to the Bliss house.

Bill said the law firm that was going to handle the suit about blocking the view had been disbanded when one of the partners was killed in a small plane crash upstate someplace. All the lawyers they had been dealing with apparently scattered to new firms.

"I still have a copy of the filings," he said to Mike, while Hugo, Gabriele, Ruth and I were listening.

Mike said he would send a courier to pick up the paperwork, so it could be read—and perhaps it might be helpful in getting a settlement from Excalibre Properties, regarding Bob Bliss's death on the sidewalk in front of that very same Excalibre building. Possibly kill two birds with one stone?

Chapter Thirteen

As it happened, at about the same time, Danny O'Toole's CSI colleagues were able to pull two fingerprints off the Beretta handgun that had been found a couple of feet from where Felipe Barrio was standing when he plunged over the edge of the building. Unfortunately, there were no matches in the system for the prints, but at least they had the prints of whoever was holding the gun the last time anyone held it.

It had also been fired recently, so the CSIs went back to the roof site to see if they could find a bullet or a casing. They found both. The casing was near the edge of the roof, not far from the railing. The railing around the roof was metal pipe on the outside of the building, but the edges of railing were wood-clad on the roof side, possibly to make it more comfortable for people enjoying the vistas. Sure enough, there was a bullet wedged in the wood at about waist-height for an adult male. No way to tell how long it had been lodged there in the wood.

It had been drizzly and rainy off and on for several nights in a row, but not the morning that Felipe went over the edge. There was no evidence of rain on the gun, possibly because it was somewhat sheltered by the low wall that partially concealed it from view in the first place.

"It's looking like somebody may have fired the gun while Felipe was standing next to the railing," Danny told us on a conference call set up hurriedly when the results came back from the lab.

"This could change things around," Mike said. "If somebody was waving a gun around, Felipe may have fallen off the edge by backing up and flipping over the railing, which would have been about butt-height for a man of Felipe's height. It would have been easy for Felipe to lose his balance if he was leaning on the railing and leaned back too far. There would have been no way for him to stop it if his upper body overweighed his legs and butt. But wouldn't you think he would have yelled if that happened?"

There were cameras in the lobby, but they were not particularly helpful at first glance. Most of the people who walked into the building the night that Felipe was on the roof were people who lived there, like Felipe and Lela themselves. Nobody was obviously packing a handgun as far as the camera views looked.

"Maybe it was someone who was already in the building," Mike said. "Even could be somebody who lived there. Was Felipe on the outs with any of his neighbors? Or was Lela?"

Ruth remembered Lela's reaction to a question about whether she was dating anyone else while she was engaged to Felipe.

"She almost smiled, but didn't," Ruth said. "I wondered if she had been flirting with one of the neighbors. After all, she wasn't wearing an engagement ring, so every guy who thought she was sexy might have been tempted to talk to her, maybe even see if she wanted to go for a drink somewhere."

Mike responded, "One of the CSIs, or maybe it was Danny O'Toole, said he thought she might be pregnant, but she kept saying she was a virgin, or that she and Felipe had never done 'it.' At any rate, she had not been having sex, because, as she said, they weren't married."

"Why would a guy think a girl was pregnant if she wasn't showing?" Ruth wondered.

"I knew when my wife was pregnant," I said. "I think it was because she would burst into tears with almost no reason to be upset," I ruminated. "At the time, it was because she showed all the signs of having something like the flu, and she complained that she felt like she might throw up. I could just tell, that's all."

"Which wife was that? You were married a few times, right?"

"She was the second one," I said, "the one in the middle. By the time I married the third wife, we were both too old for kids, and the first one—the one I eloped to Hawaii with—she would only have sex if I was wearing a condom. No babies, no how," I remember saying.

"Had to be the second wife. Her name was Mary," I said. "She had already had two kids when I met her—different fathers, and she hadn't been married to either one. She gave them both up for adoption and had no idea where they went, since adoptions were closed by courts in those days. No way to break the seals unless the adopted children were actively looking for their birth parents. Then we had babies together—all girls—and finally she had an affair with a tenor she met on a gig someplace, and wanted a separation so she could move with Mr. Wonderful to someplace closer to the Metropolitan Opera, which was apparently his goal (certainly not hers, because the idea of standing in front of an audience in a costume scared the shit out of her)."

Mary was a singer, studied voice in college in North Carolina. She couldn't do auditions, though, because she was too scared of screwing up. She couldn't sight-read worth a crap, she told me over and over. Instead of auditioning for roles in operas, she joined choral groups, where she could just sing something that she had already practiced a few times to join the group—she could sing mezzo or contralto, so her vocal range was very much appreciated—most girls wanted to be high sopranos. If she was with a choral group, wearing a choir gown, she could stand in the chorus with a choral gown on and just sing if she had solo parts or lines. She was comfortable just singing. She had the perfect voice for *Carmen*, but the whole idea of trying to convince an audience that she was a gypsy who could dance and click castanets gave her the shakes. She called herself Maria Carteret as a singer.

"Danny Boy" was one of her favorite look-at-me songs—she felt like she would knock 'em dead every time with "Danny Boy"; it fit her voice perfectly, gave her a high note that she could reach easily, and sat on her vocal chords beautifully; it also sounded classical, not pop—she could always pull it out for an encore if there was a lot of applause for something. She had a voice that had what they call 'ping.'

Ping is also called *squillo.* It's the trumpet sound in an opera singer's voice, helps it fill the house, and makes a voice recognizable after you hear it even once. Ping is a quality that allows the people in the last row of the top balcony to hear what the singer is singing. Mary once told me it originates in the diaphragm, but Caruso is said to have had the largest oral cavity of any singer ever, and the size and magnificence of his voice was said to have been because of the size and shape of the inside of his mouth. They said he could close his mouth around a hard-boiled egg without a problem. Think about that for a minute. I can gag just trying to put a walnut in my mouth. But ask any famous opera singer about ping, and each one of them will have a different idea about what it is, and where it comes from.

"But what would have clued Danny or one of his guys that Lela was pregnant?" Mike asked me in all seriousness.

"No idea, but I'd guess just crying a lot, even though her boyfriend had just died, which gave her every excuse to cry. Everybody knows that a pregnant woman has relatively little control of her tear ducts."

"The short answer is no," Mike said. "Her body, her decision. But if she is pregnant, she has to deal with being obvious fairly soon."

"What if we just told her we thought she might be pregnant, and asked her if she'd be okay taking a test?"

"Might work, might not," was Mike's reaction. "Good way to get slapped."

"What if we asked Donna if she thought Lela might be in a family way?"

"You mean, see if we could get Donna to convince her to come clean or take a pregnancy test?"

Mike smiled and nodded. "I'll talk to her, and blame my suspicions on you, most likely," he said. "If she asks you where you came up with that idea, tell her what you told me. We know she was bursting into tears right, left and center."

He pulled out his cellphone and pressed a couple of buttons.

"You have her phone number?" I asked.

"I always have the phone numbers of everybody I talk to in an investigation," he said. "Hold on, she's just answering. Hey, Donna, Mike di Saronno here. We met when we were talking about Felipe and Lela. Lela was drenching the set with tears, made my friends wonder if she was preggers."

I couldn't hear any more of what he said to her, because he turned his back on me and walked the other way. I could hear the sound of his voice a little bit, but couldn't tell anything about what he was saying.

Chapter Fourteen

Not one of Felipe's sisters or cousins was surprised to find out that Lela was pregnant.

Catalina, the Latin-looking cousin, signed onto the idea without even seeming to think about it. She had already told us that she would have given in to Felipe in a New York minute. But he wasn't interested in plus-sized girls (or relatives).

Tricia, the Caucasian-looking cousin, was slim like Lela, but with defined muscles from long years of playing all kinds of sports. For her, sex was a plus, and she was obviously experienced in romance. Lela's claim to be a virgin never made sense to Tricia. Men had needs, and women had the same needs. Being engaged was enough; you didn't have to wait to get married.

"Pipo was a total fox," Tricia said. "I would have married him in a minute if he wanted me," she said. "We're cousins, but cousins from way back, like fifth cousins, almost not related at all. No problem if we wanted to go out together, or even if we wanted to get hitched. Problem was he never came on to me, so nothing happened. He was attracted to girly girls like Lela, not athletic girls like me. No tomboys for Pipo."

Catalina said she winked at Felipe every time she saw him, but he never gave her the time of day. Maybe it was because Pipo was sexy and handsome, but muscular, and Catalina was what they would call in Brooklyn a *zaftig* of *zoftig* girl. She also had black hair. More hair on her arms than most girls, and on the nape of her neck, although she wore her hair in a pixie cut, probably to make her face look slimmer. She had a figure like a Rubens painting—generous proportions from top to bottom. Big tits.

Perfect for some guys (the ones who liked girls with big butts), totally wrong for some others (the ones who were attracted to skinny girls like Lela Swann).

Just having a brief look at Lela, it was obvious that Felipe was attracted to slim girls. Big tits were not essential for him, apparently. Lela could wear a cashmere sweater and it wouldn't look pornographic. Not true of Catalina. If she wore a sweater, anybody walking by could see her nipples.

When Tricia asked her if she was pregnant, Lela just shrugged and nodded. "I guess so, no period, or it's really late. I think I need to go to a doc to find out if there's somebody in the oven, and when I'll start to show. "

"Felipe the father?"

She nodded again. "I never was with anybody else, so it had to be him."

"Did he know?"

She nodded a third time. "I told him that same day, the day he fell off the roof."

Danny, who was standing with the two girls, asked the obvious question. "Was there a guy hitting on you around then? Somebody who might be jealous?"

"Tyrone Green," Lela said. "He was trying to get me to date him. I'm just not attracted to Black guys like Tyrone, and besides, I was gonna marry Pipo."

"Pipo?" Danny asked, looking puzzled.

"It's what everybody called Felipe," she said. "I think his mom started calling him that when he was real little, because everybody in the family called him Pipo, like it was his real name."

Danny asked Catalina if she called her cousin Pipo.

She nodded. "Boys named Felipe get called Pipo," she said. "Tricia's right, it probably came from a name his mom—my Tia Luz—called him when he was a baby."

"I'd like to meet Tyrone Green," Danny said, in a voice that was clearly meant to be heard by everyone in the room.

Catalina straightened up to look her tallest. "We all grew up with Tyrone," she said. "His family lived two houses away from where we grew up—where my parents still live, around the corner from where Pipo died. Heck, he and Pipo had the same birthday, August 8—they called it eight-eight. And they were the same age, too, so they were born on the same day, the same year. They were always best friends when they were kids, might as well have been brothers, but they didn't look alike. Ty is Black and Pipo was Latino."

She took a deep breath and exhaled it noisily, then said, "But I wasn't even going to go out with Tyrone; it would be like dating a brother or something. I would have dated Pipo, because I know we weren't too close. Just cousins, like Pipo and Tricia, but Tricia was more like a boy, the way she played sports all the time. My mom used to say Pipo and I were 'kissing cousins.'"

Mike perked up, cocked his head and edged over toward Danny.

Danny whispered something in Mike's ear, and Mike nodded vigorously. He said he had known a Black guy by the same name, but that guy had been shot in a quarrel of some kind in Queens during an Asian Hate period, when people had been taking out their anger about the COVID-19 virus on anybody with slanted eyes.

"So the guy you knew, was he Asian?"

"Nope, Black," Mike said. "Just in the wrong place at the wrong time. Bullet in the back." Mike looked up at the ceiling, then back at Danny. "I tried to recruit him to be a cop," Mike said slowly. "I don't know if it would have worked out, just like I don't know for sure whether it was part of why he got shot."

"This one is Black, too," Danny said. "Lela said he hit on her, but they never went out."

"Funny," Mike said. "Tyrone is an Irish name, but it's apparently more popular with Black families than Irish ones these days." He looked at Danny. "Ever see a play or a movie called 'Long Day's Journey Into Night'? There was a movie back in the 60s with Katharine Hepburn. Old play by Eugene O'Neill. It's about an Irish-American theater family with the last name of Tyrone."

Catalina piped up. "Ty lives about a block up there," she said, pointing up the street toward the north. "He moved out of his parents' house a few years ago, and got that apartment. He works at the pizza joint over there," and she pointed across the street to a place with a sign proclaiming PIZZA. "I bet he's over there now, can't see from here, but he's usually there."

"Do you know him?" Danny asked Catalina.

She nodded. "He likes plus-sized girls like me, but I'm like Lela, just don't want to date Black guys. I'm more attracted to Latin guys. And besides, we grew up together. It would just be super-awkward to go out with him."

"So you never went out with him?"

"Once," she said, looking at her feet. "But that was four or five months ago. We went bowling, had to wear masks to get in. I remember it well. He never even kissed me because of the masks. I was relieved." She sighed theatrically, with a loud "whew."

"But he told you he wanted to see you again?" Danny asked.

She nodded. "He's a tits and ass kind of guy," she said, rolling her eyes. "The kind that comes after me. I'm surprised he was hitting on Lela. Everybody in the neighborhood knew she was Pipo's girlfriend." She looked annoyed.

Danny pulled out his cellphone and called someone. A few second later, a uniformed Yonkers cop walked out of a bodega next to the Excalibre building, and over to Danny.

They chatted for a few seconds, and the cop walked over toward the PIZZA joint. As I stared at it, I realized there was a small sign that read "Bronx Pies." It wasn't half the size of the PIZZA sign. While I was staring at the sign, the cop walked out with a Black man in handcuffs just ahead of him.

Tyrone, I guessed.

Danny told Mike and me that Mr. Green had asked for a lawyer, but the cop was taking him to the precinct to see what he could find out about where this guy had been the night that Felipe fell off the Excalibre roof.

As the Yonkers cop put Tyrone Green in the back seat of a police sedan, a pretty Latin girl walked up to Danny. It was Maria, Felipe's sister. She was teary-eyed, but otherwise acting normally. She wiped her face with a white handkerchief. Mike and I both walked over to where Danny was standing.

"Pipo didn't like him," she said.

"You're related to Felipe?" Mike asked. "I'm a lawyer, working with the Bliss family right now. Used to be a cop, but retired a couple of months back."

"He was my brother, two years older than me, but my best friend," she said.

"How do you get along with his girlfriend?"

"Lela?"

"Does he have more than one girlfriend?"

She shook her head and gave us a very tentative smile. "He was really happy when they got engaged. He really was in love with her."

"Do you think she felt the same way about him?" Mike asked. "Is it possible that she would have been flirting with other guys on the side?"

"I like Lela," Maria said. "We're friends." She took a deep breath, and when she exhaled, she said, "Lela doesn't really flirt, at least not that I've ever seen. She's real friendly, though—and that means with girls and boys. Everybody in our family likes her. We were happy that they were going to get married. Pipo was having a terrible time with money—there just weren't enough hours in the week for him to make enough money to pay all his bills.

"If he hadn't bought that apartment, he might've been better off, but between paying the mortgage and the monthly maintenance fee, it was eating up everything he could lay his hands on."

She started to tear up again. "We all could see he was in pain, but I have to tell you that he would never, ever, have jumped off that building. Somebody pushed him. It had to be that way. He went to Mass almost every day, and took communion," she sighed. "Father Peter was a big part of his life," she said. "If he thought Pipo was depressed like that, he would have been all over him like a cheap suit, to help him feel better."

"Lela said pretty much the same thing when we talked to her," Danny said. "No way he would have killed himself on purpose. She said she was sure it was an accident. She didn't say anything about Father Peter. Is he at that church that has the picture of Padre Pio that Lela told me about?"

Maria nodded at Danny's question about the church. "Father Peter

80

is one of the priests that hears confessions on Saturdays. He teaches at one of the high schools—he's a Christian Brother. Lela wouldn't think of anybody pushing him," Maria said. "Nobody would do anything to hurt Felipe. And he wasn't the kind to trip over his own feet either. Somebody pushed him, or scared the shit out of him so that he lost his balance. He didn't fall by accident. Poor Mr. Bliss. We've known him all our lives. Nice old guy. What a terrible way to die. Nice family. Catholic, like us." She started to sob and blew her nose into her handkerchief.

Danny started to say something to her, but she turned her back.

"Did your brother know Tyrone Green?" Mike asked.

"Sure, everybody around here knows Tyrone," she answered through her hankie.

"Were they friends?"

She shook her head and shrugged like she didn't know the answer to my question. "They were when they were kids. You couldn't get a knife blade between them. They were always together, best buds. But since Felipe met Lela, they didn't spend much time together anymore. Felipe thought Tyrone was trying to hit on Lela," she said. "Not that she'd be interested. I saw her brush him off."

"Your cousin told me they had the same birthday and were the same age," he said. "That sound right to you?"

Maria nodded. "When we were kids, we always had their birthday parties at the same time. My mom used to always get them the same gift, like each one would get a sweater—different colors maybe, but same sweater. We would also make fresh ice cream to have with the cake. The kind of ice cream where you have to turn a handle to make it get like ice cream, instead of liquid. Milk, cream, sugar, flavoring like cocoa powder, and a bunch of egg yolks. Then you put it in the container in the middle of the ice cream maker, and put rock salt and ice around it. And you turn the crank until it won't turn anymore. Then you get one of the grown-ups to turn it, if they can. When the grown-ups can't turn it, it's ready to eat."

Mike nodded. "We did the same thing in my family. Every holiday, sometimes just after dinner in the summertime, to help cool off." He smiled at her. "It's funny how we have the same memories of things like that. These days we can buy any kind of ice cream at the market, in the freezer aisle. We used to have to make it at home. Either that or go to the ice cream parlor, where they would have vanilla, chocolate and strawberry. Sometimes peach, too, or butter pecan, since Grandma had pecan trees in her yard. Butter pecan is just vanilla ice cream with pecans mixed in that have been cooked in a frying pan with butter."

"My grandma always liked to put peaches in the ice cream, sometimes also with pecans or even walnuts, since she had an English walnut tree out by the garage and the chicken pen. Problem with the walnuts was that it was hard to get them open, and they would stain your fingers if you tried to open them up. We would always beg her for chocolate, but she was allergic, so we never got that. In the summer there were peaches at the grocery store."

"I guess a lot of people are allergic to chocolate, but not in our family, not that I know of anyway. Chocolate everything. Chocolate cake with chocolate icing, YUM."

"Do you think," Mike said slowly, "that there is any possibility that Felipe and Tyrone were related?"

Maria looked puzzled. "Related?"

"Catalina told us they had the same birthday, same year, everything. And they grew up together."

"But Tyrone is Black like Catalina, and Pipo had very light skin and good hair."

"They could have been what are called fraternal twins," Mike said.

Danny nodded. "We would only know for sure if we took DNA samples, but it's a real possibility. It might help us in our investigation, too. If they aren't related, it would be good to know."

"But they were different races," Maria said.

"You and Catalina are different races, too," Mike said. "And you have different skin colors."

Maria looked down at her hands or feet. She turned around and walked over to where the Barrio adults were standing. She said something to them, and several of them flashed unfriendly looks at Danny and Mike.

One of the men walked over.

"I'm Cristiano Barrio," he said. "You guys upset my niece, Maria.

Something about maybe Pipo and Tyrone were brothers?"

Danny stepped forward. "One of Felipe's cousins, a young woman named Catalina, told us that they had the same birthday, same year. It's not impossible that they could be related. Apparently, they've known each other all their lives."

"Bullshit," he said, and turned on his heel, walking back to the clump of Barrio adults.

"Only DNA would tell," Danny said as Cristiano walked away.

We could see Cristiano shrug, even though he was walking the other way.

"What do you think the odds are that the two boys were twins?" Danny asked Mike.

"How many babies are born on the same day in the same town?"

"A bunch," Danny answered. "There are four big hospitals in Yonkers. All of them would be delivering babies every day. How would we know?"

"Like you said to Maria's uncle, only DNA would tell us for sure."

"All I have to do is find Tyrone and get a warrant to arrest him, right? So I can get a swab to check his DNA?"

Mike shrugged, meaning yes.

Unfortunately, as it turned out, what looked like Tyrone being arrested and marched off to be fingerprinted was a non-starter. Something to do with a bad check he had accepted for a pizza when he delivered it. Released, no charge.

Chapter Fifteen

The Yonkers CSIs had been over the lobby and elevator videos several times, and although there were people who recurred several times, the number of them who went to the roof was not calculable, because in order to get to the roof, you had to take the elevator to the twentieth floor and then walk up a flight of steps. The final staircase had no video camera, or at least none that was powered up on a regular basis. There was no video that would dependably show everybody who walked out the door to the roof.

Danny was able to get some of Felipe Barrio's relatives to sit through the long and grueling experience of watching the videos, which went on for hours and hours—even when they were speeded up.

They saw Felipe, who got on the elevator and went to the twentieth floor at just after midnight. They also saw Tyrone Green, who walked in through the lobby in the middle of the evening, around ten o'clock, and took an elevator to the twelfth floor, which was not the floor where Felipe and Lela's apartment was. Then Tyrone got back on the elevator at the fourteenth floor, which is the floor where Felipe's apartment was at about 12:30 AM and went to the top, the twentieth floor.

"He didn't come over to see us," Lela said when she saw him get off the elevator on the video from the elevator. "He may have called Pipo, because I remember him talking on the phone. I think it was around the time of the eleven o'clock news, because we had been watching a movie that started at nine, and I think it was over at eleven. Then David Navarro and Sade Baderinwa were on the screen, and they're anchors for ABC News. I don't remember what they were talking about, maybe something about the debt ceiling in Washington DC, but I'm not sure. Then Pipo got up and left.

"I asked him where he was going, and he said he was going

downstairs to get some beer, and he'd be back in a while."

"Is there a market or a liquor store downstairs?" Mike asked. "If there is, I don't remember seeing it."

"No, it's up the block, and it's a bodega, like a deli," Lela answered. "Not a regular market."

"According to the elevator and lobby videos, he went downstairs and out the front door. He came back with a grocery bag about twenty minutes later, and Tyrone Green was waiting for him in the hallway. Then the two of them took the elevator to the twentieth floor," Danny said. He offered to play the pieces of video if they wanted to see it again.

Maria asked if they would play it for her, which they did. It was as they said. The two guys took the elevator to 20 just before 1AM. Felipe still had the grocery bag. Tyrone was wearing a leather flight jacket, and had his hands in the pockets.

"It looks like he might have something in his left hand inside the pocket of the jacket," Danny says. "Hard to tell what, but there's nothing to say it couldn't be a gun."

"No," Lela said. "Don't do it." She was whispering, but everybody could hear what she was saying.

"Who are you talking to?" Danny asked.

"Tyrone," she said.

"Don't do what?" Danny asked.

"Anything, whatever he was going to do," she said. "He was pissed with me because I wouldn't go for a drink with him."

"He asked you to go for a drink that evening?"

Lela nodded. "I told him no, and hung up. I knew he would be pissed, and I worried when Pipo went to get the beer that Tyrone would be waiting for him."

"Is your baby Felipe's baby?"

She nodded again. "I told you I didn't ever do it with any other guy. It had to be his. It wasn't the Holy Ghost that visited me, and I'm not the Blessed Virgin." She looked at her hands, and said, "I'm going to get an abortion."

Maria started to say something that started with "No," and Lela stopped her.

"Don't go there," Lela said. "I told you because I don't want it to be a secret, and I've already made my mind up, don't need advice."

Maria started to say something again, but Lela stopped her by making a noise that wasn't a word, shaking her head, and putting her index finger to her lips in a "shut up" command. "I can't raise a child," she said, "not even Felipe's child. I'm as broke as he was. All my savings was used to help him buy the damn condo. I don't even know where I'll be living after the first of the month."

"We'll all help," Tricia said. "You can stay with us until you get back on your feet."

The CSIs were able to lift two partial prints off the handgun when they dusted it—the one that had been found on the roof of the Excalibre building. Neither print was a match for Tyrone Green, which didn't necessarily mean a lot since the prints were only partials, and could have been from somebody who held the gun before or after Tyrone anyway.

Danny said they ran the prints, and it looked like there might be multiple matches, since both of the prints were partials. There were two potential matches in the FBI's AFIS (Automated Fingerprint ID System), but both of them were out of state in the Midwest, so maybe not immediate suspects.

"We'll hang onto these prints, in case we find a person of interest," Danny said. "I'm glad we went through the lobby camera videos of last Saturday (the night that Felipe fell from the roof)." He paused and said, "I can't imagine that we could get a judge who would give us a warrant for the prints of all the people who live in a twenty-story building."

"You know," Mike said, "it's not a slam-dunk that the gun was tossed that night. It could be unrelated, could have been there for days, although it didn't show any evidence of being left out in the rain, which would have been a problem, because there were thunderstorms several times in the week before." Then he had a brainstorm. "But what if we wanted to get prints from all the people that Tyrone Green works with? Do you think you could get a warrant for that?"

"Worth a try," Danny said, "although I doubt Tyrone was on the roof to harass a guy just because his girlfriend didn't want to go out with him—and we didn't see anyone walk in with Tyrone except Felipe Barrio. When Tyrone was there earlier and went to the twelfth floor, he was alone."

"Why does it have to be Tyrone Green?" Lela asked from behind where Danny was standing. Danny was startled.

"I didn't know you were there," he said. "Glad you are, though. That's a good point. It doesn't have to be Tyrone Green, of course. I had him in mind because he was hitting on you, so it made sense that he might want to confront your boyfriend, even though they had known each other all their lives."

He told her they could go over the videos again if she wanted to sit with them and watch hours of people walking around.

"There are four cameras in the lobby," he said. "They overlap each other—on purpose—but we've checked them all anyway. And there are cameras in the elevators, although they're only on in short spurts all day, twenty-four hours. If we're lucky, though, we might hit something helpful on at least one of them, especially if we run into something interesting in the lobby, where the videos are on 24-7."

He said he thought if we found something in the lobby footage, we wouldn't need the elevator images to make a case. As long as we got a good face shot, we could parlay that into a fingerprint. Somebody might recognize whoever it was, and that person could give us a print, whether it was on a water glass, or if we took a fingerprint in the usual way, with an arrest kit and a mug shot.

Chapter Sixteen

As it turned out, Tyrone Green was at home in his apartment, just a few doors up the street from the building where Felipe Barrio had lived—and died. Danny O'Toole rang Green's apartment from the intercom in the building lobby, and Green answered.

"I'm looking for Tyrone Green," Danny said.

"Speaking," the voice said.

"Yonkers Police," Danny said. "I'm a detective, and I have a uniformed policeman with me. We need to speak with you. Do you mind if we come up to your apartment? It doesn't have anything to do with that bad check thing from earlier this evening."

"If I can help you, happy to do it," Tyrone said. "Come on up." A buzzer sounded, and the door audibly unlocked to let Danny and the uniformed cop into the building. There was no elevator, because the building was only five stories tall. Danny's apartment was on the third floor.

Danny knocked on Tyrone's door, and a tallish black man with a trace of stubble on his chin, in a black T-shirt and Levis jeans opened it and welcomed Danny and Officer Spring into the apartment, which was clean and neat. The flat was apparently a one-bedroom, but it had a spacious multi-purpose front room that was furnished with a couch and a wing-chair on one side of the room, and a dining table with six chairs on the other side. There were lamps on small wooden tables at both ends of the couch. The tables didn't match, but the lamps did (they looked like they had been oriental-type vases before they were made into lamps, and they were both turned on. There was a flat-screen LED television on the dining-table side of the room, mounted on the wall like it was a painting. Two cords ran down from the bottom of the television, one to a cable connection, the other to a power plug.

The television was tuned to Channel 7, which in Yonkers was an ABC station. It was just after six o'clock in the evening, and there was news on the television, which Tyrone muted when Danny came in and sat down in the wing chair, which Tyrone gestured him to.

"Make yourself comfortable," he said.

Tyrone was sprawled on the couch with a blanket over his legs. He got up and pulled a dining chair away from the table and turned it to face the couch. The uniformed officer offered his hand and pointed to the name plate on his uniform.

"I'm Charlie Spring, Yonkers Police Department, and I'm just here because Detective O'Toole wanted me to come along to be present at this conversation." With that, he made a gesture of zipping his mouth shut, and Danny took over.

"I'm Danny O'Toole," he said, and showed Tyrone his detective's shield, which was fastened to his belt. He had a handgun in a shoulder holster under his jacket, and Tyrone could see that when Danny opened his jacket to show the shield.

"Am I in trouble for something?" Tyrone asked.

"Not that I know of," O'Toole said. "But I need to ask you about your friend, Felipe Barrio, who died recently in a fall from the roof of that tall building just down the street from here. I'm taping this conversation, and Officer Spring is going to shoot some video to document our conversation."

Tyrone turned off the television with the remote, and the screen went black.

"It'll be easier to understand the conversation without the TV news in the mix," Tyrone said.

Officer Spring reached into his backpack and pulled out a small video camera with a strap that held it firmly in his right palm. He didn't say anything, but clicked a switch on the camera, which flashed a red light to indicate it was turned on. It was so small, it was clearly digital.

Tyrone nodded and shook his head to indicate his unease with the situation.

"We reviewed the lobby cameras at the building where Mr. Barrio fell and was killed, and it appeared that you were in the building that night. Is that true?"

"Yes," Tyrone answered. "And yes, I know Felipe, or knew him, since he's dead now. I saw it on the news, like everybody else."

"There is some confusion in the Barrio family about your relationship with Felipe," Danny said. "I understand you two have the same birthday and that you and he were the same age."

Tyrone nodded his head.

"I need to get a cheek swab so we can look at your DNA," Danny said, and took a sterile tube out of his breast pocket with a cotton swab inside it. "Do you mind opening your mouth so I can just swab the inside of your cheek?"

Tyrone did as Danny asked, but wanted to know why Danny needed a DNA swab.

"We wanted to find out if you and Felipe shared any common DNA—whether you were related to each other. There was some speculation that you and Felipe might have been brothers."

"You could have just asked me," Tyrone said. "Yes, we are brothers—half-brothers. Different fathers, same mother." He smiled an automatic smile and re-opened his mouth for the swab. Danny swabbed the inside of Tyrone's cheek, slipped the cotton swab back into the sterile tube, and handed it to Officer Spring.

"So you both knew you were related?" Danny asked.

"Since we were little kids," Tyrone said.

"Why didn't you live with the Barrio family?"

"Because I'm Black and Felipe looks more White and Latino. When we were born, that meant I needed to live with my dad, and he lived with his dad, who was married to our mother, but who had obviously had sex with my dad. It took a while to get used to that part. I don't think I understood what that meant until Pipo and I were about ten years old."

"So, were you considered illegitimate?" Danny asked.

Tyrone nodded. "Yes, that's why my last name is Green. That was my dad's last name. He was Edgar, and he named me Tyrone."

"Were you on the roof with Felipe when he fell to the sidewalk?"

"No, I was not," Tyrone said. "I was in the building visiting a guy I know from the pizza and pasta place where I work. I dropped off some tortellini alfredo earlier that evening. I didn't find out what happened to Felipe until I saw the coverage on TV. I heard all the sirens—they woke me up, and I turned on the TV. That's when I found out what happened."

"Lela Swann told us you asked her out, knowing that she was engaged to your half-brother," Danny said. "Is that true?"

"Yes, that is true," Tyrone said, looking a little shaky. "Are you going to accuse me of something?"

"I don't intend to, no. You are not a suspect, just a person of interest, because you were in the building that night, and you had a hidden relationship with the man who died."

"They're the ones who didn't want anyone to know there was a Black man in the family."

"There are Barrios who are as Black as you are," Danny said. "Like Felipe's cousin, Catalina."

"I asked her out, too," Tyrone said. "She said no, and I didn't ask her again."

"Did you think Lela Swann might go out with you?"

"No, I did not," Tyrone answered. "She was obviously Pipo's girlfriend, and I'm feeling like I need a lawyer."

"You don't need a lawyer as far as we are concerned, but it's up to you. If we were going to arrest you, you would be entitled to a public defender at no cost, but we have no present intention to arrest you—we're just looking for information. We're not going to hassle you in any way. We won't be following you around, or poking into your business. But I do have two more questions, if you don't mind," Danny said.

"Have at it," Tyrone said, looking tentative.

"Did you ever own a Beretta handgun? We found one on the roof of the building, near where Felipe fell off the edge."

"I've never owned a gun in my life," Tyrone said. "Not a rifle, not a shotgun, and particularly not a handgun. I wouldn't have a handgun in my apartment if I was paid to do it. Handguns aren't for hunting; they're for killing people. The answer to your question is no, I've never had a handgun of any kind. What were you asking about? A Beretta, was that it? Nope, no Beretta. No guns of any kind."

"Thank you," Danny said. "Do you know who might have pushed

Felipe Barrio off the edge of the roof?"

"No, I do not, and I hope I never find out that somebody did that. I liked Pipo; we were friends all his life, from the time we were babies. There was never a time we weren't friends. I wanted to be his best man whenever he and Lela got married. I'm a Methodist, not a Catholic like Felipe, but I would have done whatever I could to qualify to be his best man. I know Catholic priests don't like Protestants in their ceremonies, but I would promise to help raise the children Catholic if that would have helped."

"You weren't worried about how Lela would feel?"

"No," he said. "She knew I was happy for them. Ask her; she'll tell you."

"When she told us you asked her out, she sounded like she was pissed off at you," Danny said.

"She wasn't pissed off at me, and she never has been. She told me she was pregnant with Felipe's baby, but I'm sure she didn't want me telling anybody that. She didn't even tell Pipo, much less everybody else in the world. I'll sign something about that if you want me to."

"Done," Danny said, and stood up. He signaled Officer Spring, who turned off the video camera. Danny held his hand out, and Tyrone shook it.

"Thanks," Danny said.

"Any time," Tyrone said. "Just let me know. If you want me to take a lie detector test, I'll do it. Just tell me where and when."

As Danny and Officer Spring left, Danny pulled a smart phone out of his jacket pocket and said, "Did you get all that?"

Mike answered, "Yup, no surprises there. When I found out that they were probably related, I figured they were close and that Tyrone would be totally loyal to Felipe. I don't remember interviewing anybody who was so clear, and answered so fast and with so little hesitation. I like that he's willing to take a polygraph test if we want him to. I doubt it would be necessary."

Chapter Seventeen

"That didn't tell us anything about the Beretta," Danny said. "That's something I wish we could get a hint on. People don't just chuck an expensive gun on the floor, even if the serial number has been filed off, like on this Beretta. It's still a goddamn valuable pistol."

"And they don't leave it out in the open if they do, unless the gun was never used. But in this case, we have a bullet that's been matched to that gun."

"More than matched," Danny said. "The FBI verified the bullet came from that gun, striations exactly the same. Perfect."

Mike asked if there were any interesting duplications when the CSIs went over the videos of the elevators again.

"The ones who went downstairs mostly went back upstairs at some point, but there were only a handful that went to the twentieth floor," Danny said. "One who went to 20 twice was a White guy, looked like medium height when he walked in and out of the elevator cars. Blond hair, which is unusual for adults. Most blonds are either bleached—mostly women or actors—or still kids. Blond hair usually darkens as a person gets older."

"But nobody identified him?" Mike asked.

"Not so far," Danny said. "I want to get Lela Swann and Maria Barrio to look at the videos, or maybe some stills if we can pull something out that's not blurry from the guy moving."

He said he might get Charlie Spring, the uniformed cop who had shot the video in Tyrone Green's place, to chase down the two women to look at the videos. "Charlie's a solid guy," he said. "I can trust him, and he's already been all over the videos. He may have been the one who spotted the blond guy in the first place, come to think of it."

In fact, Charlie was able to get the two women to agree to meet him at the precinct later that afternoon, to have yet another run through the lobby and elevator videos. Nobody told Lela and Maria, but what they were hoping was that the girls would recognize the smallish blond guy, whom the CSIs said had gone up to the twentieth floor several times the night that Felipe Barrio barreled over the side of the building.

I was at home in Yonkers with Gabriele, trying to take it easy, because I could feel a wave of information coming on this case. Sure enough, while I was having a turkey-Swiss sandwich and a ginger ale— Gabriele had raised his hand in a negative manner when I asked him if he, too, wanted lunch—my cellphone vibrated in my left back jeans pocket. It was Mike. I put it on speaker so Gabriele could hear the conversation.

"Sorry to bother you, Hugo," he said. "I just had a call from Danny O'Toole at the Yonkers PD. They just got another hit from the FBI on the gun that was found on the roof of the Excalibre Building."

I was anxious to find out what the news was, but it turned out to be more than I was expecting.

"Apparently, that gun was used in a homicide here in the city a couple of years back," Mike said. "Actually, in my old stomping grounds. The shooting was near Ariana, that Afghan restaurant on 9th Avenue. You'll remember it, most likely—we had lunch there a few times. Somebody used it to shoot a guy who somebody apparently thought was guilty of dealing fake pills. All of them had fentanyl inside, although they were touted as generic pills that were the same as expensive branded pills like Eliquis, which is super-expensive. The idea was that you could buy expensive brand name pills as cheap generics—when there weren't any cheap generics that were real. That would be popular with Medicare patients, because they can get stuck with very high out-of-pocket prices for prescriptions, even though they have Part D drug coverage as part of their sign-up with Medicare," he said.

"Only problem was all these pills were fakes, and poisonous. Twelve teenagers in Hell's Kitchen died when they swallowed them, because all of them were apparently based on fentanyl, which most likely came from China. The dealer had an Italian name that you'll recognize: di Benedetto, like Gabriele's cousin," he said.

"It's a common type of name in Italy," Mike said. "A name that is made from a saint's name, or in this case, all the saints. 'Benedetto' is 'the blessed' or 'the saints'; it indicates that somebody in the past was probably a baby left in an orphanage, or abandoned on the steps of a convent, which was a common way of getting rid of an unwanted child after birth. Babies like that were frequently given the last name of a saint. Names like San Carlo or Santa Maria, lots of times with conjunctions to start them off, like di San Carlo or de Santa Maria—that would indicate that the baby was left at a convent of holy nuns with some indication that its parents were well off—like a fine real gold chain around its neck, maybe, or an expensive blanket. The conjunction would have meant nothing, but the nuns might have thought it indicated nobility, so if that was the rationale, it was window decoration that was added on to make a comment about the baby's probable ancestors. If a baby had a gold chain on, the nuns would have kept it, to help cover the cost of taking care of the baby and getting it adopted.

"Dante's family probably adopted him as a foundling with no parents who could keep him. Leaving babies like that was not unusual for unmarried girls who couldn't admit to having a child. Whoever had the baby—nuns, frequently—probably gave him the name di Benedetto, which would mean 'from the blessed,' or 'from the saints.' Or it could have happened generations earlier, and his adoptive parents could have had that name from their own families.

"Could have been nuns who named the baby, or could have been the priest who baptized it. No way to tell," he said. "Lost in the sands of time, as they say. Anyway, having the same last name would never indicate a family relationship, unless it was a generation or so later, and even then it would be a maybe. If Dante became a father, the baby might have his last name—or it might have the mother's last name, if it was a recognizable family name.

"But even if the nuns named an infant Gian (or whatever—the new parents would rename babies with first names that they liked) di Benedetto, there could be others with the same name, just because giving babies last names doesn't always mean the names would be creative; they would get used over and over, especially if they were generic, like di

Benedetto. The nuns might use the same last name over and over again, for instance. Dante wouldn't have been related to this guy who was killed in Manhattan, because Dante's name was from Naples, and all the names of this type indicate that the baby's last name was unknown. His real last name could have been an Italian equivalent of Smith or Jones. Its birth parents could have been named Schnickelfritz, but if the nuns wanted it to be di Benedetto, that's what it would be."

"When I was born, my dad's last name was di Benedetto, like Dante," Gabriele chimed in. "I picked out Cortese to be my name when I was 11 years old, because it was a real name, and I knew friends—guys I liked—from school who were named Cortese. I didn't want a made-up name like di Benedetto. It was *imbarazzamte*."

"Anyway," Mike said, "this particular di Benedetto guy was apparently shot on or about July 20, 2018 on 9th Avenue near 52nd Street. Nobody was ever arrested, so it's just a cold case these days. But the bullet came from that same Beretta."

"So is Yonkers going to resurrect that old NYPD case?"

"Not exactly, although I suggested to Danny that he might want to look at any old workups he can find on Mr. di Benedetto, to see if we see any names we recognize, or who might be living near the Excalibre Building on Waterton Street in Yonkers. The gun is a real piece of evidence; it's solid and something you could show to a jury, with FBI info on the bullets."

"Did di Benedetto have a rap sheet? Any convictions?" I asked Mike.

"Danny didn't say, but I'll ask, of course," he said. "Fentanyl is no joke. It kills people, seems like every time they take it. It's one of those pills that more people die from than survive even one dose. Thank God for Narcan, because it can bring an overdosed victim back from the dead if they've taken an opioid like fentanyl."

I started going over what I had learned about fentanyl: *Totally synthetic—it's a lab copy of drugs that are made with opium, but it's cheap to make compared to drugs that come from poppy plants. The fact that it's cheap in a market where everything else is expensive is why they make it in China—it's hugely profitable because the mark-ups are huge compared to the cost of making it. It's 100 times stronger than morphine, so a few grains can be enough to kill even a young, healthy addict.*

Mike mused out loud, "The opioid crisis began around 2015, and by a year or so after the first fakes hit the streets, there were 40,000 deaths a year, every year, from the overdose. That's what made fentanyl a popular drug, because it was cheap when the brand names were sky-high expensive. A lot of oxycodone or OxyContin® users were switching to heroin, which is also an opioid, but cheaper to buy on the street than the pharmaceutical-grade pills or patches made by companies like Purdue Pharma, which is even today—after years of federal prosecution by the federal government—owned nearly 100% by the same family that founded it and made billions over the years. They made their fortunes from pills that turned hundreds of thousands of mainly suburban and rural Americans into drug addicts, and killed a lot of them because the Purdue faked clinical trials that persuaded doctors they were not addictive—not even habit-forming. Bullshit, bullshit, bullshit." He signed off, and hung up.

I tried to look up di Benedetto, but couldn't find anything helpful. I found articles on Dante—mostly recipes and cooking suggestions, but that didn't help. Too common a name, possibly, or not common enough to make it into the indices that online databases were searching.

Then Mike called me back.

"I got some info on di Benedetto," he said. "Danny has a folder on it, but so does my old precinct. I talked to John Scott, who took my place when I retired. He filled me in. The guy had been in and out of jail for twenty years when he was shot. Nobody was arrested, and my guess is that if there was an investigation, it wasn't very thorough," he told me. "The gun was never found, but the FBI reports on the bullets are still there, which is how we found out that our Beretta from the Excalibre Building was the culprit. That bullet in the woodwork did it. Bells rang at the FBI as soon as the bullet was put under the microscope, apparently. That's part of the magic of computers—AFIS computers in this case."

"Did the partial prints help?" I asked.

"Still no hits on the prints," Mike said, "although the theory that di Benedetto's death was a revenge killing could conceivably be helpful if we find out the names of any people of interest in the case. I think John will help us if he can. First of all, he's a good guy and a good cop, and second, he'd get extra brownie points for closing a cold case. Could make a difference in his career."

Mike said he was on his way over so to talk with me about other things going on with the case.

Chapter Eighteen

Gabriele needed to get back to the restaurant, so he and Mike exchanged brief pleasantries as Gabriele left and Mike arrived. Mike was making a call as he closed the door behind him and sent an acknowledging nod in my direction.

Danny answered the phone, and seemed relieved that it was Mike calling.

"I'm on speaker," Mike said, "and Hugo is here with me, because I want him to help me try to figure out how to handle this di Benedetto business. He's good with logic and taking baby steps instead of giant steps."

"Afraid I haven't got a lot to tell you and Hugo right now," he said. "We found the case in the archives, and there was some information about Mr. di Benedetto." He paused." I'm just opening up the folder, give me a minute," he said quickly. "There, got it open. He was from a large Italian family, most of them from the Bronx, but maybe from southern Italy originally, around Naples, or even south of there. Ndrangheta country, not John Gotti New York Mafia."

He paused again, and was flipping through pages.

"He seems to have been selling drugs on the streets when he dropped out of high school. He never graduated, but he was enrolled at the Mott Haven High School for three years, B minus average, played on the varsity baseball team, second base. Had fairly good grades in algebra and geometry, so maybe he was strong on math, hard to say.

"He seems to have been hanging out in the Mott Haven area, around 138th Street. He was picked up for pushing drugs several times, and spent some time at Rikers because his family couldn't post bail to get him out of the lock-up."

Another pause.

"His mother—of course her name was Maria—sang in the church choir at Saint Jerome Catholic Church on Alexander Avenue, and our guy went by the name Carlomaria, all one word. There was an orchestra conductor at the time our guy was a kid by the name of Carlo Maria Giulini, a real famous guy, but he never worked in New York that I could find out. Maybe he was from Naples, so one of his parents may have known the name. He conducted the Los Angeles Philharmonic for a while, also some time in Chicago, and he was all over Europe, including Vienna and Milan. But no way to know if that's the reason for the kid's nickname. His baptismal name was Antonio, so why he wasn't called Tony, I have no idea."

He flipped a few more pages. "He was picked up and later convicted in a bench trial of peddling heroin on the street on Alexander Avenue, not near where his mom's church was, but still in Mott Haven. He did twenty-seven months at Sing Sing in Westchester County. Maybe they put him there because he was young and his mother could visit him if he wasn't upstate someplace.

"Released on parole for good behavior, it says here," Danny said, "and he seems to have been on good behavior for three more years, and then he was released. I couldn't find any more arrests after that. Maybe the kid was smarter than you might expect. No record of who his parole officer was, or what office he was in. I probably could look it up if you need it."

"Did I tell you that my friend Gabriele was born with the name di Benedetto?" I asked Mike, but with Danny listening. Mike nodded, and Danny said something like, "not surprising. It's a common enough name. Italian, not Sicilian."

"His mom's last name was Fanucchi," Danny said, "rhymes with spooky. That might not have been his father's last name though. The mom was married several times apparently. Some of his records call him Carlomaria Fanucchi, but most of them call him Carlomaria di Benedetto, and that's the name he was buried with. Also the name his mom was buried with, but she was just Maria di Benedetto, and she's buried in Woodlawn. I think he's planted in St. Rita's Cemetery in the Pelham area, but not sure. I can find out where he is if the DA wants to exhume him for some reason."

"So why would somebody shoot him?" Mike asked, probably not expecting a response. "And why would the gun show up on the roof of that new high-rise in Yonkers?"

"Well, it's just a guess, of course, but he was probably shot by another dealer—maybe a turf issue, like being on the wrong street corner," Danny said. "The skinny girlfriend told us that Felipe Barrio was using marijuana, maybe selling it, too. Maybe somebody was waving a gun around on the roof that night to scare him. No way to tell right now, except that it makes sense that if Felipe tripped and fell, he might have been ducking a bullet, especially since there was one in the woodwork near where he was standing.

"I've been wondering if he was known more by his first name than his last name," Danny said. "Carlomaria would be a fine handle for somebody who was peddling drugs on street corners in the Bronx. It's easy to remember, and it's also Italian, which works in this part of town."

"I remember being told about a friend," Mike said, "whose father took him to see Bobby Kennedy in a parade along Arthur Avenue when he was running for the Senate, or maybe when he was running for president," Mike said.

"Anyway, my friend's dad told him that Bobby Kennedy's brother was the first Catholic president," Mike said. "My friend asked if all the others were Jews, which sounds silly today, but it made sense in the Bronx in the sixties. There just weren't any Protestants or Muslims like there are today. Irish, Italians, Puerto Ricans and Jews. Period.

"I was unusual," Mike said, "because I played basketball in a league where there was a Lutheran school, and they were good—I think they won the league we were in when I was a freshman. Manhattan was a name, not a place. Manhattan College was not in Manhattan, it was in Riverdale—the Bronx, not far from where Mount Saint Vincent's College is today. It was a Catholic school, mostly Christian Brothers.

"Anyway, the world we lived in was all Catholics and Jews. My hero was Bishop Fulton J. Sheen, who was a Catholic bishop who had a network television show, so he was a rock star, kinda. His sponsor was a television maker called Admiral TV, but my dad always called him

Admiral Sheen," he said, obviously remembering his childhood. "I guess Bishop Sheen was probably one of the first televangelists, like the predecessor of Joel Osteen, but with Catholic vestments." He sounded like he was walking down Memory Lane.

"Sorry for that," Mike said. "Long digression, my apologies. I agree that Carlomaria might have been a good dealer name. People would call him by his first name if they knew it. He was selling dime bags, after all, not postage stamps or candy bars."

"I'm going to take a chance and look up Carlomaria on Lexis," Danny said, referring to a huge computer system that had a huge database related to laws and legal issues.

"You have a Lexis terminal on your desk?" Mike asked. "We had one—just one—in the precinct where I worked when I was in the NYPD. It was in the conference room next to the Chief's office. If you wanted to look something up, you had to make an appointment."

"Things change," Danny said. "Especially things that use computers. Computers get cheaper and smaller every year. I heard that my cellphone today has more computer power than the first NASA space ships that circled the Earth back in the day. There wasn't any Internet where you could just sign onto databases like Lexis-Nexis. You had to have a terminal that was hooked up to Lexis to do a search."

"There was one at the library at Columbia when I was in law school," Mike said. "I learned how to search on it, but I doubt I could remember much of that today."

"Got it," Danny said. "Didn't take long. Carlomaria was a person of interest in a bunch of bad-guy stuff, just like that was his whole name."

"Mostly drugs?"

"Yeah, mostly, but some petty theft, too. Maybe he short-changed people sometimes, or maybe he kyped some beer from the bodega, and got caught. You'd think he'd have plenty of cash all the time from selling drugs for greenbacks all the time, but maybe he'd get cleaned out when his supplier came by to get paid. A lot of the suppliers were Mexican, and they play rough if you don't have the cash."

"You sure it's the same guy?" Mike asked.

"Physical description is the same," Danny said. "Kinda short, like

5'6", kinda fat or overweight, scruffy facial hair, pronounced foreign accent." Pause. "And there's a mug shot that looks like the same guy that was shot." Pause. "Yup, the photos are the same guy, at least it looks that way to me, for sure."

"So maybe one of his suppliers shot him," Mike asked. "Any way to find out who his suppliers were?"

"Guadalajara guys, but in those days they didn't hang out in one place for more than a few days at a time. Probably rotated back and forth to Jalisco or Chihuahua, so they wouldn't start looking familiar to the cops or the DEA undercover guys."

"If I was still a cop," Mike said, "I'd say assume the gun changed hands after Carlomaria was shot. Somebody totally unrelated probably dropped it on the Excalibre roof, maybe even fired a bullet into the wood framing on the roof level. But no way to tell when that happened, except that it probably hadn't been left out in the rain."

"I agree," Danny said. "It'd be just plain stupid to assume the gun stayed in the same hands all that time," He made a noise that sounded like a snicker. "Could be anybody that took the elevator to the twentieth floor—or it could have been left up there the night before, or a few days before. No way to tell without a witness or video camera footage."

Chapter Nineteen

Mike told me that Aristotle Costas left a message on his cellphone, and wanted to get together.

"Costas?" I said, not quite understanding, because it seemed unlikely at best. "You mean the CEO of Excalibre Properties?"

Mike nodded. "Yup, the big boss on the twentieth floor of 30 Rock."

"Did he give you any idea what he wanted to talk about?"

"He wants to talk about the Bliss family's intentions, would be my guess—but he didn't say that in his message. Just that he wanted to see if I could meet him in his office. Can you join me?"

"Odds are, he's been talking to his PR guys, whoever they are," I said. "They're probably worried about this whole deal splattering crap on the Excalibre brand. Could chase potential condo buyers away, if they think it's a hangout for druggies—or even just bad karma. You know, if there are piles of poop on the ground, you don't want to walk on it. This is the third suicide, or falling accident, since the building opened. Even though I don't think it was a suicide, based on what I've learned about Felipe, what kind of guy he was, how religious he was, stuff like that."

I walked to the station, which is not very far away, and took Metro-North to Grand Central, the subway to 23rd Street, and walked to Mike's office from there. Mike and I took a taxi to 30 Rock, and met Mr. Costas at his office on the northeast corner of the twentieth floor.

The Excalibre CEO looked nervous and acted fidgety after we shook hands.

"You wanted us to meet you here," Mike said. "Good to see you again. What can we help you with?"

"I'm Hugo, we met before," I said to Costas.

He nodded. "I remember."

Joseph Allen

"The agenda is yours, just tell us what you want to talk about," Mike said. "I presume it might have to do with the Bliss family's potential complaints about Excalibre's security with regard to traffic on the roof of the Excalibre residential building in Yonkers."

"I know you've been going over the videos of the elevators and the lobby on the night Mr. Barrio killed himself," Costas said.

"We're not convinced that his death was a suicide," Mike said. "We're more inclined to think of it as an accident, or maybe a situation where he was pushed over the edge, or got scared and lost his balance. But we're anxious to hear what you have to say."

"Look, I went over those videos myself, and I realized that my son was in the building that night," he said. "Demetrios is his name, and he's still a teenager, just a kid. He likes to visit the buildings, and since we live in Yonkers, it's easy for him to get there. Just a walk, not even a car ride. We live near the Greystone Station, near Executive Boulevard, which is where the building is. Yonkers is gentrifying, especially in the northwest part of the city around Executive Boulevard, and the potential profitability of that building is very attractive."

He was starting to sweat, and grabbed a Kleenex from a box on his desk, wiped his forehead and upper lip. I thought he might sneeze, but he looked like he was fighting it off, and it didn't happen.

"Anyway, I talked to Demetrios, and he told me he was on the roof that night. There was supposed to be a meteor shower, and he wanted to see some shooting stars, at least that's what he said."

"Did he see Felipe Barrio?"

Costas nodded. "Yes, we all knew him because he worked here in the neighborhood, and he was easy to spot—good-looking kid."

"He was an adult," Mike said.

"Still good-looking," Costas said. "And a lot younger than me, so I can call him a kid."

"Is Demetrios gay?"

"I don't know for sure," Costas said, looking uncomfortable. "Maybe, but Olympia and I love him a lot, and we don't care who he hangs out with."

"So what happened that night that you want to talk about?"

105

"Demetrios found that gun up by the side of one of the pony walls that we put up to protect the heat valves that are connected to the radiant heat system. We're required under state law to provide heat in the cold months, and we wouldn't want anyone to get burned by leaning on those pipes, or holding onto one of them. Whatever, the gun was apparently left there by someone who maybe wanted to get rid of it."

"Why wouldn't whoever left it there have just tossed it into a dumpster, or dropped it off at the police station?" Mike asked. "I think he could have gotten a couple of hundred for turning in a gun. I know you can in the city, probably the same in Westchester."

"No idea," Costas said. "No idea who left the gun or why he left it, whoever he was."

"You sound sure it was a guy, not a girl," I said.

"Could have been a girl. I just tend to think of guys holding guns, not girls," Costas said. "I have a gun in my desk, in case I need it. I have a license, and it's in a gun safe, so nobody can get at it without the combination."

"And you think Demetrios may be gay?" Mike asked.

Costas nodded.

"Are you fairly sure he might be gay?"

Another nod.

"Do you think he might have been attracted to Felipe Barrio?" Mike asked.

"How would I know?"

"You're his father. If you don't know, nobody else would—at least that would be my guess."

"Felipe was a good-looking guy, and it was common knowledge that he was going to marry that girlfriend of his," Costas said. "No reason to think he would be involved with Demetrios."

"That's not what I was asking," Mike said. "I wanted to know if you thought your son might have been hitting on Felipe, not whether Felipe would have been involved with your son."

"From what I saw on the videos, Demetrios was with his friend, Johnny," Costas said. "They go to the same school on North Broadway. And they both take Greek classes at Prophet Elias Church."

106

"Is Johnny Greek Orthodox?"

"His dad is Greek," Costas said. He pronounced Johnny's last name like "Yorgostathis," but spelled it out G-E-O-R-G-O-S-T-A-T-H-I-S. "He's a doctor, office in Valhalla at the Westchester Medical Center. Urologist, I think. But yes, they're Orthodox, and we both go to Prophet Elias on Sundays. The boys have known each other all their lives, and I think they're both queer, since that's what you were asking. So as to whether they are Orthodox or not, hard to say. You can't be Orthodox and gay at the same time."

"Even if you're not having sexual relations with anyone?"

Aristotle Costas stood up and stalked around the room, muttering to himself.

"You're disappointed with your son?" I asked him, watching him twitch and turn as he looked like he was trying to escape the conversation.

"Were you at the building that night, too?" Mike asked.

Costas turned and looked daggers at Mike for a second or two, then continued pacing around the room.

"Do you remember if you were at the building that same night?" Mike repeated. "We didn't see you on any of the videos if you were."

"I keep a studio apartment on the twentieth floor, in case I need to stay there overnight for an early meeting in the morning," he said. "I was most likely there that night, because I remember hearing the sirens outside. They woke me up the next morning while it was still dark."

"Were you on the roof?"

Costas looked confused. "Why are you asking me that?"

"Just following the conversation we were having," Mike said. "It seems to me that you're unhappy that your son may be gay, like when you said he can't be gay and Orthodox at the same time. You might be keeping an eye on him, that's all. Remember, I'm not a cop, and neither is Hugo."

"I feel like I need to call my lawyer," he said.

"Feel free," Mike said. "Do you want us to leave you alone for a while?"

He sat back down and called his secretary on the intercom phone. He was on speaker, and we could hear her answer.

"Can you find a place for these two gentlemen to wait while I make a private phone call?"

She opened the door without knocking and motioned to us. She was youngish, thirties, and pretty, but very business-like. She took us to a small conference room across the hall, and offered us some coffee or bottled water. We didn't take her up on either one, but I asked if there was a men's room nearby. She pointed to a unisex restroom, which was basically just a sink and a toilet. I went in, peed, and came back, fastening my belt while I walked

"My daughter is transgender," I said. "Not easy to be a parent of someone who's going in a different direction, but you can't have a nervous breakdown because your child has preferences that are different from your own." I was remembering my own pain after listening to Costas talk about his possibly gay son.

"I remember when they had their double mastectomy," I said to Mike. "I know that sounds strange, using the plural pronouns, but that's the way they like it. It seemed like mutilation to me when she had the breast surgery, but it was what they needed. Now they shave every day like a guy, because they take hormones. I don't have the problems I used to have because now my child looks like a guy, so it's not as painful for me when they act like a guy. I had a problem using pronouns for a while— you just shift to plurals, which takes the gender out of what you're saying. It's grammatically odd, but if it helps, it's worthwhile."

There was a knock on the door and the secretary opened it without waiting for us to tell her to come in.

"His lawyer is coming over, should be here in a few minutes, since his office is only two blocks away. When he gets here, I'll come and get you to continue the meeting."

"I wonder if it's possible that Costas had the gun at some point," I said to Mike. "We should try to get him fingerprinted, to see if one of those partials fits."

"He has a water glass on his desk," Mike said. "That could do what you're talking about if we can grab it." He showed me a pair of nitrile blue gloves and a large baggie that could easily take the water glass.

He called Danny O'Toole and told him about the conversation. Danny said he'd jump in a police car and go as fast as he could to get to 30 Rock. We were back in Mr. Costas's office when we heard the siren, and then Danny was at the door faster than you would have thought he could get there.

"We understand that you were on the roof of your Yonkers building the night that Felipe Barrio fell from the roof to the street," Danny said to Costas. "We need to get your fingerprints so that we can eliminate the potential that you might have had your hands on the gun that was up there."

Chapter Twenty

"My son was holding that fucking gun in his hand, but I saw that he was wearing leather gloves, so he wouldn't leave any prints," Costas said. "Yes, I took it from him, so my prints may be on it, and I'm happy to cooperate however you want."

"We think there is a possibility that somebody fired that gun that night," Danny said. "Did you fire the gun?"

Costas shook his head slowly. "No. I just grabbed it and held it. I probably had my finger on the trigger," he said, "but I never fired it, and it certainly didn't fire by itself. I told my son to beat it, get the fuck off the roof, and Mr. Barrio was standing by the railing. Nobody was hurt. Demetrios and Johnny scrambled down the stairs to the twentieth floor. So did I, because I knew I would be staying in the apartment that night. It was too late to go home all the way to Quogue (a town out toward the eastern end of Long Island)."

"What happened to the gun?" Danny asked. "And can you come to the precinct in Yonkers, or to a precinct here in Manhattan where we can lift your prints?"

Costas nodded, and looked at his watch. "Where's my goddamn lawyer?"

Mike had turned on his cellphone and was recording this part of the conversation.

"I think I tossed it over by the wall," Costas said. "I meant to just drop it, but I think I kinda tossed it, and then I followed the boys downstairs. They must have already taken the elevator down to the lobby, so I let myself into my little apartment on the twentieth floor. I had a scotch and eventually took a shower and fell asleep. I took a couple of melatonin pills. I keep them by the bed in case I have trouble sleeping. They're over-the-counter, not prescription drugs. I think your brain

110

makes melatonin when the sun goes down, as soon as it's dark outside. But sometimes I need extra help," he said, his voice trailing off. "I tried Unisom, but it didn't do the trick. I have trouble going to sleep. Sometimes if I read, it helps, but I can't count on that unless I have a thick book that I want to read."

His lawyer arrived. His name was Jim Sturdivant, and he looked middle-aged, like late forties. Nice-looking, nice suit, nice tie with red and yellow stripes. White guy, short haircut, light brown hair, blue eyes. I found myself thinking that Demetrios Costas, whose father told me he might be gay, might find this guy attractive. Maybe his school buddy, Johnny Georgostathis, too, since they may both have been gay, maybe even a pair.

I've never had a problem with gay guys. I'm not attracted to guys at all, was married (to women) three times and have five children. Never have done anything sexually with a guy, but I have friends who are gay. That includes my buddy, Gabriele Cortese, who is one of the most successful restaurant-owners in Manhattan. We met when he was a sex worker (escort) working in the neighborhood where I lived in the Theater District. He was a person of interest in a homicide—oddly enough, a musician who fell out a window and may have been pushed. Gabriele had been in that apartment that evening, and I was working with Mike di Saronno, who was the NYPD detective on the case. I had also been in that same apartment that same day, but was at the Metropolitan Opera when the musician flew out the window. It was a fancy apartment built over the roof of Carnegie Hall. Andrew Carnegie insisted on putting rental units on the roof of Carnegie Hall so that the theater could make some money to keep itself running. Little did he know how famous and successful Carnegie Hall would be.

Anyway, I met Gabriele while I was working with Mike on that case, and he has worked with me on a bunch of homicide cases since then—always reporting to Mike, who managed to get me appointed to a volunteer post in the NYPD. I'm am unpaid Civilian Criminalist, which puts me at the same level as the sketch artists who create portraits of people from descriptions by eye witnesses.

Gabriele was going by a different name at the time I first met him.

He was Rafaele or Rafe (also an archangel, so his feast day would have been the same: St Michael and All Angels, September 29). Most European Catholics celebrate name days instead of birthdays, so his feast day would have been a big deal. I thought he was Brazilian when I first met him, which was on the street outside one of my favorite restaurants, a place called Thalia on 8th Avenue (it's closed now, the owner moved to Tel Aviv). Turned out not only was he not Brazilian, he was Italian, from the famous Isle of Capri, not far from Naples, where his cousin and business partner, Dante, grew up. Dante was the chef. The restaurant was a huge success from the giddy-up, but it was on East 20th Street then, before it was leveled by a gas explosion in the cellar of the restaurant next door.

After they found a new location, the place really took off, and there has never been an empty table since the new place opened. Gabriele gets comped at every restaurant in New York City—all boroughs. And he never charges me for food at his restaurant. I can walk in and sit down at a time when there are people waiting literally for hours in lines outside, even in really terrible weather, like pelting rain or freezing sleet or steady snow.

Anyway, it was interesting to find out that not only was Aristotle Costas on the roof the night that Felipe Barrio died, but so was his gay son, Demetrios, who had his buddy, Johnny, with him at least part of the time. Although Costas never verified that the boys may have been involved, he didn't say they weren't. Costas said you can't be gay and Greek Orthodox at the same time, which leaned toward saying that he was planning to disinherit his son. Made us wonder if he had other children.

Costas said that both he and Demetrios had handled the gun that night, but he said Demetrios was wearing gloves, so if that was true, there would be no prints. Costas said he picked up the gun himself when he saw it, but tossed it away without ever firing it. It might have his prints on it. He agreed to being fingerprinted to see if his prints matched the partials that the forensic CSIs had found on the gun, a Beretta, which was in the Yonkers Police Department evidence locker. We also met Costas's personal lawyer, Jim Sturdivant, who didn't say a lot, but would be representing Costas on any personal issues that might involve the police.

Chapter Twenty-One

After we left Mr. Costas's office at 30 Rock, I headed home on the next train out of Grand Central. Being the news junkie that I am, I put on CNN as soon as I walked in. Mostly Beltway news that day, but then there was a Breaking News interruption, which caught my attention immediately, because it was dead center on what Mike and I had been doing.

There had been four explosions that all affected the same company, called Excalibre Properties. The first two were apparently pipe bombs that were probably remotely detonated in a building on Waterton Street in the suburb of Yonkers, in Westchester County, just north of NYC. Then, shortly afterward, there were two more explosions in 30 Rock, both in the offices of Excalibre, which was the owner of the Yonkers building. All four of the explosions started fires, and all four were on the twentieth floors of the buildings, which made firefighting complicated and difficult. But the fires were brought under control fairly quickly.

There were CNN reporters on both sites, and as I looked at the video, I saw a bunch of familiar faces, including Catalina and Maria Barrio, looking confused in Yonkers.

The Yonkers reporter had cornered Aristotle Costas in the lobby of the top floor of the Excalibre Building in Yonkers. The CEO of Excalibre Properties, who looked like he was getting close to yelling at people to get out of the building, explained that he kept a small apartment in the building, which was apparently targeted by the bomber.

"I kept the smallest apartment in the building, so I could sleep here when I had a late meeting or dinner, or an early morning meeting," he said. "My family and I live on Long Island, in a town called Quogue. We've lived there since we got married.

"Why somebody would target my apartment I have no idea—but it's totally destroyed. If somebody has a beef with me, or with the company, wouldn't you think they'd at least tell us what schmucks they think we are?" He explained that the first pipe bomb was detonated right outside of his door, which was blown into the apartment, and virtually everything in the apartment was burned or scorched." His voice got louder, and he added, "Then another explosion blew up the staircase that was the only way to get to the roof. Why the roof? Since people started moving into the building a little over a year ago, there have been three people who fell off the roof and were killed—but nobody has blamed me or the building for that."

The reporter explained that the latest suicide was more than a few days before, when one of the residents apparently fell from the roof to the sidewalk, and killed an elderly man who lived in an old house on a side street from Waterton Street, which was the address of the building where the bombs and fires were.

Mr. Costas was asked whether it was possible that the pipe bombs were related to the latest suicide.

"If they were, I don't know how there would have been a connection," Costas said. "I'm not a cop or a lawyer, so I don't have any legal opinions, but the young man who killed himself last week had been living in the building, and was getting ready to get married. That young guy worked for several restaurants here in Yonkers, and grew up within a short walk from the building that had been the victim of the bomber, whoever that might be."

"Any idea why this happened?" the reporter asked Costas.

"Makes no sense to me at all," Costas said. "A majority of the residents of the building, which is well over eighty-five percent occupied now, are Yonkers natives, and a bunch of them grew up right near here. So maybe somebody has a beef that we don't know anything about."

Costas was trying to watch the fire trucks and police cars, some of which were still arriving, with sirens and lights.

"Why would your apartment have been targeted?" one of the CNN reporters asked. His microphone had a very large CNN logo on it.

"No idea," Costas said. "It was an ugly surprise. There's always opposition to building a tower like this one, but there was nothing unusual in Yonkers. The area around this building was undeveloped until the City Council changed the zoning a couple of years back to bring in new jobs, new companies and employers, and new luxury residences. Now this building is one of the tallest in the city. Yonkers has been upgrading services, using the increased tax revenues from places like the Executive Boulevard development district—better schools, better health services, and a larger and more environmentally impactful recycling program that has become an ecological leader across the country and grows every year by leaps and bounds," he said.

"Why did this happen?" Costas said to himself in a puzzled but loudly audible voice, like he was wondering who was asking questions.

He was looking pallid and sweaty, like he might be feeling light-headed. "There was no warning, as far as I can tell, but of course we'll have a team on this, starting now, if you'll let me do my job. We need to look at all the emails that have been sent to us and every voicemail that could have been left on our telephones and information lines, but as far as we can tell, there were no threats to let us know this might be coming. This was like a terrorist attack, a total surprise to everybody, even the police and the fire department."

Costas unlocked a door to a small conference room, and as soon as he and the reporter were inside, the door to the conference room opened, and Jim Sturdivant walked in.

"Here's my lawyer," Costas said. "I shouldn't be answering all these questions. Believe me, I'm just as puzzled about all this as you are."

The elevator lobby was crowded with reporters brandishing microphones and there were flashes of light as photos were taken. It was like a riot, and getting worse every minute.

Mr. Sturdivant stood in the middle of the room and spread his arms out like a bird in flight. "Sorry to shut this down," he said in a big stern voice, "but the last thing we should be doing is talking to the media when we're victims as much as anyone. Mr. Costas's apartment was demolished. It's a thousand wonders that he wasn't hurt."

"Last night, my son, Demetrios, was here. He could have been killed by whoever did this. Fortunately, I've spoken to him, and he's

116

okay. Scared to death, but okay, like me."

Sturdivant started to herd all the reporters and videographers out of the lobby, where everyone was milling about. He was giving his card to each one of them. "I'll try to answer all your questions," he said loudly. "Just tell me what you need and I'll try to get it for you."

He walked forward and continued herding the media out of the buildings. There were still firefighters in full garb everywhere.

Danny O'Toole walked over to where Sturdivant was standing and said something to him. Sturdivant turned to the remaining reporters, which included a Dow Jones reporter for *The Wall Street Journal*.

"We'll try to put together a press conference within the next twenty-four hours, but you have to give us time to make sure that everyone who lives in this building is safe. We have to make sure there are no more bombs hiding in the building or outside," O'Toole said.

Chapter Twenty-Two

"That whole CNN coverage for the last couple of hours has been like a circus that was being run by clowns," Mike said to me on a video-conference line. "I wonder if it's as crazy at 30 Rock as it is in Yonkers."

I checked Yahoo! Finance on my phone to get the status of EXP (Excalibre Properties stock). It was down nearly eight percent on the day—a huge shrinkage in the market cap, from 800 million to 736 million. If the whole market dropped like that, it would be a crash like 1929.

"Costas is going to be in trouble," I said to Mike, "even though he was the founder, and has been responsible for its huge growth over the past five years, since they converted to a C Corp from a REIT. The remarkable part is that the dividend has been virtually the same as the REIT payout, when you consider the difference between an average REIT holding and the number of shares it would take to make an equal percentage of ownership."

My doorbell rang. I excused myself from the conversation with Mike and opened the door. It was Gabriele, who had also been watching CNN on TV. He smiled and pointed to my TV, which was tuned to CNN, but with the sound muted.

"Sorry about the sound on the TV," I said to him. "I've been talking to Mike. If Excalibre was a client of mine, I'd be calling the institutional investors one after another, day in and day out, to make sure they weren't running scared." I worried that the stability of the market cap of a small-cap company like Excalibre Properties would most likely affect the willingness of institutional investors to take meaningful positions in the stock. If they did, the valuations would most likely go up, because the float would be smaller, with institutional holdings basically removed from the float semi-permanently.

I went back to Mike's video call. "Look who's here," I said, pushing my phone in front of Gabriele so that Mike could see his face.

"Mike, I kept expecting the Barrios and the Blisses to pop up in the questions from the media,"

He smiled and said he wouldn't have been surprised if that had happened, but was relieved when it didn't come up. Obviously, the media were more interested in the physical destruction caused by the bombs and the fires. I couldn't suppress the old PR guy in myself and had to ask Mike if he had a few lines to use to respond to media if they asked about what the Bliss family felt about this attack on Excalibre Properties.

"No, I hadn't thought about it," Mike said, "although, as their lawyer on this matter, I should be ready to advise them on how to handle things."

"What you want to do is answer any questions with verifiable facts," I said to Mike, while Gabriele was listening in. "We'd do well to estimate the dollar damages at the Yonkers building—maybe an estimate from Costas's financial department or Excalibre's Chief Financial Officer," I suggested. "If reporters keep pushing for comments from the families, then we'd need to meet with Maria Barrio and Bill Bliss, to see how to put together media-ready responses. It would be good to have a couple of quotes from the families in case reporters are pushy for that sort of thing."

I told Mike my thoughts on how the family quotes might look. "The Barrio quote might be something about the grieving the family was trying to get through about Felipe's untimely death, along with a strong statement that Felipe's action wasn't suicide—it was an accident or a hefty push that sent him falling toward the sidewalk.

"The Bliss quote could start by pointing out that the bombings themselves were proof positive that Excalibre's building security was woefully lacking. If somebody could smuggle a pipe bomb in and then place two of them in precise positions to destroy the CEO's apartment and the stairway to the roof, that would prove the security system was far too easy to slip through without getting caught.

"Both of those quotes would back up the message that anything could have happened to propel Felipe over the edge of the roof—that suicide was not something to be believed without proof," I summed up. "When you're talking to the media, public relations are a real help in trying to put together the materials you need to get your message across to the people who watch TV or read the newspapers."

I flipped the TV to MSNBC, and immediately got coverage of the scene at 30 Rock. It looked like CNN had pointed all its guns at Yonkers, leaving its sister network to cover the situation at Excalibre's home office in Manhattan.

Both of the bombs at 30 Rock were targeted on Aristotle Costas's corner office and conference room on the twentieth floor. Both were close to demolished, between the two blasts and the ensuing fire.

Neither the NYPD nor the Yonkers PD had made any comments about who could have been behind the bombings. The NYC Police Commissioner's office published a written comment relative to the explosions at 30 Rock, describing the damage to the executive offices of Excalibre Properties, which was a respected and important landlord in Manhattan, as well as in Yonkers. The PC made no personal appearance on the media.

All the major networks were represented at 30 Rock, and there were plenty of videos looking at the ruins of the office suite where we had met Mr. Costas a couple days after Felipe Barrio and Bob Bliss died. One of the bombs had clearly been planted at the double doors leading into the suite, because those two doors were blown inward, and were splintered on the floor of the suite itself.

The second bomb had also detonated in the hallway outside the Excalibre executive suite on the twentieth floor of the famous Rockefeller Center landmark building. One camera on MSNBC was fixated on the office suite from ground level on the outside of the building, about where the Christmas Tree would be in the holiday season. The windows were blown out, and there were shards of glass on the cement sidewalks around what would be the skating rink from October to April.

It was late spring, so the area that would be the ice rink in lots of tourist photos was an outdoor dining area, empty of customers and surrounded by "crime scene" yellow tapes, with uniformed NYPD cops every five or six feet all the way around the warm-weather dining plaza, including guarding the gigantic golden flying statue of Prometheus bringing fire to the world, which looked to be unharmed. Television cameras were sweeping the cement around the lower level of the plaza, and found several places where there were shards of glass that might have fallen when the windows at the corner of the twentieth floor were blown out.

"I wonder if somebody's going to accuse Rock Center of having inadequate security," Mike said. "If so, that could have an effect on my ability to win damages from Excalibre in Yonkers for the Bliss family, so they can pay for the funeral costs for Bob Bliss."

I flipped back over to CNN, where the familiar face of Aristotle Costas was all over the screen again. It was a replay of some of the earlier video before Mr. Sturdivant chased the media out of the building, when Costas was looking like he might pass out, and seemed confused. The voice-over said that Mr. Costas had been taken to a nearby hospital to make sure he wasn't hurt in the explosions, when he had been in the apartment that was Ground Zero for one of the bombs. He said he had been in the bathroom, where the door was not blown out, and he was fully dressed, but he said he did need to sit down. One of the Yonkers cops found a chair in the conference room and brought it out into what had been the office area before it was demolished.

The glass windows were in pieces scattered all over, and mostly the window frames were empty, with no glass left. Walking was like picking a path through a battlefield littered with unexploded shells or landmines, with razor-sharp pieces of plate glass scattered all over the floor. The conference table was largely undamaged, possibly because the table-top was parallel to the floor, and so didn't get the worst part of the blast that blew out the wall facing Mr. Costas's office, where his family portrait was still on the wall, but without the glass covering that had been covering it before. Demetrios was smiling the smile of a happy kid in the picture. It must have been something to make Aristotle smile. A huge bookcase on that same wall was virtually empty, with damaged books all over the floor, scattered across the room, and under the desk.

But who could have been responsible for all this damage? Who would go so far as to fire bomb a residential building just to make a statement about what could have been a suicide a couple of weeks before?

Danny O'Toole didn't have a firm idea of who that might be, but he told us that they were looking to talk to members of a Mexican gang that had originally formed in Guadalajara to protect the drug trade that was making them rich. "We usually find most of the damage comes from either the Trinitarios or the Latin Kings, but those two are from the Caribbean—Dominican Republic for the Trinitarios, and Puerto Rico for the Latin Kings—no link to Guadalajara."

He rubbed his chin, and added, "That leaves us with Los Vagos, which is the biggest Mexican gang, but we haven't been seeing them causing problems for nearly a year," he said. "They have some connections to the Mexican Mafia, which has a big membership in Jalisco, the Mexican state that Guadalajara is in—and they've been a major source of opioids in New York City and Long Island. We haven't had the pleasure in Yonkers, at least until now. If it's them, we might have a real fight on our hands."

Danny's cellphone buzzed, and he pulled it out of his breast pocket. There was a text message from Costas, saying that he was being discharged from St John's Riverside Hospital, where they have a very active ER, and handle a lot of trauma cases that come in by ambulance, like Costas had.

Danny answered back with a text message, saying he was on his way to the hospital, and would get a cop car to transport him to wherever he needed to go, even if he wanted to go home to Quogue out on Long Island.

Costas replied directly to Danny: "They took blood and did tests. They said I was dehydrated, so I got a bag of saline in an I.V., and I feel a lot better. Not light-headed even if I stand up. I think it was just a reaction to the explosion. I was so scared. I peed myself without ever knowing it, something I don't remember ever doing before in my life." The tone of the message sounded like he was feeling abashed. "Secretary bringing clean jeans for me to put on. Thanks for the ride, appreciate it."

Danny showed us the texts from Costas and his own replies.

"What can you tell me about Los Vagos, if that's who you think might be responsible for this mess?" Mike asked him.

"Mexican gang, heavy into drugs," Danny said. "We haven't had them in Yonkers before, but they have been out on the Island, with M-13, but M-13 is Salvadoran and started on the West Coast, maybe around Los Angeles, around forty or so years ago. Their weapon of choice is a machete, which I haven't been able to find in reports about Los Vagos, which means something like 'the hobos' in Spanish," he said, sounding like an expert.

"You been doing some research on Los Vagos?" Mike asked him.

Danny nodded, and said, "Actually the forensic CSIs did the research. I just read what they sent me, and it makes me sound smarter than I am."

"But doesn't it seem like somebody must have put them on the scent to what happened up in Yonkers?" Mike wondered.

"Remember I'm a cop," Danny said. "You know how that is. I keep remembering that Felipe Barrio was born in San Salvador, which is the capital city of El Salvador, a teeny-tiny country in Central America. Lots of traffic between San Salvador and Mexico. Just by the way, Acapulco might be an obvious stopping-off place if they were travelling from San Salvador to Guadalajara. Lots of drug deals in Acapulco, so they'd have something in common with whoever the big bosses are in Acapulco." He added, "I think you told me that when you were in Acapulco, you met up with some of Felipe's relatives there. Am I remembering that right?"

"There was a helpful guy named Gonzalo Barrio," Mike said. "I think he was a cousin of Felipe's."

"Any chance he's in the drug business?"

"How would I know that?" Mike said. "I had a friendly conversation with the man about Felipe's death. That's all we talked about."

"Could that have gone straight to Los Vagos from Gonzalo?"

Mike shrugged. "I'd just be guessing if I tried to answer that, but he didn't impress me like a bad guy in any way." He brightened up and added, "How many Hispanics own condos in that Yonkers building?"

"No idea," Danny said. "But I bet Costas could tell us if we gave him some time to talk to his staff."

"Go for it," Mike said. "It's no more unlikely than chasing after Gonzalo Barrio in Acapulco."

Danny tapped out a text message to Costas, in case he was waiting for a cop to pick him up at the hospital.

"I hate long shots," Mike said. "They take a lot of time, can cost a lot of money, and seldom get results that are worth the cost or the effort, but if you think we should be looking at Latino gangs, finding out who the Hispanics in the building are could make sense, especially if we can get that information without a lot of hassle and time-wasting."

Costa texted back to Danny that he was getting a list of Hispanics who had bought condos in the Waterton building.

"According to the 2020 Census," Danny said, referring to the text he had just received from Costas, "the population of Yonkers is 52 percent white, and 38 percent Hispanic (defined as having a Spanish last name, not a racial grouping). The remaining ten percentage points was divided between Black and Asian, keeping in mind that some Hispanics are dark-skinned and could be counted as Blacks if the definitions were based on race instead of names (sometimes the darker Hispanics are called Blatinos, most commonly from the West Indies, like Jamaica or other islands that were mainly growing sugar cane, where there were more African slaves)."

"Interesting," I said. "Today most sugar comes from entirely different places, like Hawaii and Brazil. Before the American Revolution, the major use of sugar was in making rum, and most of that today is made either in the mainland of the United States, or in the Bahamas."

Danny announced that Costas told him that he had a list of people who had bought condominiums in the Waterton building, and who had Hispanic last names. "According to what they told me, there are twelve apartments on the average floor," Danny said, "meaning a total of 216 apartments, because floors 1 and 2 have no apartments, because 1 is the lobby, the janitor's area, some offices, a kitchen and restroom for the employees and the post office's access to the residents' mail boxes. Floor 2 is two restrooms (men and women) for residents and guests, the coin-op laundry room, and the gym, which is only open for membership to residents of the building," he said.

"So there are eighteen floors of apartments," he said with confidence. "Apparently Hispanic last names comprise thirty-eight percent of the resident owners, exactly the same as the percentage of Hispanics overall in the city of Yonkers.

"That means eighty-two apartments are residents with Hispanic last names," he said with a sigh. "That leaves 129 for everybody else. Since there are still some that are unsold, the percentages could change."

Chapter Twenty-Three

The damage to Excalibre Properties offices at 30 Rock was considerably less than the damage to their condominium tower in Yonkers, due to the heavier and more robust construction of the Rockefeller Center building, which had more steel rod reinforcement, more concrete, and several feet of baked bricks that blunted the explosions. A lot of glass was shattered in the Rock Center offices, more from the blast noise and the shockwave than from flying debris, which had done a lot of damage in Yonkers. Mr. Costas's small apartment was almost completely destroyed, except for the blank walls, none of which had windows, due to the way the apartment was situated with regard to the outside walls of the building.

The Barrios and the Blisses had similar reactions to the fire bombings at Excalibre Properties—something close to amusement that the landlord had been punished, one way or another, for what had happened on their watch.

"You can't let yourself or anyone in the family say anything to the media or the cops that makes it look like you might be on the side of the bombers," Mike said to Bill Bliss. "Don't even smile when you're answering questions about the bombing, and make sure everybody in the family understands that they need to look serious and emotionless all the time when the media is watching, and especially when they're asking questions. That goes especially for that radio reporter, Caroline Kashevsky, from 2020 WINR."

Mike put his sternest look on his face. "That Caroline woman is like a tropical storm over warm water, just getting ready to rip into dry land with floods, tornadoes and straight-line winds way higher than 100 miles an hour. She'll unplug your electricity faster than Hurricane Ida did." He allowed as how CNN and MSNBC reporters had a reputation for being more careful to look for the truth, while Caroline would do almost anything to get a lurid headline that would run in big letters on the top

126

half of any newspaper.

He turned to me and said, in a very soft voice that was clearly intended not to be heard by anyone except me, "I wonder if Gonzalo could have anything to do with this mess that Excalibre is in. I mean, we talked to him about Felipe, and they knew each other, but they also hadn't seen each other in years, and Gonzalo didn't read like a crook. How could he sic the bombers on Costas—why would be do it even if he had the connections?"

I had no idea how to respond, and told him so. "Gonzalo seemed like a straight-up guy to me," I said. "Not like somebody that was going to whip out a dime bag from his backpack."

"Your impressions are interesting, but they're not evidence," Mike said. "It wouldn't affect my work for the Bliss family, because I can't summon Gonzalo to be a witness in any court proceeding in the United States. As far as I know, he's not only a Mexican by birth and by residence, he's a citizen of Mexico, too."

"If you think he could be involved," I said, "tell Danny O'Toole. He's more likely than anybody else I can think of, to be able to find a trail of bread crumbs from Acapulco to Yonkers."

Mike tapped out a number on his cellphone, and Danny answered on the second ring. "Hey, Mike, where are you?" he said in cheery voice. "I've been poking around in the list of Hispanics in the building on Waterton Street, and there are several—eighteen or so—with rap sheets and names that could be Central American. Not Puerto Rican or Cuban."

"Hugo and I were just wondering," Mike volunteered, "if it was possible that Gonzalo Barrio could have been part of a chain of people that sparked bomb explosions in the Excalibre building—and maybe in their Manhattan office, too."

"Great minds," he said. "Just where I was going. He could have started a snowball rolling without even intending to do it, would be my guess," Danny said. "Acapulco is a long way from New York, but all you have to do is dial a phone to talk to anyone anywhere. We're all just a telephone number away from almost anybody in the world. If you've got the right number, you might eventually end up talking to the right person. Gonzalo Barrio is a person of interest with the FBI with regard to a kidnapping near Acapulco." He wondered if Mike had spoken to any of his connections in the NYPD about the Rock Center bombs.

Mike said he had called John Scott, the detective who was his own replacement since his retirement. But they hadn't connected yet. "I left a text message last night after he was probably having dinner at home, but no response yet. I expect I'll hear from him pretty soon. I can push him if you want, but your FBI intel would help me get the wheels rolling faster."

"The sooner the better," Danny said.

Mike tapped out another text message and sent it. Then the phone chimed to indicate an incoming call. Mike answered it on speaker.

"I'm on speaker," he said, "because Hugo is here with me, and I've got Danny O'Toole from the Yonkers PD on the other line. We've been wondering if the Mexican part of Felipe Barrio's family could be involved in these bombings."

Mike paused, then added, "Danny says the FBI is interested in Gonzalo Barrio about something that happened in Mexico—a kidnapping, he said, but he didn't say why the FBI is involved. Gonzalo's a cousin of the Yonkers Barrios, and I think he told us he spent time with Felipe when they were both living in Los Angeles some years back."

He continued, "We had a talk with Gonzalo when we were in Acapulco, where he lives these days. I gotta say, he seemed like a straight guy. None of that Guadalajara or New York street thug crap about him, no machete in his belt, no grab-ass stuff about girls. Just a lot of smiles, and nice things to say about Felipe, who was probably ten or so years younger, but still family. That whole family was hot to have Felipe buried in Catholic soil in a real cemetery."

Danny answered, "The FBI interest was part of an investigation about a junior American diplomat that disappeared while he was in Acapulco a little more than four years ago. According to what they told me, he's still missing, might have been a Los Vagos grab, since the diplomat had been a DEA guy before he was drafted into the State Department, where he was an analyst, but with fluent Spanish. Los Vagos has had both feet in the drug biz since forever, and they're probably still the largest gang in Mexico. Not puny or easy to ignore in New York either."

"That's interesting," Mike said. "I told Hugo and Ruth that I thought going to Acapulco was like looking for a needle in a haystack— but maybe I was wrong. Maybe Gonzalo made a call to somebody that got this war going. Mexican gangs wage full-sized wars against the cops around the big cities, and on major highways, like the one from Mexico City to Acapulco and Taxco, which is still the center of silver mining and sales in the whole country. I guess I was wrong, because this seems like important intel. Los Vagos could be a kingpin in this whole bomb thing."

"I think I'll try to get in touch with Mr. Costas, to see if he has had any contact with Los Vagos," Danny said. "I'll get back to you after I talk to him."

Chapter Twenty-Four

I called Lela Swann and left a voice message on her phone when she didn't answer. She got back to me about half an hour later.

"Thanks for calling me back, Lela."

She showed up to meet me in the lobby of the building, and we sat down on a sofa in front of the big empty space near the elevators that was obviously intended for visitors.

"No biggie. I've been trying to find an apartment to move into, now that Pipo is gone," she said. "I've been through four apartments today so far, and I have a list of three more. I don't need a lot," she said, "a studio would probably do, as long as it's not too tiny. I need a closet to put my clothes in, and I'll be moving some of Pipo's stuff to wherever I move. His sister, Maria, will be taking the bedroom furniture and the kitchen stuff, like plates and flatware, because a lot of that was gifts from their mother, who died after she gave those things to Pipo."

"Sorry to change the subject, but Mike has had me working on what happened to Felipe, what happened to the Bliss family, and what happened to Excalibre with the fire bombs," I told her, then laying down a blanket of silence for a short breather. "We went to Acapulco and met with some of his cousins, in particular a guy named Gonzalo. I think they were cousins, him and Felipe."

"Yeah," she said. "Pipo talked about Gonzalo. I think they knew each other when his mom and Pipo and Maria were living in Los Angeles when he was in high school. Gonzalo's probably nearly twice Pipo's age, but I never met him, so I don't know for sure. Pipo really liked Gonzo a lot. Always said nice things about him."

"Apparently there's some possibility that he was at some point in his life, part of a street gang called Los Vagos."

She frowned. "I doubt that," Lela said. "I know what Los Vagos is, mostly drug dealers, and real thugs, kinda disgusting to be around. B.O. and probably covered with germs, and constantly getting in trouble with the police. Not at all like my Pipo."

"From what you and everybody else told us, Felipe was a regular guy, church-goer, always on the straight and narrow," I said. "You told us at one point that he may have been smoking some grass once in a while, but there's nothing wrong with that. For sure, the cops don't care anymore, unless you have a shopping bag full of it, trying to sell it to kids or something gross like that."

"He didn't sell any drugs to anybody," Lela said, like she was a catechism teacher telling me something to memorize for my Confirmation.

"I didn't mean to say anything like that about Felipe," I told her. "But Gonzalo may have not been so squeaky clean. He may have run with the Crips for a while when he was a kid, and at some point moved over to Los Vagos. But then he moved to Los Angeles, and maybe had a girlfriend who wanted him to straighten out, so he did," I said, just making guesses, but trying to be on her side of the street.

"I know you met Gonzalo in Acapulco. Pipo always told me he was a nice guy."

"Seemed like a nice guy to me, too," I said enthusiastically. "We all had dinner together at a place where they had a Mexican-Thai fusion menu. I had some Thai noodles with chicken and mole poblano. Heavenly. I think it was probably one of Gonzalo's favorite places; it certainly would have been one of my favorites if I lived anywhere near there. The food was really fabulous. I think it was expensive, but everything there was expensive. I think he probably lived south of the city, near where our hotel was, which was right in the middle of a really nice residential area, full of palm trees and flower gardens. Lots of Spanish colonial houses, some of them gigantic, and one of them belonged to some famous Hollywood actor who apparently gave money to a lot of local children's charities and cancer hospitals, according to what Gonzalo told me."

"Pipo certainly thought Gonzalo put the stars in the sky," Lela said. "And I thought Felipe put those stars in the sky himself. He wanted to save up to buy me a fancy engagement ring, but he didn't live long enough."

She started to tear up again.

"So you never heard anything about Los Vagos?" I asked in a low voice.

She shook her head. I was recording the conversation on my smartphone in the breast pocket of the light jacket I was wearing. "I take it that means no, is that right?"

She nodded again.

"That's what I thought," I said for the transcript that would eventually be done. "I think any connection with Los Vagos would have been through Gonzalo. I thought that then and I think that now. No God-fearing guy like Felipe would be holding hands with thugs like that."

"You should talk to Maria," she said. "After all, she knew Pipo for a lot longer than I did."

I indicated that I would try to get together with Maria as soon as she could make time for me.

"You work for that lawyer, right?" she asked me.

"Yup, I work with Mike di Saronno, who is a lawyer," I said. "Right now he's working to get a settlement that would help the Bliss family pay for Bob Bliss's funeral. If he gets a settlement, I think it'll come from the company that owns the building. It's called Excalibre, and I think the firebombing proves that their security wasn't good enough. There was even a handgun on the roof the night Felipe fell. Nobody knows where it came from, or who left it there. It was just on the floor, wedged up against a low brick wall that was part of the boiler system that was responsible for the hot water in all the apartments."

She gave me a wide-eyed look, and said, "I never heard about that. Really? A gun? Was somebody pointing it at Pipo while he was on the roof? That could have scared him over the edge. Oh, poor man!" She moaned.

"I doubt anybody was pointing it at him, because it would have been hard to miss him when the gun was fired, which it apparently was, and the bullet lodged in a piece of wood that was lining the inside edge of the railing around the edge of the roof," I said. "The FBI ran the prints that were found on the gun, and it had been used in a homicide about three years earlier, a drug dealer, as it turned out. Nobody was ever arrested on that murder," I said, adding that, "we went all over the videos taken by the cameras in the elevators, and never found any thug that looked like he might be trying to rob somebody. Not that night or any other night. Almost every person on the elevator videos that night was a resident of the building, as a matter of fact. Even Mr. Costas, the CEO of the landowner company, was on the elevator to the 20th floor that night, but that's because he kept a small studio apartment on that floor for when he needed to sleep over instead of going to his home out at the end of Long Island, which would have been longer than an hour and a half of driving."

"Makes sense, and he probably didn't have to pay anything for the apartment, because it was his building."

"If he took the apartment for himself, it would have meant that he wasn't getting any money from somebody who might have bought it. I think a studio in this building goes for a good price," I said. "You and Felipe were living on the 14th floor, I think, so I doubt Felipe paid a bargain price for the apartment you lived in."

She said "Ha!" like a theatrical laugh. "No bargains here. And the monthly maintenance fee was high, too, and didn't include anything helpful."

"Usually there are property taxes in maintenance fees, so that would be tax deductible for you and Felipe, but you're right that there was probably nothing extra in the maintenance fee. You probably had to pay extra for parking, for instance."

"Felipe parked on the street, and moved his car whenever the alternate-side rules were in effect," she said. "Me? I don't have a car. I ride my bicycle to the store when I need something."

"I know how that is," I said. "I pay $65 every month for parking under a car-port type of roof where I live, also here in Yonkers. At least I get heat in my apartment—radiator heat—but it's included in the maintenance, and all the hot water I use, for no extra cost. I have to pay my own electricity bill, internet bill, and cable TV bill, not to mention telephone and stacks of quarters to use the washing machines and dryers in the basement. And if I want to use the swimming pool, I have to pay an annual membership fee for that, too."

"Are you in a condo?" she asked me.

"Co-op," I said.

"So you don't even own your apartment," she said.

"Exactly," I said. "I own shares in the building, and I get an apartment because I own part of the building. It's like a condo, but legalistically more complicated. Also the Board can restrict who I can sell my apartment to if I decide to sell—or if I die and my daughter, who inherits my estate, decides to sell it. That part hasn't been a problem in the past, as I understand it, but the Board is elected each year, so things could change any time."

"Good luck to you," she said, standing up and stretching. "I'm going upstairs to get on the computer and see if I can find some other places with apartments for rent." She turned and walked toward the elevator in the lobby.

Chapter Twenty-Five

Danny called Mike back, and Mike added me to the phone call with Danny's permission, making it a three-way conference call.

"I spoke with Aristotle Costas," he said, "and it turns out he probably did have some conversations with guys from Los Vagos."

Mike was in his office, but I could imagine him perking up and putting away whatever he was working on so he could concentrate on what Danny was going to be telling us. Mike and I have been friends for years.

"He was a little confused when we talked, so I had to kinda piece things together, but here's what I think he told me," Danny said. "We can arrange a face-to-face meeting to go over this again, if that will help you, or if you think it could help the Yonkers PD move this case along."

"Go ahead, Danny," Mike said. "Costas was acting confused yesterday when he was talking, so I sympathize with what you're telling us. I'd guess he's trying to sort things out, but he probably knows what he's talking about, just having trouble explaining it."

"Anyway," Danny said, "apparently a pair of LatinX guys showed up at his office in Manhattan after he filed the plans in Westchester for the Waterton Avenue building, and when they were grading the land to get ready to start construction. They were planning for a ceremonial ground-breaking, and they had apparently hired all the construction companies that would be working on the building until it was mostly finished. At that point, interior decorators would take over, and then the finishers would put in paneling, bathroom fixtures, window trims, and the marble kick-plates at the doorways inside the apartment.

"When it was time to polish the model apartments, there would be crown moldings and decorative touches like fake-antique glass doorknobs, ceiling fans and ceiling light fixtures, as well as kitchen appliances and basic great-room furniture, including dining tables, sofas, living room chairs and end-tables, master bedroom and second bedroom furnishings, and in the case of the few three-bedroom floor plans, nursery furniture for the smallest bedroom."

Mike said, "That sounds normal, so what were these Latino guys after?"

"The summary he gave me was a description of an old-fashioned Mafia security scam, one of the most common scams in organized crime. They get paid without actually doing anything. It's like you pay us, and nothing bad will happen to your building. Don't pay us, and you'll regret it, including graffiti, thefts, broken windows, and trash everywhere, plus whatever else we decide to do to your building and your employees. But a lot of harassment that doesn't break the law, or at least not felonies. Cops aren't likely to chase after somebody with a can of spray paint that's been writing obscene words on windows."

"How did Costas know this was Los Vagos?" Mike asked.

"Apparently, he didn't. He sounded confused. When I explained who Los Vagos was, he said that was who was giving him the runaround, picking his pocket, whatever kind of swindle they were trying to get by with. They had Hispanic accents—although he didn't know from where—and they looked what he called 'Mexican,' which he explained meant shiny black hair, dark eyes, light brown skin tones, some tattoos on their forearms, and jeans that were too tight and looked like they'd been poured into them, like they didn't fit."

From what I remembered, that could be a description of Costas himself, although he was bald and had a light complexion and hazel eyes. He had a neck like a tree-trunk, arms that complemented the neck, and clothing that was as tight as another layer of skin or two, including his suit-pants, which showed every ripple of thigh muscle on both legs.

"And they were hostile, like they didn't have time to waste. Like 'just sign the fucking paper; we'll leave, and you'll be safe'."

"So, do you think it was Los Vagos?" Mike asked Danny.

"It was either them or somebody like them. What Costas was sure of was that they were what he thought of as Mexican, which fits Los Vagos as we know them from the past. It also fits the FBI description of

Los Vagos in other states. This security scam is a favorite of theirs, too."

"Did he sign up?" Mike asked.

"Hard to tell. He was unclear about that. I think he wanted to look like a leader, a strongman," Danny said. "But what I took away from what he said was that he didn't sign up, tried to put them off. They left, and didn't come back."

"But they could have been the bombers, easily enough," Mike said. "Only they wouldn't have bombed the Rock Center offices. They would have just been after the Waterton Avenue building, which, as we know, is now nearly 40 percent LatinX anyway."

"If they did it, they could have been playing off what was being called a Latino suicide. They'd have been acting like the public would blame the building, instead of feeling sorry for them."

"Was there any other vandalism on the street?" Mike asked.

"Nope," Danny said. "Not even any graffiti on the bus stops."

"Not helpful to me. If it looks like Los Vagos was involved, it would be hard to convince a jury to award the Bliss family a settlement based on Excalibre Properties' negligence with regard to security on the roof," Mike said.

"Not my problem, counselor," Danny said. "I'm gonna have to tell the media that Excalibre may have been on the wrong side of Los Vagos; everybody and his brother is going to assume that this was a gang-related crime. It'll obliterate any accusation we might level at them of negligence or total lack of security, even with no locks on the freakin' roof door, and railings around the roof that were just thigh-high on a man of average height, and wouldn't have stopped a fall under almost any circumstance."

"Sounds like you might want to consider talking to the ADA about security negligence while Costas is still acting confused," Mike said.

"From my point of view," I said, "I'd advise you to get the Bliss and Barrio families to act on what they have in common. Felipe loses his balance and falls, and Bob Bliss is killed accidentally because of the negligence of the building owners. And you should make note of the fact that Costas's son, Demetrios, was on the roof that night."

"How do *you* know that?" Mike asked in surprised tones.

137

"I went over the elevator and roof stairway videos several times," I said. "And I saw the photo of his son on the wall behind his desk. That kid got a little older and was on those videos going up to the roof. That probably means Costas himself was on the roof that evening. How much do you want to bet that would be enough doubt to swing a jury?" I asked.

Since we were talking on the phone, I couldn't see the expressions on their faces, but I could hear the silence.

"Remember that Costas was fairly sure that his son was gay, and didn't seem comfortable talking about it," I added. "And remember that Felipe was a good-looking young man waiting on the roof for something. Maybe Demetrios was making a play for him. I wonder if Felipe would have been thinking about blackmailing Costas. If he said something to Costas, would Costas have pushed him over the edge?"

"You're out of line," Danny said. "You don't have any proof of any of that."

"The videos will uphold what I said about Demetrios, and probably what I said about Costas himself following his son up to the roof. From what Costas told us, I believe I remember that Demetrios had a friend with him—maybe a boyfriend type of friend. How embarrassed would Aristotle Costas have been if that came out?"

"How old do you think Demetrios Costas is?" Mike asked me.

"I don't know, well into puberty anyway."

"And how old was he in the photo in Costas's office?"

"Again, I don't know, but maybe ten."

"And why did you recognize him?"

"He was platinum blond in the photo in the office, and his hair stayed that color until the night that Felipe Barrio went over the edge," I said, "and the features matched. We know because Costas told us that the boy was gay, and that Costas was plenty annoyed because of that."

"Do you suppose that Los Vagos would have known that Demetrios was gay?" Danny asked.

"No idea, but I wouldn't put anything beyond people like that. Wouldn't you want to know if there was some kind of blackmail letter that landed on Costas's desk?" I asked. "If it was Los Vagos and they did know about Demetrios being gay, and that his gay friend, Johnny

Georgostathis was there with him the night of the latest suicide, I wouldn't put it past them to try to turn that knowledge into cash, especially if they knew that Costas himself was embarrassed by his son's sexuality."

"How many suicides does a building have to have before it goes to unusual standards to keep people away from the edges of the roof?" I asked Danny and Mike.

"No idea," Mike said. "Some months there are a handful of suicides from the George Washington Bridge, but so far the MTA hasn't done anything architectural to prevent them."

"Did Carlomaria have any relationship with Los Vagos?" I asked the cop and the ex-cop.

"Carlomaria was both Hispanic and a drug dealer," Danny said. "Odds are he had some interactions with Los Vagos people—like maybe they supplied pills at times—they used to be big on synthetic opioids like fentanyl—and with the opioid-addicted population growing in leaps and bounds every month, that might be an important part of Carlomaria's trade. Or maybe Los Vagos would deal directly with his users to get paid or do the face-to-face work of buying off the uniform cops on the street corners he needed to use. There are lots of things that need to be done if you want to both run a sales business and be invisible at the same time."

"You mean somebody had to bribe the cops?"

"Not necessarily bribes, no," Mike said. "Somebody might talk to the cops on the local beat to see when they were planning to be monitoring the particular street corner where Carlomaria was planning to meet buyers. Maybe Los Vagos would be able to supply intel from their own experience on how long uniform cops might hang out around a specific street corner, or when they would get bored and start moving on to some other street corner. Or maybe somebody had to convince the uniform cops to keep a closer eye on an area two blocks away from where Carlomaria would be pushing pills." None of those things is illegal, and none of them involves bribes. And, as we know, Carlomaria got shot anyway, so maybe he didn't listen carefully to his handlers, and that was the problem, not nosy cops."

"Isn't it racist to say that Carlomaria must have had interactions with Los Vagos if he was pushing pills?" I asked the two of them.

"Maybe," Danny said. "But we don't make decisions based on racism, at least not when we're aware of what's going on. As a matter of fact, drug peddlers who are people of color frequently sell to users who are White. One of the ways PD detectives find places to hang out is to find where expensive cars drive real slow through areas of town where you wouldn't expect them to be. So if you found a new BMW 7 series car creeping along the curb on 135th Street and Broadway, that would be a good place for cops to look for law-breaking transactions."

"Are there more White addicts than addicts of color?" I asked.

"Maybe, because the White population is more likely to have been addicted by getting prescriptions from doctors," Danny answered. "That's how most addicts end up on the street. They get started on oxycodone or some other painkiller, and graduate eventually to street drugs, which are cheaper, and easier to get when you're strung out."

"When you arrest a user, is he usually strung out?" I asked.

"A lot of times, yes. It makes them less careful in who they're doing business with. And where they are," Danny replied. Mike grunted his agreement.

"And is it likely that somebody like Felipe would be graduating—to use your word—from grass to something harder, like heroin?"

"Not usually. If the marijuana isn't going where the user wants, he's more likely to drink alcohol than to buy coke or smack," Danny said with a sound of certainty. "You can buy vodka anyplace, and it's cheap, especially if you buy the cheapest brands. If you buy horse or crystal meth, you're going to be out a lot of cash."

"And if somebody is a drunk, are they more likely to upgrade to pills?"

"Hard to say," Mike interrupted. "You need to ask a specialist in substance abuse if you want an answer to that one."

Chapter Twenty-Six

I have a hard time with long phone calls. It's like after a while I can't follow where the other people are trying to go with their conversation. Maybe I just stop being able to concentrate. Whatever.

When I was a teenager, I had real problems doing the kind of long girlfriend phone calls that all the other guys were into. I always had girlfriends, and usually spent a lot of weekend time with whichever girl I was dating—swimming, surfing, sometimes hiking if I could get the family car to drive someplace where there was a trail I wanted to try. But I would break into a sweat if the phone rang and it was the girl of the day wanting to talk on the phone. I could tell what the call would be like from what she would say. Either she would ask me about the homework assignment from some class we were both taking, or she would say something lovey-dovey—and that's when I knew I was going to fall asleep while she was talking.

Maybe it was because we were on a party line at home, and sometimes one of the neighbors might be listening in, which worried me in case we got gooey for some reason. But mostly it was because I couldn't find ways to keep the conversation going. I had a hard time if she started to complain about the other girls, because some of them were probably girls I had dated at one time or another. Most of the girls would complain about guys, though—especially football players, because the girls always treated them like goons. If I had to lead the conversation, I'd wander off into talking about baseball or football, because my friends were mostly athletes. It wasn't like you needed to be like Mickey Mantle to play on the school baseball team, and you sure didn't have to be in line for a college scholarship from football for the coach to welcome you to the team. Not me, never me. I was a klutz from the word "go," and the coaches knew it. I couldn't run fast, jump high, and never learned to throw a football without it going end-over-end uncatchable. It seemed to me like girls only wanted to talk about movies and whatever music was popular, or how so-and-so other girl was such an idiot and didn't know how to use make-up without looking like a floozy. They all had crushes on singers, and I couldn't even remember who the singers were—even on the number-one hits.

My favorite song in high school was when I was a senior. It was called "Runaround Sue," and I nicknamed one of the girls at school after that song. Oddly enough, she was a girl I never dated, but she was one of the "popular" ones—and pretty. Her name was Arlene, and if she had called me, I would have had to tell her that I was on my way out the door to go to the market for my mom, because I wouldn't be able to stay on the phone without feeling like I was going to go berserk and start to laugh uncontrollably.

That same thing still tends to happen to me on Zoom calls, or on conference calls like the long palaver I had just been through with Mike and Danny. For me, I wanted to go over to 30 Rock and see if I could barge into Aristotle Costas's office and ask him what the heck he thought was going on. I can talk to a person all day, but talking to a voice on the phone makes me feel like I have insects crawling all over me.

I called Costas's cellphone number, which he had, probably mistakenly, given to me on the card he handed me when Mike and I were in his office. It was chilly outside, and I was wearing a wool sweater, even though I was indoors. Feeling cold is, for me at least, as much psychological as physical. If I look outside and it's cold and rainy, or—God forbid—cold and snowy, I start to shiver just looking at the weather. When I was in high school, we had a dog (a part-Labrador mutt) who used to sit on the rug in the living room and look out the picture window at the snow on the ground when we were in the mountains in the winter—and he would shiver, even though it was warm in the house or the cabin where we were staying.

Same with me, just like my buddy, Duke the dog.

I left a voice message on Costas's cellphone, and he called back very quickly.

"What can I do for you?" he asked.

"I'm working with Mike di Saronno, the lawyer who's representing the Bliss family. Tall guy, getting old, thinning gray hair, usually with a baseball cap."

He grunted a "Yup."

"I just got off a long call with Danny O'Toole from the Yonkers PD, and Mike, the Bliss family lawyer," I said. "They were talking about whether a gang of thugs that goes by the name Los Vagos was involved with the bombings that your company experienced over the last few days."

No response.

"Are you familiar with Los Vagos?" I asked him, with nothing but silence on his end of the line. "I can come over to your office in Rock Center if that helps, or I can meet you at Waterton Street, since I live in Yonkers."

"I'm at Waterton Street today," he said. "We've got some guys trying to patch up the damage the fuckin' bombs did." He paused. "I'm using a small office on the street level, behind where the concierge desk is in the lobby."

"You want me to come over?"

"It's easier to talk to a real person than to talk to a voice on the phone, when I can't see how you're reacting to what I tell you," he said. "Come on over. I don't have a schedule today, pretty flexible. I'm just hoping that they can make my little apartment livable, because I feel like I'll need to spend a lot more time here than I usually do for the next few weeks."

"I just want to talk about Los Vagos, which is an organized crime syndicate that's involved in anything that's illegal. They're Mexican in origin, but they have a lot of things going on here in New York. We think they may have been involved in the damage to your building," I said. "I talked to a relative of Felipe Barrio who we think used to be a part of Los Vagos and could have sparked some of the timing of what happened because of his cousin's fall from your roof."

"Who's 'we'?" he asked, with some vague traffic noises in the background of the call.

"I'm affiliated with the NYPD, although I'm a civilian, not a cop—no badge, no gun, no night-stick," I told him. "I think I told you when Mike and I came to your office once before. Mike used to be a detective with the NYPD, but he's retired now, took his pension after twenty-five years. I'm helping him because we're friends. He's representing the Bliss family following Bob Bliss's death on the sidewalk outside your Excalibre residential tower."

"So why do you think one of the Barrio boys was part of Los Vagos?" Costas asked, point blank.

"Felipe's cousin, Jose-David, told me that Gonzalo Barrio—also a cousin of theirs who spent part of his life in Los Angeles, but who's now living in a fancy area of Acapulco—used to be in the drug business when he lived in California a bunch of years back," I told him. "Jose-David told me he went to visit Gonzalo in Acapulco and was creeped out with some of the thugs he met with Gonzalo there.

"We were able to get in touch with Gonzalo Barrio before we got to Acapulco," I said. "When we were getting ready to go to Acapulco, we asked around the family and got a phone number for him. When we called, he wanted us to have dinner together when our group was there.

"My impression of Gonzalo was that he was very cool and collected," I said, "like ice wouldn't melt in his mouth. He was wearing super-expensive clothing, like brown Gucci loafers that probably cost upward of $1,000.00. He was one of those people who you could tell was made out of self-confidence. He was also obviously overflowing with cash.

"My colleague, Gabriele Cortese, who owns one of the most famous restaurants in Manhattan, told me during dinner that Gonzalo acted like an Italian gangster, and he wouldn't be afraid of anything or anyone," I told Mr. Costas. "Gabriele said Gonzalo had the evil eye and was probably 'Ndrangheta (which is like Mafia)'. He made that hand-gesture with his thumb poking through his fingers to ward off what they call *maloik* (Calabrian slang for evil eye).'

"Gonzalo is clearly well-off, living in an upper-class area full of mansions," I told Costas, "and also featuring a huge-walled estate owned by a famous Hollywood actor who does action movies, kinda like James Bond with magical cars that can fly or turn into boats or whatever."

I decided to tell Costas that, "As far as we have been able to tell since we got back, he doesn't have a job of any kind, and he certainly didn't inherit a fortune from his family—his father was a bus driver, and his mother cleaned houses and at one point had a nearly full-time job in a downtown hotel, making up rooms when customers checked out.

"For a guy who never went to college, and apparently never had a regular job, he did pretty well financially—at least it looks that way," I said with a sense of finality.

"Well, if he had anything to do with Los Vagos, then he's part of the mob that tried to kill me, and other people in this building," Costas said in a tense voice. "Those two thugs that tried to sucker me into paying them to keep my building from being trashed were Los Vagos men; they threatened me and my company, and then those goddamn fire bombs exploded on our penthouse level here in Yonkers, and totally destroyed an apartment that I was renting for my own use when I had to stay in Yonkers overnight, and blew up the stairs from the penthouse level to the roof.

"They also scared the living shit out of the fine people who bought apartments and live in the building," he said. "Then they tried to destroy our executive offices in Manhattan, which fortunately weren't damaged as heavily as the Waterton building in Yonkers—the two buildings were designed and built differently, and the Yonkers building was more glass, while the Rock Center buildings are more steel and brick, and didn't get the kind of structural damage that the Yonkers building got.

"My own office in Manhattan was completely trashed, along with the Board Room next to the office, which was turned into shards of glass and splinters of expensive Board Room furniture, including a custom-made conference table that seated the whole Board—twelve directors and me, I'm the Chairman. Our financial department estimates that the damages done to the two buildings will total nearly five million dollars to bring them up to the way they were the day before the fire bombs were detonated.

"I'm completely convinced that this was associated with the security scam that those two Los Vagos guys threatened me with before we even started construction on the Waterton building—a building where nearly 85 percent of the apartments are now owner-occupied. If we start losing families because of what happened, the cost of getting back to the way things were last week will go up and up and up."

He pointed at me, and said, "I'm gonna need a lawyer, and I can pay. Let me know if you're interested, because I like the way you work, and I think I could trust you, too."

"Like I said before," I told him wearily, "I'm working with Mike, who's representing the Bliss family, and may be filing a suit against you and Excalibre Properties. It would be an unforgiveable conflict of interest for me to sign on with you. Sorry. I'll be happy to help out unofficially whenever I can do it without causing damage to Mike or the Bliss family."

Chapter Twenty-Seven

Mike called me and said he thought it was time for us to get in touch directly with Demetrios Costas, since he was on the videos the night that Felipe fell off the roof. "What if he was attracted to Felipe?" he asked me.

"Gay men aren't known for hitting on straight men," I said. "I've been friends with Gabriele for years, and I know a lot about his lifestyle. He's totally gay, you know, even though it seems obvious to me that most people couldn't tell that from the way he acts. He doesn't seem to get hit on in the restaurant, and that's as low-pressure and friendly as any bar in Manhattan."

"I'm not suggesting that Demetrios dropped his pants, or backed Felipe off the roof or anything like that," Mike said. "I was just thinking that if Felipe was on the roof because he was trying to come up with some answers to his financial problems, he might have put up with Demetrios making suggestive comments, just because of the power Mr. Costas has over anyone living in the building."

"I don't think he's eighteen yet," I said. "His dad or his mother would have to be present if you were asking him questions."

"Yup, got that."

"I was going in a different direction in my mind," I said. "I was thinking I should get in touch with Jose-David again, to see if I can get any more detailed info on Gonzalo. If Gonzalo has any connection with Los Vagos, and if the two security salesmen that were harassing Mr. Costas were Los Vagos guys like Costas thinks, that could affect the outcome of everything that happened, including that gun on the roof, Felipe's fall, and any settlement that the Blisses might get as a result of the building's negligence."

"Interesting how close Los Vagos is to Las Vegas," I said.

"Maybe not just a coincidence," Mike said. "A lot of people have a sense of humor, maybe even a drug thug sometimes."

"I like Jose-David. I think he'll tell me what I need to know about Gonzalo."

"Morals don't run in the blood," Mike said. "Everything we know about Felipe tells me that he was the opposite of what we think Gonzalo might be like. Maybe Jose-David is like Felipe. I say that although I don't think I've ever spoken to him—but you seem to have a favorable impression of him."

"I think the way people grow up and their morals come from the way they were raised, not the DNA they were born with," I said. "Maybe Gonzalo had a hard childhood, or parents who didn't teach him the kind of things Felipe's parents taught him. Felipe didn't get to be a devout Catholic because of the way his brain was shaped or whatever DNA might have given him. It came from his mom and dad, had to."

"Go for it," Mike said. "I don't think I've met Jose-David, or even spoken to him, but I'll buy your judgment any day of the week."

"I don't know where he lives, exactly, but I know he lives in Yonkers, because he put together a family meeting for me. That's how I met Catalina and Maria and Tricia. Even Felipe's brother, Rodrigo, was there, although I don't recall him saying anything about Felipe. Jose-David is a close relative, like I think their mothers were cousins and grew up together in El Salvador, or something like that. But I feel sure I can get in touch with him. I probably still have his number from when I first talked to him. I think Lela gave me his number."

I was right; I did still have the number in my contacts on my phone, where I had called him right after Felipe fell off the roof.

I dialed the phone, and—lo and behold—Jose-David answered on the first ring.

"Hello?" a male voice said like a question.

"Hi, Jose-David. This is Hugo Miller," I said. "We met when I was poking around with Danny O'Toole from the Yonkers PD about Felipe's fall from the roof of that building."

"I remember," he said. "I got a bunch of Barrios together at your apartment. You live near St John's Riverside Hospital, right? Lotta nice paintings, I remember. I think you had a hefty bunch of bottles of wine where I could see them, too."

"Yup." I nodded like he was there in the room with me as I answered his question. Nice guy; I remembered him better when I heard his voice—not that it was so distinctive, but it helped me fish up a picture in my mind. Medium height, maybe 5'9" or 10", black hair, good symmetrical features, well-developed upper body, looked like he spent a fair amount of time at the gym. "Any chance we could get together again?" I wanted to know. "I'm trying to put together some intel on your cousin, Gonzalo, in Acapulco. The owner of the Waterton building thinks he may have been involved with Los Vagos. You know what Los Vagos is?"

"Yeah, sorta," he said. "Mafia, drugs, that kind of thing. What does that have to do with anything?"

"You heard about the bombs that were set off in the Waterton building?"

"It was on the television news, but I didn't do any deep dive into the news to find out what happened. What does it have to do with Gonzalo, who lives all the way in Mexico?"

"Maybe nothing, but two thugs tried to pressure the building owner to pay them off to protect the building from being attacked or damaged," I said. "Mr. Costas said they were Mexican, and from what he said, it sounded like an organized-crime-type security scam.

"And he thinks Gonzalo might have been involved?"

"All he told me he was that these two guys tried to get him to give them fifty thousand dollars for protection for the building—and then there were these two fire bombs that virtually destroyed part of the penthouse floor of the building," I said, "including a studio apartment that Costas himself was using when he had to hold over in town instead of going home to Long Island."

I wished I could see him, to know what his reactions were to what I was telling him. "I remembered that you had a low opinion of Gonzalo, or it seemed that way to me. I haven't mentioned Gonzalo to the building's managers or anything. I'm just trying to help Danny O'Toole, who is the PD detective on the case. He knows we met Gonzalo when we were in Acapulco."

He said he would come over in a few minutes. "I live on Lake Street, right near Roberts Avenue," he said. "I can walk over to your place; it'll take me ten minutes, maybe less. That work for you?"

I told him to call me when he was downstairs and I would buzz him in. "I have Cokes in the fridge, or a bottle of Italian red on the table."

"I'm more a Coke guy than a wine guy," he said. "You got OJ?"

"Sure, no prob. I'm a juice fan, got pomegranate juice, too, if you want."

"Maybe mix 'em up," he said. "See you in a few."

"I told Mike that Lela introduced me to you," I said to him when he got to my apartment.

"More like Maria," he said, correcting my memory. "She was real close to Pipo."

"Anyway, I met Gonzalo when we went down to Acapulco to see what we could find out about Felipe's family background," I told Jose-David. "Gonzalo wanted to pay for everything, like he wanted us to know he was floating in cash, but he did seem real well-off, wanted to pay for dinner for everybody at a fancy Asian Fusion restaurant he took us to."

"He's got a lot of money," Jose-David said.

"Must be a smart guy," I said, "to make a lot of money so young."

"More well-connected than smart," he said. But he didn't volunteer anything more than that.

"I thought from where he lived, maybe he was into real estate."

"Nah," Jose-David said. "I wish, but nah."

"What do you mean?"

"He hangs out with wise guys," he said, using a slang name for Mafia thugs. "I don't think he's doing anything illegal these days, but he sure went through a period when he was just out of high school in LA. He was pushing a lot of drugs, and making a lot of money. That was while he was in Los Angeles, and all of a sudden he moved back to Mexico, like overnight. I always wondered if he was trying to get away from being arrested for drug crap. He's fucking rich, doesn't have to do anything dangerous these days. He's got what he needs to do whatever he fucking wants. These days he's a gentleman, has everything he needs."

I noted the obscene words, and thought that sounded unusual. From what I remembered when I first met Jose-David, he wouldn't ever have used those words, especially with women in the room. Of course, it was just him and me sitting in my living room, no ladies to offend.

"Sorry about that," he said, watching me with what I thought was a serious look on my face. "I usually watch what I say better. It's just that Gonzalo has done things that none of us in the family wants to know much about."

"Mr. Costas, the owner of the Waterton building where Felipe and Lela were living, thinks he was being harassed by Los Vagos," I said, and stopped.

Jose-David nodded. "Possible," he said. "Gonzalo isn't dealing these days, but I know he knows the Vagos people. You don't ever get a chance to quit Los Vagos. Once you're in, you're in forever. It's like being a Catholic—you're a Catholic for life. You might fade away from the business part like Gonzalo has done, but you never get away. They know everything about what you've done, and you can't get rid of that either. They can sic the law on you there in Mexico, but they can also break your legs, if they're really pissed off, or take your kids or your wife or your mother."

"Are you saying that Gonzalo is involved with organized crime?"

"Nope," he said. "I said nothing of the sort," he said curtly. "But he got his money from someplace, and it wasn't the Lotto. Nothing that he would want to talk about these days, now that he's respectable."

"That must be difficult for other people in the family."

"We're mostly poor," he said. "I mean, we get along, but none of us is rich, and none of us is on the wrong side of the law."

That was what I wanted to know. I gave Jose-David a tall glass of orange juice, and he drank it down like he was thirsting to death. Then he got up and left.

I called Mike and told him what Jose-David had said, to the best of my memory. "He was careful to say that Gonzalo is respectable now," I told him, "just that he maybe got his hands dirty at some point earlier in his life."

"Tells me a lot," Mike said. "Also may mean that Felipe had more on his mind than we knew about, especially since Lela said he was maybe selling grass to people he knew."

Chapter Twenty-Eight

"So Gonzalo Barrio did a hitch with Los Vagos," Mike said when I told him when we got together in his new office on 5th Avenue and 20th Street. "If I'd've known, I would've asked him some questions myself, when we were having dinner that night."

"From what Jose-David told me, Gonzalo probably isn't a blabber-mouth about things he doesn't want people to know."

"Hey," Mike said. "Yes, I used to be a cop, but I'm also Italian— and I had relatives growing up that were what we might call colorful today. Most of my family were first-generation Americans. I was the first one to go to college, and certainly the first one to get a law degree. I wasn't the first cop in the family. A lot of my cousins who were around the same age as me went to the Academy and became cops."

"I'm not surprised about any of that," I said.

"For years I was worried that I would be on a case where one of my relatives was on the other side," he said.

"Like Jose-David and Gonzalo, you mean?"

"Kinda," he answered.

"You've got a nice conference room here," I said. "These chairs are comfortable, and they have arms that are easy to adjust up and down. You must have spent a lot of money on this stuff," I said. "Table looks custom-made, too."

"The table and the chairs were both catalog items," he said. "Nothing custom-made, nothing particularly expensive. I didn't even spend a lot of time looking through the online catalogs. This stuff all came from Overstock, and that includes the sofa in the office. Office furniture isn't cheap no matter what you get, but nothing here is something that Aristotle Costas would have in his office."

"Funny you should mention Costas, since he's the one who says he got hit on by Los Vagos front men," I said. "And Felipe Barrio's cousin turns out to have been close to that same syndicate when he was living in California. You're one of the people who told me not to believe in coincidences like that."

"Well, it wasn't a bunch of teenagers that set those fire bombs off," Mike said. "It fits Los Vagos like a glove."

"I keep going back to Aristotle's son, Demetrios, and his buddy that were taking the elevators the night that Felipe fell off the building," I said. "Not that I think a pair of gay teenagers pushed Felipe over the railing, just that it's peculiar that they were all there at the same time. And then somebody destroyed that staircase and the apartment next to it—which belonged to Aristotle—almost immediately after what the coroner called a suicide."

"But which we're inclined not to think of as obviously a suicide by a super-Catholic young man who was going to Mass on weekdays, not to mention every, every Sunday," Mike said. "Line all that up and see what it looks like. Los Vagos, Gonzalo Barrio and his cousin Felipe, Aristotle Costas and his gay son—all maybe involved in the same series of events. That's a series of coincidences that make me smell something putrid," Mike said. "I wonder if Aristotle had any threats that the bombing might happen. I wonder if Demetrios knew his father was in on his secret about liking boys. I wonder if they had argued about it. I wonder if Demetrios had been looking at pipe bomb sites on the Internet, or maybe if his friend, Johnny had. There's nothing to say that gay boys couldn't be the fire bombers. From what the Yonkers CSIs said, there may not have been much of anything in those bombs that couldn't be found at Home Depot—even the explosives could have been made from ammonia-based fertilizer."

"Your mind has been busy," I said to him. "Maybe it's time to lay this all on Danny O'Toole, to see if he wants to get a warrant to bring in the boys and Aristotle Costas, to see what they have to say about what happened."

"Kids can be more clever than most people expect," he said. "I wouldn't put it past Demetrios and his buddy to make those bombs, and it wouldn't be any trick for Demetrios to plant them by his father's apartment and his office in Manhattan. He wouldn't have any problem getting admitted to both buildings."

"I kept wondering," I said to Mike, "how Los Vagos would have been able to target Aristotle Costas so exactly in two locations that weren't even in the same city. The boys could have had access to both of them easily."

"I think it's time to talk to Aristotle and see if he would be willing to arrange for us to talk to Demetrios," Mike said. "Given the two locations, we need to investigate where Aristotle himself was at the time the bombs were planted, and where his son was, because both of them would have known exactly where to plant the bombs to do the most damage to Costas and the company he started."

"He's going to want Jim Sturdivant to be in any meeting we might have," I said. "As I remember, Sturdivant told the media he would put together a press conference once Mr. Costas had been checked out at a hospital to make sure he was okay, and hadn't been injured in any way, since he was in his apartment on the 20th floor when the bomb by his front door destroyed a lot of the apartment."

"I think I remember," Mike said, "that Costas was in the bathroom when the bomb went off, and although he may have been hit by a shock wave, he wasn't burned or hit by shrapnel from the explosion, in spite of the fact that the main room of the small apartment was almost totally demolished, and the door to the bathroom was partially blown in, so that it was inoperative when the firefighters got there."

"Did the firemen have to bash it in?"

"I think so," Mike said. "I wasn't there and I haven't been there since then, so I haven't seen it, but I remember it that way from what Danny O'Toole said that morning."

The phone on Mike's desk rang, and he answered it, and almost immediately said out loud, "Speak of the devil." He put his hand over the mouthpiece end of the telephone, and said to me, "Danny O'Toole," then pointed to the phone.

"Hey, Danny, Hugo's here in my office, and if we're going to talk business, I'd like to put the phone on speaker, so Hugo can join us in the conversation. That okay with you?"

Apparently, Danny said "yes," because Mike pressed the "Speaker" button and I could hear noises on the other end of the call.

"Hey, Danny, it's Hugo," I said. "Hope you're having a good day."

"I just had a call from Olympia Costas," he said. "Aristotle's wife, and the mother of their son, Demetrios."

"That's odd," Mike said. "I figured Aristotle was married because he had a kid, but I had no idea what her name was. She lives out on the Island?"

"Quogue," he said. "At least that's what Aristotle said."

"So," Mike said, "what's up that his wife called you of all people?"

"She said Aristotle wouldn't get out of bed this morning, and she ended up calling 9-1-1. The EMTs took him to the hospital. Seems like he's had what we used to call a nervous breakdown."

"Is he going to be okay?" I asked.

"I'm not a doctor, but I don't think I've ever heard of anyone dying from a nervous breakdown," Danny said. "I know it's not a real medical term, but I've been thinking he was talking and acting strangely. So in a way, this isn't surprising. I was thinking to myself that he might be having PTSD, since he was in that apartment when the bomb blew it up."

"So, what did Olympia tell you?" Mike asked.

Danny cleared his voice. "Apparently, he's in the ER at St John's Riverside in Yonkers, right near where the Waterton co-op building is."

"Near where I live, then," I said. "If he's having mental problems, I bet he ends up at New York Presbyterian in White Plains."

I was busily looking up "nervous breakdown" on my phone. "I just looked it up on the Internet," I told the two of them. "I think you're right, from what I just read on Web MD. It's not a real medical term, although it was used for years to describe what has happened to a person who can't function normally. Maybe tied to anxiety or depression, but it makes sense to me that it might be caused by post-traumatic stress—or any kind of stress, for that matter."

"Has his wife seen him since they took him away?"

"She was at the hospital when she called me," Danny said, "but I didn't ask her if she had seen her husband. She said Demetrios was there with her."

"He'd be about what age?" Mike asked.

"I'd say late teens, like seventeen going on eighteen," I said. "I think I remember Aristotle saying the kid was on the roof smoking a cigarette, so maybe he's old enough to buy a pack. That would make him eighteen, I think—but I don't smoke, so I'm not sure. When I was a kid in California, the smoking age was sixteen, but now I think it's eighteen everywhere."

"I wonder what happens at Excalibre if the CEO is in the hospital," Danny said slowly. "Who would be in charge?"

"Depends on the way the corporation is set up," Mike said. "Most corporations there would be somebody who would be like a Vice President in Washington—who would step in and take over the day-to-day job of CEO when the CEO is incapacitated. Like a lieutenant governor in a state capitol."

"But not always?" Danny said in response.

"Could be that everything reverts to the Board of Directors or the shareholders. If it's the Board, it would mean the Board would probably appoint an interim CEO, like promoting the Chief Operating Officer temporarily in a case like this. In the meantime, the Chairman of the Board would probably be in charge. All depends on the way the by-laws are written."

"And if it's the shareholders?"

"Then a majority shareholder would have the last say, if there was a shareholder who held control like a majority of the stock."

"So if Aristotle owned more than half the stock, maybe his wife would be in charge?"

"Could be," Mike said. "But remember that Excalibre Properties is listed on the New York Stock Exchange. If there is somebody who can take control, it would be in the Annual Report or the 10K." He sat down at his desk and turned to his computer. "Going on EDGAR," he said, "to pull up the latest 10K. There should be a section called 'Management,' that would give us the answer."

"I suspect that lawyer, Jim Sturdivant, would have a say about how to interpret the by-laws."

"Wait, it's more cut-and-dried than that," Mike said, staring at his computer screen. "I'm looking at the 10K, dated April of this year, and as of this filing, the Costas family has a simple majority of all the shares issued and outstanding."

"So that means Mrs. Costas is in control?"

"Probably, but it depends on the family," Mike said. "They could have an agreement on who does what to whom if Aristotle is off his game. He built the company, after all. He has a brother on the Board, named Socrates, naturally." He kept reading on the computer screen. "It says here that Socrates Costas lives in Bronxville, not more than a couple of miles from the Waterton building. Interesting."

"I'd like to meet Socrates," Danny said. "I'll try to get on that right away."

"Wait," Mike said. "Olympia is on the Board, too. Her middle name is Costantinos, so two of her initials are Cs. One of the big bond-holders is also called Costantinos. Costantinos Incorporated, as a matter of fact. And guess who's on the Board of Costantinos! Aristotle, Olympia and Demetrios Costantinos."

"I wonder if Costas is a contraction of Costantinos. That could be the real family name—a variation of Constantine the Great, the founder of Constantinople, the city now called Istanbul. Could be this Demetrios is their son, the gay boy who was maybe on the roof smoking when Felipe Barrio went over the edge."

"I wonder if there is more than one Demetrios in the family," Danny said.

"I nominate Hugo to get on a train and go back to Yonkers, where he lives these days, to meet Mrs. Costas at St John's Riverside Hospital. Maybe we can get some current info on Aristotle."

"I can poke around on that part of the puzzle," Danny said, "but I'll welcome Hugo's help, if he doesn't mind me tagging around after him."

I smiled and started to say something smart-ass, but decided not to.

Chapter Twenty-Nine

Olympia was the opposite of her husband, physically. When I got to St John's Riverside's ER entrance, the front desk told me where to find her, on the fourth floor in a single room where Aristotle had been admitted.

She was tallish for a woman, probably taller than her husband if they were both standing up. The blond son was there in the room, too, and he looked eighteen, and like he got his genes from her, not from Dad. He looked taller because of his posture, although he probably shorter, and slim as a willow tree. His complexion was untroubled by the acne that a lot of teens suffer from, and his eyes were as blue as the summer sky.

"Welcome," Olympia said, when she opened the door to the hospital room. "This is a difficult time for us, but Demetrios and I are really pleased that you are here to help us out, or hold our hands—or both."

She was pretty in a standard way: light-colored hair, probably from a bottle because it was too much the same all over. Natural blond hair, like her son's, varied a bit, with some strands of brown here and there, and some strands of platinum blond balancing them. She clearly got a lot of exercise. Her calves were round and muscled and spoke of bicycle riding. She had a big smile and big, round hazel eyes. Very pretty, and she was wearing a silken shirtwaist dress that showed off her curvy figure, and especially her small waist, which also went with the exercise that shone all over her.

"No, there's no other Demetrios in the family," she said, "and yes, Costas is a short version of Costantinos. Ari started the company when he was still hiring carpenters to do construction jobs," she said. "He wanted to name it Costas Construction, but it ended up being Excalibre Properties. It had a kind of sound to it that he liked."

"What happened that made you call 9-1-1, if you don't mind my asking?"

"He wouldn't get out of bed this morning," she said. "That was the opposite of what he usually is like. He would always jump out of bed like he had stuck his finger in an electric socket. But today he wouldn't even let me turn down the covers to help him stand up."

"That's because he peed the bed," Demetrios said eagerly.

She nodded, and said that was actually the impetus behind her calling the emergency number. "We were staying in one of the model apartments that are being used to show people what the apartments look like when they're furnished. It's hard to sell apartments when they're just empty. They need to look a little like homes, but without any clutter. The apartment we were in is a two-bedroom, so that Demetrios could be with us. We had food from the pizza place across the street, and I brought a bag of coffee from home, so we could have coffee when we wanted it. You could smell the pee when you got near the bedroom. I didn't know what to do. He smelled bad, too, like he hadn't been showering for a few days."

"You mind if I ask you a question that's off the subject?" I asked the young man.

He shrugged and said, "Okay."

"Your father told us that you were holding a gun that night on the roof," I said.

He nodded. "There was a gun on the floor by one of the short walls that hide the heating pipes," he said. "I picked it up to look at it."

"Your fingerprints weren't on it. The cops who came to see what happened when Mr. Barrio fell off the roof, and they found it. They took it back to the station and we dusted it for fingerprints."

"I was riding my bike around the park up the street, and had gloves on," he said. "I usually wear gloves when I ride my bike, because I tend to grab the handlebars right, and I can get blisters pretty easy if I don't wear gloves. I just wear lightweight winter gloves, the kind I would wear if we were going out to eat, not the kind I'd wear if we were going tobogganing, or building a snowman. When it's really cold, I always wear gloves that are stuffed with down or Kapok, and are waterproof, so my

160

fingers don't freeze," he said.

"What did you do with it?"

"The gun?" he asked.

I nodded.

"I put it back where I found it. It was heavy and felt like a real gun. I was kind of afraid of holding it."

"Did anyone else pick it up?"

"My friend, Johnny, was there, but he didn't want to get near it, but Dad picked it up and had a look."

"Did anybody pull the trigger?" I asked.

He nodded. "Dad did, but it didn't hit anything when he shot it," he said. "That man who was standing next to the railing looked scared, but it didn't hit him or anything. He looked like he was trying to figure out how to get back downstairs, but he stayed where he was, next to the railing. He looked really scared."

"Was there anyone else on the roof at the time? Maybe smoking a cigarette?"

"Nope," he said. "I smoked a cigarette, but only a couple of puffs. My dad would crawl all over me if he saw me smoking, so I threw it on the floor and stamped it out before he saw me."

"What kind of cigarettes do you smoke?"

"Marlboro Lights, but I don't smoke very much, usually not even a pack in a week. People don't like smokers these days. I hate having people make faces at me, like my friend Johnny does when I light up." He pointed to the hospital bed. "Or Dad, who would bite my head off if he had a chance."

"What happened after the gun fired?"

"We left, went back downstairs to the lobby and waited for Dad to come down so we could ride with him back home."

"So you took the elevator?"

He nodded. "The stairs down to the Penthouse Floor, then the elevator."

"Did your father drive you home?"

He shook his head negatively. "I think he decided to stay in his little apartment overnight. Maybe it was too late, or maybe he had an early meeting the next morning. I don't know, but he sent me a text message to call an Uber car to get home. Johnny stayed with us in Quogue that night."

"Are you and Johnny dating?"

He frowned and shook his head. "I know people think I'm gay, but I haven't ever had sex with anybody, no girls, and certainly no boys."

"So when he stays with you in Quogue, you guys don't sleep together?"

"Right, we don't. We wouldn't. I don't think he'd be interested any more than I am."

"If you don't mind my asking, why do people think you might be gay?"

He shrugged, "Not sure, maybe I don't act as much like a guy as they're used to. I don't like football, even on TV. But I'm not swishy, and I don't hang around with feminine guys. I have dates with girls like other guys, but I haven't ever touched a girl someplace I shouldn't touch her."

"You think you plan to marry and have kids some day?"

He nodded, but not eagerly. "I guess so, that's what people do," he said. "Right?"

I nodded. "That's what I did," I said. "I have five kids and two granddaughters. My wife died a couple of years back, but we were married for a lot of years, and we were always close. I hardly remember a day when we didn't talk to each other, even when she was living in California and I was living in Manhattan after I started my New York office."

I should put Demetrios in a room with Gabriele, I thought. *That'd be an acid test about whether he's gay or not.* I didn't feel like I could take him at his word about being straight. He seemed to me like me might be partial to men.

Gabriele tells me that he is super-attracted to me, which I consider a compliment, but I'm not into guys at all. Truthfully, I'm not much into girls these days either. Too old to be interested, and too old to be horny in the way that men get horny. Gabriele's super-handsome and built like the proverbial brick shithouse: muscular, tallish, broad shoulders, well-developed arms and legs, pectoral muscles that pop out if he's wearing a T-shirt, or a fitted dress shirt. People stare at him wherever he goes, like he was Brad Pitt or something. He's not Brad Pitt at all; he's Italian, with black shiny hair that's wavy but stays combed, skin that always looks slightly tanned, and perfectly symmetrical facial features, with deep brown eyes. I met him when he was looking for johns in my neighborhood when I was living in the theater district—he was a person of interest in a potential homicide case that I was working on with Mike di Saronno when he was still a police detective.

Anyway, he's one of those people who has very dependable gaydar, which means he can tell if a guy is straight or gay or both.

I found myself wondering if Demetrios was just fibbing about not being gay, or whether he was deluding himself for religious reasons—I kept thinking about his father saying you can't be gay and Orthodox at the same time.

I wanted to ask him if he and Johnny came back and planted the pipe bombs, but I thought he would hold it against me if he thought I was accusing him of something.

Chapter Thirty

After I left the hospital, I called Danny and asked him to do some further snooping on the elevator videos, and sure enough, Demetrios and Johnny took the elevator to the 20th floor just after midnight before the explosions. They weren't carrying bags, as far as we could tell, but they could have had pipe bombs or weapons inside their puffy jackets.

"I could try to get a judge to give me a search warrant to look through the house in Quogue and see if there's any indication there was explosive anyplace there," Danny said.

"Not a bad idea, but not the only thing we can do to move this along," I said to him. "We could talk to Mrs. Costas, you know. Women are reputed to be more open to dealing with gay men than straight men are. I remember reading that if a gay man tells his mom, she's likely to be sympathetic, but if he tells his father, he may be angry, or maybe even violent in some cases. I bet Aristotle was nasty with Demetrios when he thought the boy was gay."

"He didn't write off Demetrios from his will, and the boy is on the Board of Costantinos, which is the major owner of Excalibre Properties bonds," I said. "That doesn't sound like a guy who's going to disinherit the boy. Maybe his pique is for show. Have you thought about that possibility? That he may be reacting to what other people think and showing them that he wouldn't tolerate if his boy wasn't sticking to the straight and narrow."

"I wonder if he played with dolls when he was a toddler," Danny said. "Or if he was making motor noises and running toy trucks around the living room, like other boys."

"Do you have kids, Danny?"

He nodded. "Two boys and two girls, all of them straight."

"How old are they?"

"Youngest is seven, oldest is seventeen."

"And if you went to the boys' Little League games and one of the fathers thought they were gay, what would you do?"

"Punch him, maybe."

"Punch who? The father or your son?"

"Not sure, it never happened, so I'd be guessing anyway."

"And what would your wife do in the same situation?"

"Probably hug them and tell them everything's going to be okay."

"There it is," I said. "That's why I said we should talk to Mrs. Costas."

"A lot of kids don't have a clue about sex," Danny said. "I wouldn't have known what to say if any adult started asking me about what I liked when I was a teenager. I went through having crushes on the star athletes in my school, but I wasn't thinking about sex, just being one of the popular kids. If Ricky Rounsavelle, who was a star football player, was my friend, there wasn't a girl in eighth grade who wouldn't go out with me. And not one of them would have thought I was having impure thoughts about Ricky—because I wasn't. What did we do with our friends when we were teenagers? We had sleep-overs, like kids do today. Doesn't mean we were playing doctor, and we didn't have co-ed sleepovers, just to be clear."

"But who made snacks and tucked everybody in?"

"My mom, of course. Dad was always working on proposals or whatever. Didn't have time for my friends from school."

"Does Dad tell you what the business is like? What he worries about? What makes him want to whoop and yell like a winner?"

"Sometimes he tells me what he's planning to do, but he never tells me about problems, only about things that he's proud of."

"How do you feel about what's going on with Mr. Costas now?"

"It would make me sad, but I know boys don't cry."

Chapter Thirty-One

Mrs. Costas, Danny O'Toole, and I were in the Yonkers PD station where Danny was officed, sitting in an interrogation room with a big table in it—looked like a conference room in a commercial office. Of course there was a large mirror on the wall, behind which there would be an observation room, where people might be watching and listening to what went on.

Our greetings had been cordial, and Mrs. Costas seemed relaxed and not particularly anxious about what direction the conversation might take. She had been sitting in the hospital for many hours, worrying about her husband, Aristotle Costas, until Danny asked her to come into the precinct for a more formal question and answer session after my brief conversation with her and Demetrios there earlier.

"He wants Demetrios to take over the business when he gets old," Olympia said when I asked her. Danny was sitting across the table from us, and smiled real big.

She looked a little like a mom from a 1950s sitcom. She was pretty, had a nice figure, and couldn't resist the opportunity to hold hands with her kids and most likely her husband, too. She was wearing jeans, but not tight-fitting, and a Peter Pan collar blouse with a sweater tied around her waist by the sleeves, so the navy-blue sweater itself covered her rear end.

Danny asked her an obvious question. "Did you grow up in a Greek family?"

"No," she said. "My family are of northern European extraction, I think. I was told when I was a child that the family has been in the United States since before the American Revolution. My family name was Best. There used to be a department store called Best & Company, but we weren't related. My dad was a postal service letter carrier, and my mom stayed at home and took care of her children. I have three brothers and two sisters, so we were three and three, boys and girls. Anyway, mostly British and Dutch, which is why I'm tallish and light-skinned, unlike Aristotle. We met when we were students at City College of New York, and hit it off from our first date, even though we didn't look like we'd be a couple. People said that to me all the time, still do sometimes, although I think these days we look more like we belong together than we did when we were young."

I decided to just go ahead and ask the big question. "Does Aristotle think Demetrios is gay?"

She smiled and shook her head to say no.

"All young boys have some girl in them," she said. "They're born that way. I grew up with brothers—three of them—and they all went through times when they wanted to try on my clothes—not my underwear, but my blouses, and my skirts. I think all three of my brothers tried on my ballet tights and tutus. It's normal, just like boys wanting to try on what girls wear, girls want to put on those shoulder-pads that boys wear when they play football—and probably their helmets, too. We all learn what works for us, and I wouldn't be surprised if one or two of my kids were gay. There are predictable percentages of people who are gay in the population as a whole. I have been told that ten percent of boys are gay, although some part of them never act on it—but it hangs over in hero-worship. Guys would follow their heroes to hell and back. Think Tom Brady, Derek Jeter, Brad Pitt. But some predictable percent of boys are going to fall in love with other boys, and be willing to pursue it. I had girlfriends when I was in middle school who would hug and kiss each other on the mouth. Most of them turned out to be normal; they were just trying things out to see how they felt."

"But Demetrios in particular," Danny asked. "Do you think he might be gay?"

"He might be, but he's not there now, not yet," she said. "Yes, Ari worries that since he doesn't want to be a football tackle or a Greco-Roman wrestler, he'll end up being a florist in Chelsea or a Rockette. But most boys don't go that route, even though some of them may be programmed so that could have been a possibility they could have sex with another guy, they just don't—probably most often because of religious reasons. All Christian religions see homosexuality as being on the dirty side of life—nobody more so than Orthodox priests.

"But there's a real pull to wanting to have a family. My grandmother used to say babies bring their love with them from the womb, and it's true. If you bond with a baby, that baby is yours forever. We all grew up in families, and we expect to repeat that family experience as parents, watching kids turn into regular people," she said. "And then, of course there are grandchildren, which I don't have any of now."

She stood up and looked out the window, like there was a great vista to see there, when there was really just salt grass and sand. There was a time when cattle were driven to places like Galveston to feast on the salt grass and fatten up. There's even a Saltgrass Steak House in Galveston to this day.

"Demetrios has some great ideas about Excalibre Properties," she said, musing at the salt grass and sand. "Remember, he's from a different generation than us adults. He's growing up with greenhouse gases choking up the atmosphere from jet planes and the cars we drive to church. Kids today have to live with climate change, floods, once-in-a-century hot summers, droughts and water shortages. We grew up with four seasons that were all about the same length; you could predict what the weather would be like in March or July or October—not like today, when it could be 75 on Halloween, and freezing on the 4th of July. Demetrios is growing up with the Kardashians as role models, not to mention actors who are married to same-sex partners, and playing Brady-Bunch people on television. Think about that program called *How I Met Your Mother*. There was a male actor in that—a male actor who was a headliner—who was not just gay, but married to a guy in real life. Not only that, but his character was a ladies' man from start to finish. Half the laughs that came from that show were based on shenanigans by this gay actor, and comments that reflected his idea of a horny man who wanted to screw every pretty woman he met. Sometimes it takes an outsider to be funny about things like that—and that actor was certainly an outsider to male-female relationships."

She shifted her position and leaned over the edge of the table toward Danny. "That's real different from what was on TV when Ari and I were kids—maybe it was the same with you."

"I used to look forward to *Bonanza, Gilligan's Island*, and *The Beverly Hillbillies*," Danny said. "That's not anything like what kids watch on TV today. Think about *The Simpsons*, *Miami Heat*, and what kids see and hear on social media these days. Heck, kids can be kidnapped by crooks and thugs from social media pretending to be twelve-year-olds, or middle-aged priests or whatever."

"They're going to grow up different from us. And, yes, some of them will be gay. Some will be tree-huggers. Some will be vegan to save the planet from methane poisoning by cows, goats and sheep. If they don't start doing these things, Earth will be devastated like Mars in a couple of hundred years. There won't be any oxygen to breathe—so where will we be then?" I said.

"Don't get me wrong, Mrs. Costas," I offered. "I may not be gay, but my brother is, and so are lots of my friends, including Gabriele Cortese, whom I hope you will meet. He's the handsomest man I've ever known, and also the most successful restaurant owner in Manhattan. Probably rich as Croesus, given the lines of rich people who stand outside his restaurant waiting hours for a table.

"Gay doesn't mean chorus boys and florists anymore," I added. "My brother ran his own rural newspaper in the Midwest for a couple of decades, then started a newspaper in Los Angeles County, and spent his time selling ads for real estate in beach communities in the South Bay. You can't tell which guys are gay these days, because it doesn't matter to them, just like it doesn't matter to most people anymore. If I was going to buy a home in Manhattan, I would for sure look in Chelsea, because I want to live in a gay neighborhood, where it's safe, well-maintained, and friendly, with great shops, bars and delicatessens every place you look."

"So let me ask you again, Mrs. Costas," Danny said. "Do you think Demetrios is gay?"

"He might be," she said. "It's too early to tell. I'll wait until he partners up with somebody, and see who he's picked out to spend his life with. Remember, I fell in love with a short, heavy-set man named Aristotle. If you'd've asked me when I was in college whether that was a possibility, I'd've said you were crazy as a loon. I wanted a man who was tall and handsome, not built like a fireplug. But since Ari asked me to marry him, I've never looked back. I trust Demetrios; I think he has his head screwed on straight. He'll be what he will be, and I'll love him no matter what."

Chapter Thirty-Two

"I can't get over what an odd couple those two look like," Danny said while we were still sitting in the interrogation room after Mrs. Costas left to go back to the hospital to sit with her husband.

I felt the same way, but of course you can't judge a book by its cover, as they say. They apparently had been real happy over the years, and she was obviously a very loving mother for Demetrios. I didn't ask her if she went to Mass at a Greek Orthodox church, but from what Aristotle had told us, it seemed like the whole family followed the Orthodox religion.

"Demetrios looks like his mother's son, but no way he looks like he's related to dear old Dad. The kid looks like he's a foot taller than Dad already, and he might be still growing. According to what Olympia said, he's eighteen. I grew nearly two inches when I was in college," Danny said, "so it's not impossible that he would be towering over his father even more when he gets to be his full height."

I said maybe Aristotle's father was taller, so maybe the boy takes after his grandpa.

Danny said he wanted to see Demetrios's birth certificate. "I think she said he was born in Manhattan, so the CSIs should be able to fish his birth certificate up fairly easily. After all, Demetrios Costas or Costantinos must not be a common name. He stood up and walked over to the door, stepped out and beckoned to one of the cops sitting at desks outside.

When he sat back down, a female uniformed cop walked in. "You were looking for me, sir?" she said to Danny.

"This is Officer Edna Stryker," he said to me. "Edna, say hello to Hugo Miller. Hugo lives here in Yonkers, not far from the hospital where Mr. Costas is being treated as of now, and he is a Civilian Criminalist with the NYPD. He used to work with Mike di Saronno when Mike was the lead detective in the New York PD, and now he still helps Mike out, since Mike retired and decided to open his own law practice in Manhattan.

We bumped elbows, which is what you're supposed to do these days instead of shaking hands—so we wouldn't spread germs that could cause something like the flu or COVID-19.

"Edna," he said to her, "I need your help with finding a birth certificate and any doctor discharge papers from when Mr. Costas's son, Demetrios, was born. He's either seventeen or eighteen, but I don't know his birthday. You could probably find it in the DMV database. I just want to find out what it says on the birth certificate. Mr. Costas was the victim of that bombing on Waterton Avenue up in the Executive Center. He's the CEO of Excalibre Properties, which owns the building that was bombed a couple of days ago. And it's the same building where a guy fell off the roof several days ago, and hit an elderly man who was out for a walk at the wrong time. Originally, the coroner labeled it a suicide and accidental homicide, but now we're inclined to think the fall wasn't a suicide after all. Maybe there was more to it than that."

Danny wrote Demetrios's name, and his parents' names on a yellow tablet from a short stack of tablets sitting on the corner of the table, and handed it to Officer Stryker, who took it and left.

A few minutes later, Officer Stryker was back with a piece of paper she handed to Danny. "Birth certificate, sir," she said.

"It's just a regular birth certificate," Danny said. "Doesn't say anything to indicate that Aristotle wasn't the biological father, so I guess Demetrios Andreas Costantinos is biologically the son of Aristotle, like it says."

She walked back to her desk, and picked up another piece of paper off a printer, then brought that back. "There's this, but I don't know what it means," she said.

It was a court order addressed to James Francis Best, who had apparently been a willing sperm donor to his cousin, who is now Olympia Costas, and Demetrios's mother. It looked like it said he could claim to be the biological father if he filed the appropriate forms. It didn't appear that the forms had been filed, because the petition had been invalidated as of a month later.

"So maybe Aristotle isn't the biological father of Demetrios," Danny said, handing the paper to me to look at. He pulled out his cellphone and tapped out a telephone number, which was answered by Olympia Costas. He had his phone on speaker, so I heard him say to her, "We just had a look at the paperwork from when Demetrios was born," he said.

"And you found out that my cousin Jimmy was the biological father," she said, finishing Danny's thought for him.

"That's what I wanted to ask you," he said. "What happened?"

"Ari and I had been trying to have a baby, but I never seemed to get pregnant. He had bladder cancer at one point, and had some chemotherapy that might have made it impossible for him to inseminate me. We never found out for sure, because he didn't want to give the doctor a sperm sample to test, to see if he was, as they say, shooting blanks."

"So the reason Demetrios looks like you is that your family's genes are his genes 100 percent," Danny said. "No Costantinos genes in his body."

No answer, but I imagined a grim smile on her pretty face, sitting next to her husband in a hospital bed.

"Does Aristotle hold that against Demetrios?" he asked.

"Never," she said. "He believes he's the father. We had been trying to get pregnant for months, and he believes it finally worked. Meanwhile I had an IVF procedure that I never told him about—what they call a turkey baster—and I got pregnant," she said.

"The birth certificate lists Aristotle as the father, and he is the father, always has been. That boy is the most precious part of his life. He loves Demetrios more than he loves me," she said. "Please help me. Demetrios doesn't know about this, and we don't want him to know. He thinks of Ari as his Dad, and he's right. Ari is his Dad, always has been, always will be."

"None of what we found will be in our records, and I won't be telling anyone other than you what your cousin's petition said. It was cancelled anyway, so we presume it was wrong to start out with.

"Does this have any effect on how you feel about your son?" Danny asked her. "I'm on speaker here, and Hugo is still sitting here with me."

"You have to understand," she said. "Ari wanted a son more than he wanted anything else in life. His parents died early, so he was pretty much alone, no brothers or sisters, and although there are some relatives in Greece, he's never been over there to meet them. Now it's looking like he's not going to be traveling a lot for a while. Demetrios is his life. He built Excalibre Properties for Demetrios. That's why Demetrios and I are both on the Board of Directors, even though there was a struggle with the New York Stock Exchange when they went public about having three family members on the Board. That's why there are fifteen directors instead of the twelve that there were when we filed to go public, so that the family directors wouldn't be able to outvote the independent directors."

"Does Demetrios know about any of this?" I asked, speaking directly to Danny's speaker phone.

"Not a word of it," Olympia said. "And he has a copy of his birth certificate in the family files, proof positive that Ari is his father."

"Does he know your cousin Jimmy?" Danny asked.

"They've met, but Jimmy lives in Virginia, near Charlottesville, so we seldom see him and his family," she said. "They have a big piece of property, almost twenty acres, I think, most of it forest land. But they have a huge vegetable garden in what would have been a back yard. Looks like a truck farm there."

"Your cousin has a family?"

"He and Susie have been married for nearly thirty years now," she said. "They have six kids and two grandkids. They still have two kids at home, Brandon and Maggie. Maggie's the baby of the family, still in pigtails. Like Demetrios, blond and light-skinned, but her hair will probably darken as she gets older. Her dad was blond when he was a kid, and now he has brown pepper-and-salt hair, with some white or gray shining through."

"So Demetrios has a lot of relatives he doesn't know about?" I asked.

"He knows about all of them," she said. "He just doesn't know he's more closely related to them than just being cousins. And I don't intend for him to find out, either. They've been to Quogue for Thanksgiving a couple of times. I have a lot of the family china and silver, so it seems like when we were kids in some ways, especially when the table is set, and the turkey is in the middle."

"He told us he might want to marry and have kids," Danny said. "He told us that when we were talking about sexual preferences. He said he goes on dates with girls, but he didn't say he was in love with a girl. I remember when I was a teenager, I thought I was in love with Sonja Anderson, who I dated for two years in high school. I didn't hear anything like that from Demetrios."

Olympia said she thought if Demetrios knew the whole story, he might be more inclined to be gay.

"Why do you say that?" Danny asked.

"I think he'd find it more complicated than it actually is," she said. "A relationship between two men would be a lot simpler in some ways."

"My friend, Gabriele, who has always been gay, was married to a lesbian girl who lived in Ohio," I said. "He told me that she helped him get his green card, but they never had sex—neither one of them was interested. The immigration authorities visited them and they acted like newlyweds when they had to, but they never went all the way. He helped her pay for her college costs, and she helped him become a citizen. Now he's a regular voter in New York City, lives in Brooklyn, and carries an American passport, although he was born in Italy."

"If Demetrios married a man," she said, "I'd hope they would find a surrogate who would carry a child for Demetrios. I want to have grandkids. If they could adopt an infant, that would probably be just as good—as long as I could hold the baby when it was still a newborn. I think adults bond with babies in a serious way. I think one of the reasons that Ari is a little strange sometimes is that his parents both died in a car crash when he was a toddler, so he didn't have that parental love that molds most kids. It certainly had a lot to do with Demetrios becoming who he is today."

"He's a nice young man," I said. "I really don't think he's gotten to the place where he's looking for a mate—never mind male or female. I think he'll be open to either one when he meets the right person."

"Bless you," she said. "I hope the same, but I suspect he'll end up being a Mr. and Mr. partnership. Just a hunch."

Chapter Thirty-Three

"I wonder how heavy it is on Aristotle that he thinks his son might be gay," Danny said. "I have boys at home, and I don't know how I would feel if one of them turned out to be gay. I hope I would be okay with it. I love my kids—all four of them—two boys and two girls. I'd love it if one of them was a gay artist—maybe a writer or a painter -- just like I'd love it if one of the other boys was a star quarterback on his high school football team."

"Brothers have a unique relationship with each other," I said. "My brother and I fought like wet cats when we were little, but we've become really good friends as adults. He married a girl and had a daughter who has been a real bright spot in all our lives, especially his. He's a grandfather now, of a mixed-race boy who's in fifth grade, memorizing multiplication tables, I'd guess—although I'm not sure kids still memorize things like we did when I was in elementary school."

I was at home in my apartment in Yonkers after leaving the Yonkers PD precinct on Lake Street, and feeling like I ought to be able to walk over to St John's Riverside Hospital to say hello to Aristotle and his wife. My place is about a ten-minute walk to where he was being treated. When I was in my early twenties, I accidentally got hooked on taking Librium and drinking scotch at the same time. That's a combination that actually killed Marilyn Monroe—I remember that, but I never realized that I was doing the same thing.

My parents lived in Westchester County at the time, because my dad had been transferred by his company to the Manhattan home office, from a factory position in southern California. I ended up at UCLA, but was stranded in Westchester one summer, without enough money in my pocket to fly back to California to go to the fall semester of college. That was when I got the prescription for Librium from a psychiatrist I started

Splat!!

to see when I was worried about being drafted and sent to Vietnam.

Long story short, I ended up in a mental rehab hospital for substance abuse, and had treatments that aren't used much anymore, like electroshock therapy. Wouldn't you know that when I got out of the hospital, I managed to go to a new Broadway show called *One Flew Over the Cuckoo's Nest*, which starred Kirk Douglas as the lead patient who also had electroshock therapy.

Honestly, I don't remember my therapy. I remember that I was strapped down on a bed with leather straps, but that's about it. Whatever it was like, it worked. I was back to normal by the time the spring semester rolled around—and my worker's comp insurance had accumulated enough money in my account that I could not only get back to California, I could put a deposit down on an apartment to live in. All's well that ends well, as Shakespeare said.

Anyway, I wanted to walk over to the hospital to see Aristotle and Olympia. Maybe I'd see Demetrios if he happened to be there. I asked Danny if that would be okay, and he said it would be fine with him, but he'd like to meet me there, and listen to what was said.

That was all right with me.

As it turned out, Mr. Costas had been transferred to the Westchester Medical Center, which is north of Yonkers in a town called Valhalla. It's about a twenty-minute drive, so I met Danny in the front lobby there, and we made our way to the room where Mr. Costas was staying. He was hooked up to an intravenous line, and was getting some kind of medication that was hanging on a tree next to his bed.

"Tylenol," he said. "It's amazing how fast it takes effect when they give it to me through my I.V.," he said. "They tell me that I was dehydrated, and they've been giving me saline water pretty steadily," he said. "I also got a blood transfusion, because I was anemic when they did my blood work. I need to pee pretty constantly," he said, pointing to several translucent plastic urinal bottles that were hanging on the side of his bed. Each one of them had a yellowish or brownish liquid in it.

Mrs. Costas was sitting in an easy chair that would have tilted back to accommodate Aristotle and his I.V. if he had preferred sitting instead of lying flat in bed. "I've been helping him when I can," she said,

178

"but he seems to be getting better."

"Has your son been here to visit?" I asked Aristotle.

He smiled broadly and answered with a big "Yes, he's been to see me several times. He's on his way back here from Quogue now, I think," he said, looking questioningly at Olympia.

She nodded and said that yes, Demetrios was in an Uber car at that very minute, but it was a long drive from Quogue to Valhalla.

Danny and I were both sitting in straight chairs that looked like they belonged at a desk. He stood up and asked Olympia if she thought it would be okay if he asked Aristotle a question about what happened.

She nodded again. "He's getting better. If he doesn't feel like he can answer, we'll just forget it. Okay?"

Danny nodded, and said, "Demetrios told us that you had a look at that handgun that was on the floor of the roof level, and that you weren't wearing gloves. Do you remember that?"

Aristotle nodded, and said, "Demetrios was wearing gloves, because he had been riding his bicycle, and he gets blisters sometimes. He saw the gun sitting on the floor, and picked it up, looked at it for a minute, then put it back down."

He took a deep breath and said, "I was standing by the door down to the 20th floor, because I had been working on some documents in my apartment there, and had just followed the boys up to the roof. Johnny was standing a foot or so away from Demetrios. I walked over to where the gun was. I remember my shoes crunching on the pebbles or whatever-you-call-it that were on the floor. I picked up the gun and turned it over a couple of times. I'm not a gun kind of guy, and it was strange to have one in my hand.

"While I was holding it, I heard a popping sound, and my hand jerked," he said. "I realized the gun had fired, but it clearly didn't hit anything or anyone. I put it back where I found it, and thought I should call the police to come and pick it up. I asked Demetrios to run downstairs and see if he could get the concierge to call the police. I saw that Latino fellow standing next to the railing, looking like he was scared. He probably knew the gun had been shot. I went back down to my apartment and called the concierge's desk. The guy on duty said there were cops on the way over."

He was looking tired, like he might fall asleep.

"This is getting difficult," Olympia said, and walked over to the bed, started stroking his arm, saying to him, "It's okay, you're going to be okay. Don't worry about anything. Close your eyes if you want to. Do you want to read?" She was holding a book about Constantinople.

"I brought this from your bedside table at home," she said. "Thought you might want to read some of it. There's a business card that looks like a page marker here, if you want to go to the last place you were reading." She handed him the book, which was called *Constantinople: Capital of Byzantium*. "Maybe this isn't what you want to read, though," she said. He reached out toward the book, which was a bright shade of blue and had a picture of a minaret on it. She handed it to him.

"Thanks," he said, and opened the book. "Kinda boring," he said, looking at the book. He was looking around for something.

"Looking for your glasses?" she asked.

He nodded.

"They're hooked onto your hospital gown," she said, and handed them to him. He smiled, and opened the book to where the business card was.

"Istanbul," he said. "Wonderful place. It's the real center of Greece. Athens is just a tourist trap; people go there to see the ruins. People go to Istanbul to see the churches, like Aya Sofya. It was the first Christian city in the world. The old Greeks called it Roma Nova, not Constantinople. Foreigners called it Constantinople."

"Did you hear the sirens when the cops came?" Danny asked him.

Olympia looked at him like she was expecting him to ignore the question. He didn't ignore it. He nodded.

"They didn't come because of the gun, like you probably thought," Danny said. "They came because that Latin guy fell over the railing and died, and happened to fall on an old man who was out for a walk. He died, too."

"He was probably scared by the gun going off," Aristotle said. "I was scared, too. That's why I left to go back down to my apartment."

"He's still got brain fog," Olympia said, smiling at her husband and putting her hand on his forehead. She leaned over and kissed him on the middle of his brow.

Chapter Thirty-Four

"So, according to what Aristotle told us, not only had the boys gone back downstairs, he had left before Felipe fell over the railing," I said to Mike when I got him on my cellphone. "I wonder if he tripped and fell because he was so rattled by the gun being fired. The bullet hit the wood next to where he was standing, so he may have thought somebody was shooting at him."

"Or he may have jumped off the edge, like the cops originally thought," Mike said, "although he hadn't been climbing on the rail, and the rail was probably high enough to keep him from falling over it by accident." He said to himself, "I wonder," but didn't finish the thought.

"You wonder what?"

"I wonder if he fell over backward. If he was leaning on the railing, he could have over-balanced fairly easily, and without trying, especially if he was scared."

"Do you suppose the cops came to see the gun and ran their sirens?" I asked Mike. "That might have scared him, after the gunshot. He could probably see the gun from where he was standing, especially if he was leaning with his back on the rail."

"I wonder if there was somebody else who saw what was going on," Mike said. He told me was going to try to get Lela Swann on the phone, and disconnected from me.

I was trying to imagine what Felipe was seeing from where he was standing. He would have been facing the door from the stairway up from the Penthouse floor. But as far as we knew, there was nobody else on the roof. It was late and anybody who was there probably vacated when the owner of the building was there. Nobody wants to tangle with the landlord, especially Felipe Barrio, who was having trouble making his maintenance payments. I wondered if he had been late, or missed any payments completely.

I called Danny and asked him if he had Felipe's bank statements.

"We have about six months of bank statements," Danny said, "but I don't have them myself. The CSIs are supposed to be looking at them."

"See if he missed making any of his maintenance or mortgage payments, if he was in arrears on anything major."

"Okay, I'll talk to the CSIs. That's exactly what they're supposed to be looking for," he said. "If he was a suicide, all that would be evidence."

"I'm thinking in a different direction," I told him. "Just a shot in the dark, but maybe it'll help us figure out what really happened."

Mike called me back and said Lela was still living in the Waterton building, but was moving to the 14th floor. "Can you make it over there to talk to her?" he asked me. "She told me she went up to the roof to see if Felipe was there, because she didn't know where he was and it was the middle of the night."

I told him I could be there in ten minutes, if she would buzz me up, or if Danny or one of the Yonkers cops could meet me there and let me in.

"But I don't think I'm the right person to do this," I told him. "I feel like I need to be with somebody who's more official than me. If I go over there and talk to Lela, I could testify to what happened while I was there, but anything she told me would be hearsay, and I can't believe any lawyer would let me get by with that."

Mike said he would jump in a car and drive up to Yonkers.

"Sorry, but I think you might have the same problem with hearsay," I said. "I think we need Danny O'Toole to make this work. He might have to take her in as a person of interest. That might make it possible to get her testimony on the books."

"You're right," he said. "I'm too used to being a cop, and as we know, I'm not a cop anymore. And even if I was, I wouldn't have any jurisdiction in Yonkers."

I was wearing house slippers and had to put on outdoors shoes, but otherwise I was okay to go. I always need to pee, but that doesn't take long. I grabbed a surgical mask, because I try to avoid getting infected, especially with the flu. I had the Fluzone High Dose Quadrivalent shot, which is the version that is given to people over 65—but it only protects you from four types of flu each year. So it's worthwhile to wear a surgical mask, to ward off germs that might be a problem.

It took Mike a little over half an hour to get to my apartment. I offered him a cup of coffee, which he accepted, and then we started for the Waterton building.

It was a short drive to the Waterton building, and we had to drive right by St John's Riverside Hospital to get there.

"I was thinking we could see Aristotle and Olympia there at St John's, but you told me they were transferred to Westchester Medical Center, so that wouldn't work," I said. "But it's only about twenty minutes from here to there if we need to talk to the Costas family afterward." I was careful to drive well under the city speed limit, and tried to miss the huge potholes that the roads are pock-marked with all over Westchester. A car was pulling out from near the pizza joint just up the street from Lela's building, so I was able to park fairly easily.

Mike told the concierge we were there to see Lela Swann, and we were working with the Yonkers police and Mike was a lawyer representing the Bliss family. He let us through to the elevator bank without calling upstairs.

I rang the bell and Lela answered the door.

"You were talking to Mike?" I asked her. He stuck his hand out for a shake.

"Hey, Lela, good to see you; thanks for making time for us."

She nodded and opened the door widely in an invitation to come in.

The room was very neat and clean, and looked less crowded with furniture than it had the other time I was there.

"The apartment's on the market," she said. "The real estate agent got rid of most of what was in the front room to make it look more spacious." She waved her hand around the room. "Looks like we ought to be having a party or something."

"So," Mike said as he sat down on a straight chair that looked like it belonged with a desk. "We were talking about the night that your fiancé was out late, and you wondered if he was up on the roof looking at the stars."

She nodded again. "He liked the nights when it was clear enough to see stars. He was always looking for shooting stars. He kept talking about a story called something about a little match girl."

"That's a story that kids read. It's a tear-jerker," Mike said. "It's about a little girl who sells matches to buy food. She sees a shooting star and she believes that when there's a shooting star, it means that someone is dying and going to heaven. In this case, it happens to be her, since she's outside in the cold."

"Did you find him on the roof?" I asked her.

She nodded. "I crossed paths with Mr. Costas, who was on his way down from the roof. I knew him, but he didn't say anything to me," she said. "I don't think he saw me. I was probably looking down at the stairs, because I always worry that I'll trip and fall on stairs."

"Tell me what happened. You know we're trying to prove that Felipe wasn't a suicide, that he didn't jump off the roof. Did you see him up there?"

"He was on the roof, over on the side of the terrace area where people would go to smoke. That whole area is covered with cigarette butts, because it's a no-smoking building—you can't even smoke inside your apartment, and you have to make sure that anyone that's visiting doesn't smoke, too. But the roof was okay, probably because there was almost always a breeze up there, and the air would stay clean and not smell like smoke.

"He waved at me, and said that Mr. Costas had just been there, and there was a gun lying on the floor about two feet from where Felipe was standing.

"He told me Demetrios, the owner's son, had been looking at the gun first, but he just put it back on the floor where it was lying when he saw it," she said. "Then apparently the old man came up the stairs, and saw Demetrios with the gun. When he put it down, the old man picked it up, and it accidentally went off, either while he was holding it, or when he dropped it on the floor.

"He said the boys and Mr. Costas left, all at about the same time."

"Boys plural?" Mike asked.

"Demetrios and his friend that he's always with. Every time I see Demetrios, he's with the same kid. They go to the same school and they probably get bullied, because the other boys think they're queer, so they probably get beat up. Boys are really mean to each other. So are girls, but girls are meaner without actually hitting each other. I think his name is Johnny something."

"Do you think Demetrios is queer?" I asked her.

"No, I think he's just immature; he acts like a kid. He's tall but he looks like a baby, and so does his buddy," she said.

"What happened then?" Mike asked.

"Nothing," she said. "I asked him when he was coming downstairs, and he said in a few minutes."

"He didn't fall?" I asked her.

She shook her head. "Not while I was there," she said. "It was starting to drizzle, looked like it would be raining hard pretty soon. There weren't very many stars because of the clouds that were blocking everything, so I figured he'd be giving up on finding shooting stars and would be back home."

"So he didn't go back downstairs with you?" Mike asked.

"Nope," she said. "I figured he'd be downstairs pretty quick, because it was going to rain. I went back to the apartment, and by the time I got there, I was hearing sirens. Our apartment is in the back of the building, so I couldn't look out and see what was happening on the street in front of the building. I figured it was EMTs, somebody slipped and fell. I didn't know it was Pipo, though."

Chapter Thirty-Five

Where I live is real close to the building on Waterton, where Lela had been living with Felipe, but Mike was in Manhattan when we spoke on the phone the next day, at his office at 5th Avenue and 20th Street. He said he would take a squad car to my place, and we could drive over together.

"I can still get a ride when I need it," he said. "Once a cop, always a cop, you know."

I almost said "Liar, liar pants on fire," because he was constantly reminding me that he was no longer a cop, but a lawyer, whose sole goal was the satisfaction of his clients' needs. But I bit my tongue, and said nothing.

It was close to forty-five minutes before he texted me that they were in Yonkers, and he would be at my place in a few minutes. I've lived all over lower New York State. When I first opened my office in Manhattan, it was at 30 Rock—a small, crowded place, but with a perfect address. I found an apartment within walking distance, so I could get to work without having to drive or take a taxi. That apartment was in the Theater District, just across the street from Morgan Stanley's headquarters, which was one of the buildings that made the Theater District respectable and safe again. Before that, 8th Avenue was called the "Minnesota Strip," because there were so many street-walkers, and they were legendarily teenagers from the Midwest.

Mike arrived, and it was still before noon, so I turned on the coffee maker, and was able to pour him a cup when he got upstairs to my place. I told him that the drive to the Excalibre Properties building would only take about five minutes, so we were in no rush.

When we got there, however, the place was buzzing with cop cars, lights flashing, and a fire truck with an ambulance and EMTs in front of

Splat!!

the building. There were sirens in the distance, obviously on their way to where we were.

Danny O'Toole was there already. He shook hands with Mike and me, and told us that Lela Swann had been attacked, apparently in the elevator.

I asked if there were any clues about who did it. He told me that it was apparently Demetrios Costas, who tried to wrestle her to the floor so he could rape her. Just as he was telling us what happened, a pack of EMTs were rolling out a gurney with Lela lying on it. There was blood on the gurney, so she must have been manhandled one way or another.

"She was fighting back," Danny said. "Apparently there is some flesh under her fingernails, so there is probably some DNA that can be introduced in an arraignment or a trial."

"I thought he was queer," I said.

"Rape isn't sexual nearly as much as it is just violent," Danny said. "He could still be queer and get off slapping or punching a girl. This one was pregnant, and seems to have aborted a fetus as a result of being punched in the abdomen. That might have really made him excited."

"Where is he?" Mike asked.

"He was flat on his back in the elevator lobby area of the 14th floor, which is where the victim's apartment is," Danny said. "Lots of blood coming out of his mouth."

Just about then, another one of the elevators opened, and another gurney rolled out, this time with Demetrios on it—and there was indeed, blood all over his face. He was choking and moaning, but it was hard to feel sorry for him, knowing he had punched a pregnant woman in the stomach, and she had miscarried her baby as a result.

"What happened?" I asked the EMT.

"No idea," she said. "But it looks like the woman stuck her hand in his mouth to try to force him away from her. She speared the back of his mouth. I think they told me there was flesh under her fingernails. The back of his mouth is all torn up, so that makes sense." She picked up a syringe and fed its contents into the I.V. in his arm. "Painkiller," she said.

Two separate ambulances took the two of them to St John's Riverside Hospital, which was the closest ER to where we were.

Demetrios was handcuffed to the rail on the right side of his gurney.

"Did anybody call his mother?" I asked Danny.

He shrugged and said, "If somebody calls her, I'd prefer it not be me."

"She'll be at Westchester Medical Center in her husband's room," I said. "It's gonna be really hard on her that Demetrios has done whatever he did. This guy is the only child of the CEO of Excalibre Properties."

"I just hope the young woman is okay," Danny said.

"Her vitals are strong," one of the EMTs said. "Doesn't mean she's okay, but it means she's fighting back at what happened. Good BP, good blood oxygen, no fever. We're giving her some morphine, but I think she'll be able to get by without it when she gets to the ER."

I looked in the contacts on my cellphone and found Mrs. Costas's cellphone number.

"Do we know who the woman's next of kin would be?"

'The only thing I know about her is that she was engaged to Felipe Barrio. She's Catholic, like he was, but I have no idea where she's from. I think she may be local, because they met in school, and Felipe was local—most of his family lives close to the Waterton building, in the house he grew up in. They both go to St Anthony's Catholic Church—she told me that, so if you call the pastor there, he may know more about her family."

"How is Mr. Costas doing?" Danny asked me. "Have you seen him in the last couple of days?"

"Mike and I saw him, but most of the conversation was with his wife, who is glued to his hospital room. I don't think she's been home to where they live in Quogue since he went downhill and was admitted to St John's. Then they sent him to Westchester Medical Center, because they have a psychiatric department, and they thought that was what he needed."

"Is he capable of talking?"

"No idea. He was talking when we were there, but only to Olympia, not to us. She had taken him a book he was reading at home, something about Constantinople. He's very Greek Orthodox, and said he thought Istanbul is the center of the Greek church—not Athens," I said.

"I think he's from a first-generation American family. His parents were probably from someplace where they speak Greek. Maybe in Greece, maybe in Turkey someplace. In ancient times, everybody in that part of the world spoke Greek. All of the New Testament, including the gospels, were written in Greek. And for most Greeks, Constantine is a saint, because he recognized the Christians and made Christianity the state religion of the Roman Empire."

"Is the wife Greek?"

"Olympia?" I asked. "Probably at least part Greek. As I remember, she told us that her family was all northern European, maybe she said mostly Dutch, which is why she's tall for a woman. She has blue eyes and light-colored skin, too. Like the opposite of her husband. If her family is all from Denmark and the Netherlands, I'd guess she was brought up either Lutheran or Calvinist. But I bet she converted to Orthodox when she married Aristotle Costas."

"What kind of a name is Costas?" Danny asked me. "Is it Greek? It looks Spanish to me."

"It's not anything," I said. "It's a short version of the last name he was born with, Costantinos, which is really Greek, a version of the name of the emperor Constantine 'the Great.' The son is Demetrios Andreas Costantinos, the one who is now under arrest for beating up and maybe sexually assaulting Felipe Barrio's girlfriend, Lela Swann. Everybody thought he was gay. This was a nasty way to find out he had eyes for girls."

"She was going to marry that Mexican guy that jumped off the roof, right?"

"Wrong," I said. "He was born in El Salvador, not Mexico, and he spent most of his life in the good old USA. He does have a darker skin color than I do, but I'm mostly British and Dutch and German, which is probably why I have blue eyes too. He was a different mix, and he had deep brown eyes. I have a granddaughter who's Latin. Her father was from Costa Rica, which is where he went back to while my daughter was pregnant with his child. When they did her DNA with Ancestry, it turned out she is part Native American. That's something to be proud of, and I feel sure Felipe Barrio was proud of being Latin too, although I don't believe I ever met him when he was alive.

"Felipe was a really devout Catholic. I've been told that he went to Mass during the week, not just on Sundays. He did a novena of First Fridays each year to get indulgences that'll help him avoid Purgatory and get into Heaven when he died. So maybe he's up there with the saints now, while we're talking. I've met a lot of his family—nice people like his sister Maria, and his brother Rodrigo. He has a ton of cousins, including a wealthy one I met in Acapulco, where he moved when he got tired of living in Los Angeles, apparently.

"The whole family are well-adjusted, and they all speak at least two or three languages, and they seem intent on going to college—all of them. Felipe graduated from City College with a degree in Culinary Arts. He wanted to break into the restaurant business, and my friend who owns a super-successful Italian restaurant in TriBeCa said the chefs in Yonkers were real high on him. Felipe met Lela while she was going to City College, too, studying finance and accounting. She works for a big CPA firm, and looks like she'll be making a fortune when she gets her CPA license."

I felt like I was on a roll, especially since Danny had made some comments that sounded real redneck.

Chapter Thirty-Six

It didn't seem like we were any further along than we had been at the beginning. Several people had seen Felipe standing at the railing, but nobody saw his fall or jump, or even saw his feet fly out from under him when he lost his balance on a slippery floor.

Danny O'Toole and I were in his station, using an interrogation room for a conversation, and planning to call Mike di Saronno to bring him up to date.

"You know what we need to do?" Danny O'Toole asked. "We need to see if there are any slippery areas of the roof floor, especially over by the corner where Felipe was standing."

He stroked his chin, like he was checking to see if he ought to shave. "My mom wears graduated compression stockings because she had blood clots in her legs a few years back," he said out of nowhere. "Her stockings are made out of latex and they squeeze her legs and feet so that they don't have the kind of flexibility that they had before she was wearing the compression stockings." He paused, and then continued, like he was talking to a doctor. "She can slip and end up on her ass just walking across the kitchen if she's not wearing rubber-bottom shoes like Nikes or Vans. Leather-soled shoes are like ice skates under those circumstances."

Danny said he was beginning to think, "Maybe Felipe slipped when it started to drizzle. Maybe he fell by a total accident. Maybe he wasn't startled by a gunshot. Maybe he wasn't pushed. Maybe he was just wearing new shoes with slick soles on a roof terrace floor that was turning slippery with the rain. Not suicide, just slick-bottom shoes on a slippery floor."

"We need to see if we can find out how slippery that roof floor was the night that Felipe Barrio fell to the street from the roof," Danny said.

Danny dialed Mike's number on the phone that was sitting in the middle of the conference-style table in the interrogation room. Mike picked up

"Hey, guys," he said. "Hugo, you there?"

"Yup, here," I said. "Hope you're having a good day. We've been talking about what happened on the roof that night when Felipe Barrio fell off the edge."

Mike started talking, and sounded like he knew what Danny had been saying, about the fall maybe being an accident after all. But he was still focused on getting what he could for his clients, the Bliss family.

"If the roof floor was slippery, then all the more reason to say that the building was negligent in taking care of people who were allowed on the roof," Mike said. "The Blisses were victimized by Excalibre Properties' negligence if the floors were slippery enough for Mr. Barrio to lose his balance and fall to his death. Bob Bliss, who was just out for a night-time walk, should have been able to trust that if there were people on the roof of the building, Excalibre would have taken steps to make sure that nobody was hurt."

While we were talking, Danny's cellphone buzzed.

"Wait, guys," he said. "Tamara, the Medical Examiner, is calling me. I gotta take her call; she only calls when she has something important. I'll put my phone on speaker, so you can hear."

"I think I may have a handle on what happened to your guy that fell off the roof," she said.

"My colleagues, Mike di Saronno and Hugo Miller, are both on a conference call with me in the interrogation room in my station, so they can hear you."

Mike and I both said hi, and "Glad to meet you on the phone."

The City of Yonkers doesn't have a Medical Examiner. When they need one, they call on the Westchester County Medical Examiner, who is officed in Valhalla, about a twenty-minute drive north from where we were at Danny's station. Yonkers is a real city, but they'd be hard-pressed to keep a Medical Examiner busy most of the time.

"Anyway, gents, I'll say it again," she said. "I think I may know what happened to your boy, Felipe Barrio, when he fell off the roof."

"A light in the darkness," I said. "We've been puzzling about that, so we're happy to hear what you have to tell us."

"Sorry you can't see the X-ray I have on the light box in the morgue, which is where I am calling from," she said. "But I think your guy was dead before he fell off the roof."

"How so?" Danny asked.

"If you could see the X-ray and CT scans, I'd show you two places on the back of his head where either somebody hit him or he fell and banged his head on the edge of the roof, but before he fell off the building."

"How can you tell?" Mike asked.

"There was internal bleeding at these two places on the back of his head, but his heart stopped and there wasn't any real bleeding from the other injuries that his body had from the fall. Does that make sense? We only bleed when the heart is beating. Once the heart stops, bleeding stops."

"There was blood on the sidewalk," Danny said.

"That was from the impact when he fell," she said. "You don't want to look at him. He landed on his stomach, and virtually every bone in his body was broken. The skin burst open all down his front and all over his face. I tried to stitch him closed, but I had trouble finding a way to make the stitches stay in."

"So, how could he have been hurt in the back of his head?" Mike asked.

"Well, I can't tell you exactly what happened, but there are basically two ways he could have been injured like this. First, but not very likely, somebody could have hit him with a baseball bat a couple of times. But more likely, he slipped and fell, and hit his head on a railing and then on the floor."

"Why do you say a baseball bat?" Danny asked.

"Because whatever hit him, at least the first time, was rounded," she said. "A lot of railings are rounded, and so are baseball bats, which is why I said what I said."

"When his girlfriend left him on the roof after they talked, she said

194

he was leaning with his back against the railing," Mike said.

"Okay, so on to the next part of my theory," she said. "He only had one shoe on, and it's now covered with a layer of dirt, which would have been mud in the rain that night. The other shoe is probably up there on the roof, if I'm right."

"One shoe meaning?" I asked.

"His other shoe came off," she said. "Probably when he fell against the railing, so that's probably where it is now. His other foot was just a sock, and it was covered with mud, too."

"What kind of shoes was he wearing?" I asked.

"Penny loafers," she said. "Brown or cordovan, not sure which, because the one he still had on had been polished with different types of polish, it looked like."

"Have you ever fallen when you were ice-skating?" she asked us.

"I sure have," I said.

"Where did you end up?"

"The time I remember most, I fell and hit my head trying to learn how to do a hockey stop on the ice. I knew I had to turn my feet so they were sideways compared to the direction I had been going. Then I had to dig the point of one of my skates into the ice like a brake, to slow down and stop myself. But instead of stopping, I pitched over forward and fell. My head hit somebody else's skate, and it cut a hole in my eyebrow. I guess there was a lot of blood, because my sister called our mom and told her I was dead."

"You weren't dead, obviously," she said. "But you were flat out on the ice, right?"

"Yes, as far as I can remember. I woke up on the ice, and there were two guys helping me to the side, and firemen waiting to put me in an ambulance."

"So they took you to the hospital?"

"No, I was awake, and then my mom and dad drove up and took me home. It was Thanksgiving Day."

"Well," she said. "Mr. Barrio was dead on the floor. If he fell so that he was partly hanging off the edge of the roof, he probably just slid over and the next step down was the sidewalk."

"How are you going to say he died?" Danny asked.

"Accident," she said. "His body probably slid off the edge of the roof under the railing where he hit the back of his head. But he was already dead when that happened."

"Why wouldn't somebody have pulled him back onto the roof when he started to slide off?"

"Was there anybody there when he fell?" Tamara asked. "If there wasn't anybody there, there wouldn't have been anyone to try to pull him back. But like I said, he was already dead by then anyway."

Epilogue

The Barrio family were all smiles to find out that Felipe's fall was totally accidental, not even a possibility it was intentional, according to the Medical Examiner. His sister, Maria, put up a little memorial table in the living room, with some of his ashes in a metal vase, and several potted orchids in bloom. There was an antique prie-dieu next to it for anyone who wanted to say a prayer, and there was a big photo on the wall behind the memorial of Felipe in his soccer uniform, smiling and waving.

"He was such a good person," his brother, Rodrigo, said to me, pointing at the soccer photo. "That's how I remember him, he loved playing soccer, and he played on the St Anthony's team. I don't know anybody who was more loving and went to church all the time like he did. I know he always gave money to St Anthony's, too—even when he was flat broke and couldn't pay his bills—which was most of the time. Fortunately for him, he had a guardian angel who made sure he had enough to make ends meet before things caved in. He always managed to pull the fat out of the fire, as my mom used to say."

Lela recovered from her pummeling by Demetrios, and Olympia Costas paid all her hospital bills. Both of them were morose about losing the baby, especially since Felipe was gone, and the baby would have been like still having part of him around.

"I think Demetrios is having mental problems like his dad," Lela said. He hadn't raped her, although he had worked her over like he was fighting with her, so she was initially afraid that she might not ever be able to get pregnant again. Maybe it wasn't his fault anyway, she told Olympia and Danny, because she was already feeling the miscarriage when she opened the door and it was Demetrios, yelling at her.

"I was already starting to bleed before Demetrios knocked on my door," she said. "So it wasn't his fault that the baby died. Maybe God wanted the baby to be in Heaven with his father."

Danny O'Toole saw to it that Demetrios was being treated by a psychiatrist at New York Presbyterian's campus in White Plains, where the specialty was mental problems. Demetrios begged Lela to forgive him, and said he didn't have any idea what came over him.

"I was pissed off that my dad was turning into a vegetable," he said. "And I got really mad at everybody. I'm so sorry I took it out on you. I never hit anybody before, and I never will again."

Lela told him that his mother was covering all her treatments. "The doctor told me I'll still be able to have children when this is all over, that is, if I ever meet a man I want to have children with, and he wants to be with me. I was so in love with Pipo; I still can't believe he's not going to come home anymore. I keep his picture next to the bed, and I hope every night to dream about him. Sometimes I do."

Felipe's cousin, Catalina, gave Lela a copy of the Padre Pio portrait that Felipe had loved at church. She put it in the front hallway of the apartment, and her CPA company gave her a raise that meant she could stay in the apartment instead of looking for a new place to live. Felipe had left his entire estate to her in a handwritten will, so that made her the owner of the co-op shares anyway.

Gonzalo sent a blanket of white roses to the church in time for the memorial service since that gathering occurred after the funeral. He also paid for a bronze plaque that was affixed to the outer lobby of St Anthony's church, in remembrance of Felipe Barrio.

Aristotle seemed to sink further and further into dementia, and the doctors didn't seem to think he would come back to be anything like his former self. He was afraid of everything and everybody who came near him, except his son and his wife, whom he recognized as soon as they came into his hospital room. He threatened the nurses with his fists, and of course, he was built like a brick shit-house, so they were scared of him. He let the doctors and the male nurses treat him, and he responded like a child to haloperidol, which was a sedative that kept him in bed and helped him sleep most of the time.

Olympia was named CEO by the Board of Directors of Excalibre Properties. One of the first things she did was to put a sign on the

Waterton building as the Costas Memorial Building. Then she founded a mental health walk-in clinic on the ground floor and hired a full staff that was affiliated with St John's Riverside Hospital. She put aside an endowment of a hundred million dollars for the clinic, and reserved seven no-charge studio apartments in the building for homeless people with schizophrenia, severe depression or other serious mental problems, and saw to it that they were in the care of psychiatrists. As time went on, she also subdivided several two-bedroom apartments and dedicated them to patients of the clinic as well. Because of the work she did on the building, Aristotle was able to stay there, instead of being held in a mental hospital someplace else. As a result, she was able to have lunch with him most days. He liked Chinese food, and could still use chopsticks to eat.

Demetrios remained on the Board of Excalibre Properties, in spite of his attack on Lela, who forgave him for everything that happened. He pleaded guilty to sexual assault, and submitted to being chemically castrated for three years. Then he married Johnny Georgostathis and they were happy together. Johnny became a gourmet cook and eventually wrote a cookbook of Green Fusion recipes. They bought the old Bliss house around the corner from the Costas Memorial Building, which had been put up for sale after Mike got a big settlement for them from Mrs. Costas and the Board of Excalibre Properties. He refused to accept any part of the settlement as a fee for his work, so I never got paid either.

About the Author

Joe Allen's first success in "trade" books (books for retail buyers) was *Sandcastles: The Splendors of Enchantment* (published by Doubleday & Co in 1981), followed by *The Leisure Alternatives Catalog: Food for Mind & Body* (A Delta Special from Publishers Inc).

His first mystery novel, *Rocky Point Road,* was published by Rogue Phoenix Press in 2015, followed by *The Monteverdi Manuscript: A Hugo Miller Mystery* (2016), *The Hanging Man: Hugo Miller Mysteries 2* (2018), *A More Perfect Union: Hugo Miller Mysteries 3* (2019), *Fools Playing Fools: Hugo Miller Mysteries 4* (2020), *The Coniston Curse: Hugo Miller Mysteries 5* (2021), and *Just a Scream at Twilight: Hugo Miller Mysteries 6* (2022). His family saga, *Where All Past Years Are,* was published by Rogue Phoenix Press in 2018.

Joe is also the author of five nonfiction books, including *Effective Business Communications: A Practical Guide*, published in 1979 by Goodyear Publishing, now a part of Prentice Hall, a subsidiary of Savvas Learning Corporation. His *Systems in Action: A Social and Managerial Approach,* was a text published by Goodyear Publishing in 1978. It was an advanced problem-solving text used in several MBA programs, including the UCLA Anderson School of Management. He contributed chapters to two Aspatore (Thomson Reuters) books on investor relations.

Most of Joe's business career was with Bozell & Jacobs and then at Allen & Caron Inc., a consulting and investor relations firm he founded in 1981 in Irvine, California. Under his leadership, the company worked with clients in the UK, Ireland, France, Belgium, Sweden, Denmark, Italy, Greece, Germany, Poland, Switzerland, South Africa, Singapore, Australia, New Zealand, Brazil and Argentina, among other countries. Allen & Caron maintained offices in Irvine, CA; Manhattan (NYC); and London (UK). The firm was merged with a Chicago-based investor relations firm in 2015, and Joe retired in 2017

Joe served on the boards of several small companies, was vice president of the United Way in Orange County, California, has written on a variety of topics for numerous leading magazines and newspapers, and has published interviews with financial luminaries on SeekingAlpha.com.

Joe studied Classical Languages and English Literature at UCLA in the 1960s, prior to becoming an editor of scholarly journals at Sage Publications, and was then a marketing manager at Benziger Bruce & Glencoe, a college publishing subsidiary of Macmillan. He was married for forty-seven years. Now widowed, he has two children (John and Angus) and two granddaughters (Isabelle and Xixi).

Other Books by the Author
at
Rogue Phoenix Press

Rocky Point Road

When his ex-wife drowns in a hot tub in California, Denis Rosa sets out to bury her and sell the house. He confronts her philandering history and her fixation on young Chicano boys and is the victim of a vicious attempted murder without ever knowing why. The house on the cliffside on Rocky Point Road holds a ghost, a hidden treasure of some kind, and decades of memories for the Rosa family. When Detective Sue Mason is assigned to the case, her son and his soon-to-be husband and two dogs move into the house with Denis to protect him from further attacks. Is it drug-related? The wife was alcoholic and smoked grass, but nothing hard. Denis confronts his ghosts as he finds himself attracted to Sue. The key to the plot is found when Denis slides off the edge of the cliff.

The Monteverdi Manuscript

The action revolves around the death of a famous musician who hits the pavement outside Carnegie Hall from the window of his apartment seven stories up. He has recorded keyboard versions of a lost opera by Claudio Monteverdi, the man who "invented" opera. Set in New York, London and Venice, action includes a kidnapping, drug use, prostitution, LGBT characters, one character who comes back from the dead, and three classic New York detective characters led by Hugo Miller.

Where All Past Years Are

Starting on Thanksgiving Day 1954, the Chadwick family encounters wars, financial crashes, 9-11, and the Great Recession. As a family with a WASP history they discover the wider world that is America, marry across religious, racial and ethnic lines, live, love, laugh and celebrate Thanksgiving and Independence Day at the Old Home on the shore of Lake Champlain near the Canadian border in New York.

The love of husbands and wives, the closeness of relatives who are an increasingly rainbow-like group, the touching beauty of the Old Home on the Lake as some family members move back to the property into new cottages—all are major themes. Children running a three-legged race watch the young man, Gray Chadwick, drop to his knees to beg his pregnant girlfriend, Melissa, to marry him. Births, deaths, burials, 4th of July fireworks, boating and bass fishing, and the strengthening power of love lead to a final surprising and unexpected reunion of two branches of the family for the first time in over three hundred years.

A More Perfect Union

Former ADA Eddie Hill, divorced African-American father of two, plans to marry Jimmy van Gelsen, wealthy gay man who, like Eddie, has been unlucky in love. Eddie is injured in a car accident on the NY Thruway, and Jimmy is shot in the forehead, killing him instantly. Was it Eddie's gun? If so, with Eddie in the hospital upstate, who pulled the trigger? Hugo, Ruth and Gabriele sort through a thicket of clues—a stolen Bentley, a shabby vacation home on Antigua, a multimillion-dollar co-op in Greenwich Village with fabulous art. Major political demonstrations with thugs and tiki torches, reminiscent of the Charlottesville riots with protesters battling in the streets—one at a prayer vigil, one a "Million Woman March" down 5th Avenue, another outside the Copley Plaza in Boston. Eddie runs for Congress from a mixed-race district in Brooklyn. Jimmy's will left a fortune to Eddie, who doesn't want any of it. Is it a right vs left murder? A gay-bashing murder? A robbery gone wrong? The answers are close to home.

When wealthy investment banker Luigi's body is found hanging from the crossbars of the George Washington Bridge, it is immediately thought to be a Mafia hit. Is it? Not according to a Catholic bishop with a diplomatic errand from the Vatican and an out-of-control Twitter account. As the truth unfolds, the reader meets a mad dwarf who eats insects and small rodents, a long-dead candidate for canonization, a deceased gangster who owned The Cotton Club in Harlem, and a tribe of mis-shapen males whose lives have been spent in tunnels under Hell's Kitchen.

Explosions, whispers coming from walls, mysterious billionaires from Grand Cayman, Luigi's terrified young wife with a suckling baby at her breast, treasure-hunters looking for buried gold in the basement— provide a frightening backdrop to a mystery that literally goes deeper and deeper into Manhattan as the story develops.

Hugo Miller, Ruth the Sleuth, handsome Gabriele Cortese and stalwart NYPD detective Mike di Saronno pool their considerable resources to solve a series of crimes that may hark back as far as seventy-five or one hundred years.

www.ingramcontent.com/pod-product-compliance
Lightning Source LLC
Chambersburg PA
CBHW051951220626
47052CB00004B/902